A ROGUE FOR SIÂN

WELSH REBELS

VIRGINIE MARCONATO

OLIVERHEBERBOOKS

Prologue

"Cousin Iorwerth is even tinier than our brother Rhys," Siân whispered. How was that possible? Rhys was tiny; his head was hardly bigger than the ball she liked to throw for her dog, Crumpet, and his hands were smaller than the umbrellas of wild carrots.

Her uncle Matthew laughed softly, careful not to wake the baby in his arms. "That's because he was born slightly before his time and this only three weeks ago, whereas Rhys is already more than six months old. That's a big difference, you know."

He was right, she supposed. But a difference in age was not always so significant where size was concerned. After all, she was only nine years old but already as tall as her mother. Well, she could almost reach to her shoulder if she lifted her chin. Well, almost.

Just then, the babe opened his big black eyes and looked straight at her. Siân leaned in, instantly captivated.

"Would you like to hold him?" Branwen asked, seeing her reaction.

Her *aunt* Branwen, Siân reminded herself. It still felt odd to think of her mother's best friend being married to her uncle.

The uncle who had become her uncle only when his brother, Connor, had married her mother, Esyllt, a couple of years earlier to replace her real father, Gwyn. And now Siân had a sister, Jane, who did not share either parent with her, a brother, Rhys, and a sister, Gwenllian, who both had the same mother as she had, and a baby cousin, Iorwerth, who lived in England.

It was all very complicated, as things were wont to be where adults were concerned.

"Oh, no, I can't hold the baby!" He was so small. What if she hurt him? Or, worse, dropped him? It didn't bear thinking about. He was bound to be fragile, being so small, more fragile than the vase she had broken only the other day when she'd placed it back on the table too roughly. "I wouldn't dare."

"I would like to hold him, please."

Jane, always bolder than she was and less clumsy, held out her arms to Uncle Matthew, who handed her the bundled-up baby.

I want children when I grow up, Siân thought as she watched her sister cradle the little boy against her chest. *If they are mine, perhaps I will not fear holding them.*

Yes, that was a good plan. Except she had to find a husband. But how did one go about doing that? Husbands had to please their wives; they could not be just anyone.

Later that day, as the guests started to arrive for the banquet given in Iorwerth's honor, Siân was relieved to see that finding a pleasing husband would not be as hard as she'd feared. A blond boy had just walked in through the door, a boy who instantly drew her attention. When their gazes met, she inhaled sharply for she had never seen eyes like his. Surely, it was a sign, a way for her to recognize who fate had in mind for her?

He smiled, and a strange feeling swept through her body. Everything became clear.

Yes. She would marry *him*.

Chapter One

England, Christmas 1299

ere he was again.

Heart thumping hard in her chest, Siân stared at the retinue in the bailey. The boy who had captured her imagination the last time she had come to England—her future husband—had just ridden through the gate. Except this time, he looked more like a man than a boy. In two years, he'd grown even taller and broader, even more handsome. Was it the black stallion he was riding that made him appear like a knight about to charge at his opponent in a joust?

No. The horse was admittedly magnificent, nothing like her own, slightly too-plump Welsh pony, but the imposing bearing of its rider was all his own.

Though the change in him was drastic, Siân knew it was him at first glance. She could not have mistaken him for anyone else, not with those eyes. No one she had ever seen possessed eyes like his. Up until the previous year, she hadn't even known it was possible to *have* eyes like his.

At first, she'd thought a trick of the light had made her see one eye lighter than the other. Perhaps the candle placed to his side was illuminating one while the other remained in the darkness. But no, his left eye was indeed blue, whereas his right was deep brown. The effect was most striking. Not that he would have been anything other than striking without that. It was hard to say what appealed to her the most. Perhaps the mane of hair the color of ripe wheat falling over his strong shoulders in thick waves. Or the jaw that seemed to have been cut with an axe and was enhanced by the first traces of stubble. He reminded her of her uncle Matthew. Her adoptive father's milk brother was one of the men she loved most in the world, and the resemblance between them seemed to suggest that the boy on his black horse would indeed be perfect in the role of protective husband and loving father.

"Look over there," she told Jane while he jumped off the saddle with impossible grace.

She would ask her sister, who had lived in England for seven years before coming to Wales, whether she knew who he was. The question would surprise her, but Siân could not keep thinking of the man she wanted to marry as a stranger. She was almost twelve; she had to start planning ahead. Her mother and father kept telling her she had plenty of time to think about such things, but it was not that simple. *She* might have years ahead of her, but her future husband was older than she was, perhaps as old as fifteen or sixteen, by the looks of things. It would not be long before he started looking at women, perhaps even bedding them. What if he fell in love with one of his conquests? What if his parents thought he was old enough to be married off to a rich heiress in the new year?

The opportunities for disaster were endless.

She had better start planning without delay.

Jane looked in the direction she was indicating and let out a little gasp. "How did you know?"

Siân frowned. She had known as soon as she'd seen him that he was the one she was destined to marry, but surely, that was not what Jane meant? "Know w-what?" she stammered, feeling caught out.

"To warn me he was here."

Warn her? What was Jane talking about?

Her bewilderment must have shown on her face because Jane answered, lowering her voice to a whisper. "That's Lord Ashton's grandson, the horrid boy I told you about." She cocked her head, considering. "Well, I guess he's not a boy anymore even if I'm certain he's still as vile as ever."

Siân's heart skipped several beats. *That* was Christopher Harrison? Her future husband was her sister's enemy? Surely, Jane had mistakenly thought she had pointed to another man in the retinue? It had to be a mistake because if he was Christopher Harrison, everything was about to get more complicated. Over the years, she'd heard all about the boy who had made Jane's life a misery when she'd lived at Sheridan Manor, and she refused to believe that the man who had captured her imagination was none other than that nasty persecutor.

As if to settle the matter once and for all, the boy chose that moment to approach them with what bore an uncomfortable resemblance to a victor's swagger.

"Well, if it isn't little Jane Hunter." A smile that, deplorably, could have been described only as mocking uncovered a row of shiny white teeth. "How long has it been since we haven't seen one another?"

"Not long enough," Jane answered drily. She was *not* impressed, and Siân wasn't sure what to think. There certainly was animosity there. So ... was he really Lord Ashton's grandson? Or perhaps her sister had more than one enemy?

That slim hope, if hope it was, was dashed when a knight slapped him on the shoulder and asked, "Will Lord Ashton be joining us today?"

"No. My grandfather is unwell. He won't be coming."

So he *was* Christopher Harrison; there was no doubting it anymore.

Siân forced herself not to despair. All could not be lost. It had been years since Jane had left England. Perhaps he had changed in the meantime? The victor's swagger and the mocking smile didn't have to mean anything. She sometimes swaggered, as she imagined everybody did, and her own smile, with its regrettable crooked tooth at the front, might well appear mocking at times. Yes, perhaps.

The boy—*man*—Christopher—threw Jane an appraising glance. "Still as neat as ever, I see. That dress doesn't have a single crease on it, and your hair is perfectly pinned in place."

More dismayed than ever, Siân ran a hand over her gown. It was creased, and earlier that afternoon, she had noticed a stain on the bodice, just above the waist. As to her hair, it was most certainly not pinned in place, perfectly or otherwise. It was far too untameable, so she usually let it loose. Because of that and her unfortunate clumsiness, she looked as wild as her sister looked neat. The contrast between the two of them had always been stark. It usually didn't bother her, but she could have done without looking so ruffled since Christopher seemed to admire neatness in a woman. Surely, he would not want a wife who could not keep her clothes clean and her hair securely contained?

But when he spoke again, she understood that, far from praising Jane, he was only mocking her, just like he had done when she lived in England. The weight crushing her chest became near unbearable.

"Do you ever do anything that might land you in trouble?" he asked, eyeing her sister up and down.

"Of course not. No need to ask if *you* do that."

His smile widened, going from mocking to dangerous. Siân

wasn't sure it was an improvement. "No need. I think you have already guessed the answer."

"Indeed."

He crossed his arms over his chest and tilted his head. He really was quite manly for his age. Having learned who he was, she knew him to be four years older than she was. Which was to say, almost sixteen. She also knew he was the last person she should have taken a fancy to.

Except it was not a fancy. On the contrary, it was deadly serious.

The two of them were supposed to marry.

She knew it not only because he had appeared in front of her mere moments after she had understood she needed a husband if she was to have children but also because, upon returning to Castell Esgyrn, she had asked old Myfanwy at the village if she could see what type of man fate had in store for her. The woman was renowned for her powers of divination, and she had told Siân she was destined to marry a man with two identities. The prediction had made no sense at first, but then Siân had understood that it had to refer to Christopher's two different-colored eyes, each presumably betraying a different aspect of his personality. It did make sense. Hadn't she often heard her mother remark that her husband's green eyes appeared to change color depending on his mood?

No, unfortunately, she knew she was supposed to marry Christopher Harrison, and nothing anyone did or said, him included, would make a difference. Fate knew what she was doing.

"Do you know," he said when the silence between them was in danger of becoming awkward, "someone told me the other day you lived in a place called Bones Castle now. Is that true?"

"It's called Castell Esgyrn, actually."

"Yes, but unlike you, I don't speak Welsh, do I?" He waved the comment away. "I assume it means Bones Castle?"

"It does."

"Well, then." A scoff. "I cannot get the image out of my head of Perfect Little Jane Hunter lying in her bed at night surrounded by pile after pile of cracked old skulls and dusty skeletons waiting to topple on top of her. How many people the savages had to kill to be able to build a castle out of their carcasses is anyone's guess."

"The castle is not actually made of bones," Siân couldn't help but retort, piqued. "It is made of stone." That was her home he was talking about. She could not let him disparage it thus. He sounded as if he imagined walls constructed of long white bones and doorframes adorned with hollow-eyed skulls. It was a terrifying image.

Christopher turned to her and looked at her for the first time since she had decided they would marry and arched a brow. It was the one over the blue eye, and she found herself shivering. Dear, oh, dear. At that moment, she felt like a child about to be scolded.

"Normal castles are made of stones, I will grant you, but one can never know what these Welsh people are capable of."

Siân's heart fell to the bottom of her stomach. His first-ever words to her, and they were to tell her he despised her people. He had called them savages earlier, but she had hoped it was just a way of adding to the image of the castle he was creating. It was not.

How could their first meeting be so disastrous? What had she done to deserve that? Why did the man she was destined to marry have to be the one her sister hated because of his high-handedness and cruel taunts toward her? Having met him, she could see that Jane hadn't been lying or even exaggerating. He was … She hesitated, knowing a woman was not supposed to think such a thing of her husband but still unable to repress the thought.

He was horrible.

"Do you know many Welsh people, then, to know what they are capable of?" Jane replied, taking her defense the way she always did in front of people making scathing remarks about her countrymen.

Because Siân spoke English without any accent, people didn't immediately identify her as Welsh or hesitate to voice their worst prejudices out loud in her presence. She had not imagined she would hear such insults out of her future husband's mouth, however. In just a few moments, Christopher Harrison had been exposed as her sister's tormentor, a braggart, and hostile to the Welsh, believing them capable of building castles out of the bones of their enemies' corpses. He'd barely spared her a glance because of her age and shown himself to be imbued with his self-importance, mean-spirited, and proud of it.

It was an inauspicious beginning, to say the least, and she wondered whether she had better set her sights on someone else. He was not like Uncle Matthew at all. Surely, a man like that would not make a good husband or supportive father?

But ... Old Myfanwy had never once been proved wrong. However odd her predictions might have sounded, they always ended up being surprisingly accurate. A few years ago, she had told them that Bethan, Gwenllian's best friend, would soon transform into a chicken. It had sounded so ludicrous that everyone had dismissed the prediction as mad ramblings. But the following week, the little girl had fallen headfirst into the vat where the cook of Castell Esgyrn collected the soft feathers from all the fowl she plucked to make a blanket for her daughter. When poor Bethan had emerged into the bailey covered in downy feathers, she had looked just like a chicken, as predicted.

So what was Siân to think? *Was* she destined to marry Christopher or not?

Perhaps he would grow up and forget all that nonsense when he became a man, because, black stallion notwithstanding, he had only just turned sixteen.

Yes. That had to be what it was.

"Let me introduce you to my sister Siân," Jane said, sounding very pleased to be able to put him back in his place. "She's Welsh."

Of course, he was not in the least perturbed by the revelation. "Is she now? She looks rather normal, I have to say. Except perhaps for her hair. I've never seen such a wild mane before. At least not on a person."

When he finally walked away, his swagger definitely that of a victor, Siân realized, to her shock, that she was glad to see him go.

Their first meeting had been a disaster.

Chapter Two

Eight years later—England, Spring 1308

Siân skidded to a halt and almost dropped the puppy she was holding. Fortunately, she had become somewhat less clumsy than she'd been as a child, so the poor beast wasn't hurt, but it had been a near miss. In front of her was the last person she had expected to see in the bailey. Christopher Harrison. And today, there was nothing left of the boy in him. His body was unmistakably that of a man; the tight tunic and hose did nothing to hide the fact that he had fully developed. His face had lost all traces of youthful roundness, and the copper-colored stallion next to him was even more enormous than the black beast he'd ridden eight years earlier.

He was a knight in all his splendor.

What was he doing here? Couldn't he have chosen to come at a better moment, when she was wearing a more elaborate dress and carrying something other than a filthy pup in need of a bath?

Oh well, at least he was here. She had been racking her brain to find a way to contrive a meeting with her future husband since she'd arrived from Wales two days earlier.

Because she was now nineteen and it was high time she started putting her plan to execution.

She released the puppy, who scuttled away as quickly as his legs could carry him. It was as if he'd known she'd been on her way to the tub of water.

"Lord Ashton," she whispered, dropping a quick curtsy.

Having heard through Uncle Matthew that both his grand-father and father were dead, she knew she could call him by his new title.

The greeting seemed to surprise him. "I'm afraid you have the advantage over me, my lady. You seem to know me, but I have no idea who you might be."

It was a good thing she had released the puppy because this time, she might well have dropped the animal.

How can you not know me? We've already met three times, she wanted to scream. *Once at Iorwerth's christening, where we admittedly didn't exchange a single word, and then at Christmas the next year when cousin Rhian was born, when you told me I looked rather normal for someone who lived in a house made of bones and had the wild mane of a beast.*

The third time, when the family had come to Sheridan Manor to meet their third cousin, Eirlys, Christopher had told her she was rather small for her age. Since then, she had not seen him once.

Siân would have liked nothing more than the opportunity to rectify her first disastrous impression of Christopher Harrison. He could not be that scathing, insufferable man. There had to be a reason for his loathsome attitude.

Well, here it was, the long-awaited chance to make him redeem himself in her eyes.

Except ... the first thing he had told her was that he had no recollection of ever having seen her. It was hardly encouraging.

But why was she even surprised? He was certainly not the

first person to overlook her. She had always been the shy sister, the one who stayed in the background while the more self-assured Jane led any conversations. People tended to address her only when they had something specific to ask her or no better option. It was even more the case here in England. As soon as they were told that she was Welsh, English people tended to consider her a simpleton barely worth the effort of talking to even if they could hear that she spoke their language as well as they did.

Usually, she didn't mind, as it suited her temperament to be hidden. But not with Christopher Harrison, the man she had thought about for years, the man she was hoping to marry one day.

"I'm Siân, Jane Hunter's sister," she said, knowing that the name, at least, would mean something to him. He would not have forgotten the girl he'd so dearly loved to rile once.

"You are?" The incredulity in his voice matched the disbelief in his eyes.

"Well, stepsister really. We were raised together from a young age, you see—seven or so—but we don't have the same mother or father. My father, Gwyn, died when I was six years old. I hardly remember him at all. Lord Sheridan is the man I consider my real father, and Jane and my mother created a bond the moment they met. We have two sisters now, Gwenllian and little Seren, and a brother. My uncle Matthew always jests that Rhys must be another man's child, as he knows for a fact that Connor Hunter is only capable of fathering girls. It is true that Jane had two—"

Siân stopped her blabbering abruptly. Had she really been about to mention the two sisters Jane had lost before leaving England? Thankfully, she had stopped before she'd revealed such intimate and painful information to a man who could not be trusted with it.

Christopher crossed his arms over his chest in a gesture she remembered, highlighting the fact that he had indeed grown larger since they had last met. From such close proximity, he seemed huge. Then again, it was hardly surprising. He was a man of four and twenty, at the height of his potency. It was becoming urgent that she did something about her intention to marry him. It would not be long before another woman wanted him.

"So you share no blood with Jane?" he asked calmly.

"No." Any fool could have guessed that Jane was taller, more generously endowed. She had black hair that fell to the middle of her back in one sleek sheet and piercing green eyes, like their father. By contrast, Siân was petite and slender, her honey-colored hair fell in a profusion of curls that refused to be tamed, and her blue eyes were too pale to ever be called piercing or anything else.

"I see." He smiled the smile she remembered. The dangerous one. "*Now* it makes sense."

It seemed to Siân that Christopher's blue eye twinkled while the brown one remained cold. Was that even possible? She didn't know. But that was what she thought she'd seen.

"W-what makes sense?"

"If you do not share blood with Jane, I understand why you are so pretty."

"Oh!" Siân recoiled in outrage. "You cannot be serious. My sister is the prettiest—"

"She is no such thing. She might be beautiful, but she is too perfect not to stir people's animosity and too haughty and imposing to ever be called pretty. You, on the other hand, are lovely."

She stilled. Too busy being offended on Jane's behalf, she had not noticed he had called her pretty before. But he had. And now, he was calling her pretty again. What should she make of it? Was he teasing her? Unfortunately, experience told her it was not impossible. Regardless, he *had* called her pretty. To be complimented thus when men usually ignored her was flattering, undeniably, and went some way toward soothing the disappointment of not having been recognized. Hearing Jane being disparaged for being haughty was painful, though, because she was nothing like that.

"Yes. I am so pretty, apparently, that you've no recollection of having spoken to me," she couldn't help but mock. "Both times."

Christopher was suitably confused by the sally. "When did we speak, pray tell?"

"Once eight years ago and a second time two years later."

Far from being chastened, he let out a bark of a laugh. "Why, you would have been a child then. That is why I cannot recall our encounters. I am not in the habit of lusting after infants, you know."

Lusting? He'd called her pretty, which was an acceptable compliment, but then he had said he was lusting after her, which anyone would agree was much more scandalous. Though lust was not the emotion she'd hoped to provoke within him, she couldn't help a surge of ... she was not sure what it was, but she knew exactly where it was located.

Between her thighs.

"I was hardly an infant," she whispered. "I was fourteen the last time."

"A child, then, which is much the same thing." He shrugged. "I only ever take an interest in people I can either fight with or f—"

Instinct had made her raise her hand before he could finish the sentence, and she was mighty glad she'd been able to stop him before he could utter the word. He took an interest in only the men with whom he wanted to pick a fight and the women he sought to lure into his bed, and she fit in neither category.

"What are you doing here anyway?" She had to regain control of the conversation, and fast. Nothing in her somewhat sheltered life in the Welsh hills had prepared her to face a man like Christopher Harrison. "I see no reason for you to be at Sheridan Manor today of all days."

For good measure, she looked around. Today was no one's christening. There were no Christmas festivities to explain the presence of a guest in the castle, and she knew the members of her family didn't hold him in much esteem. It was doubtful they would have invited him.

The smile Christopher gave her was carnality itself. He leaned in to whisper in her ear, something that required him to lower his head by at least a foot. "You wouldn't see the reason for my presence here, as Elsie is currently lying on a bale of hay in the stables, recovering from my ... attentions, shall we say."

That was such a shocking thing to tell a woman that Siân stared at him for a long moment. Had she heard him right? Were the "attentions" he'd just mentioned what she thought they were? Had he just told her he'd been to the stables to—

There was no avoiding it. Her first impression of him, formed the day he had gone out of his way to mock her sister and disparaged Welsh people, had been the correct one. It had not been an unfortunate misunderstanding, and he had not, contrary to what she'd hoped, grown wiser in the interim. He was a rogue, through and through, and that was all there was to it.

Her heart broke at the same time as her temper exploded.

"You, my lord, are positively ghastly! I'm sure with such abhorrent behavior, you can goad plenty of people into fighting with you. As to your other urges, it is a marvel you can find any woman willing to indulge them."

A stunned silence followed the declaration. Then Christopher barked another laugh. "'Positively ghastly.' I'll be sure to remember it. Of all the things people have called me over the years, this has to be my favorite. You see, usually, people try to mitigate their outrage; they do not dare tell me what they really think, so they always end up making rather bland observations that fail to pierce my thick hide." There was another laugh, this time more like a chuckle, a rather unexpected sound coming from a man so virile. "But you did me the honor of not sparing my sensibilities."

"That may be because I assumed you had none."

"Ah. Very wise. Another mistake other people make is assuming that I will take offense if they tell me what they think. I never do for I care not what they think as long as they don't ignore me."

To Siân's intense surprise, he took her hand and placed a kiss on her fingers. She should have pulled away, but she couldn't. It was the first time they had touched, and all she could think was that she didn't want it to be the last.

For ten years, she had waited for that moment, and now that it had finally come, she could do nothing but enjoy it. Then she stiffened, remembering what he had just told her about tumbling another woman in the hay. She could not let him believe he could unsettle her and get away with it.

She had to retaliate.

"Oh, and just so you know, my lord, we Welsh do not live in houses made of bones."

The look of bewilderment on his face was ample reward for her efforts. "Bones?"

"Bones." Let him mull over what she meant. If he didn't remember their previous encounters, he had only himself to blame. And it would do him good to be the one unsettled for once. It was not hard to guess that it didn't happen to him often.

But, as could have been predicted, he recovered quickly enough. "If you'll excuse me, my lady, I have some pressing arrangements."

"Another tryst, perchance?"

His throaty laugh made her shiver. So masculine ... "No, I don't think I will bed another woman until at least tonight. A man has to get things done, you know."

Siân watched the copper horse thunder away. Jane had been right all along. Christopher Harrison was an insufferable rogue, debauched, provoking, and arrogant. But even worse, none of that was enough to change her mind.

In spite of it all, she still thought she would have none other as her husband.

Christopher brought another cube of cheese to his mouth and chewed it without noticing the taste. The little firebrand who'd caught him red-handed coming from the stables after his encounter with Elsie was Jane Hunter's sister?

This he had not seen coming, because she was everything Connor Hunter's poised, elegant, intimidating daughter was not. In fact, he would have gone as far as calling her unassuming. Had she not walked straight into him, almost dropping the puppy she'd been holding in the process, he would most likely not have noticed her. Which would have been a mistake. Once he'd stopped to look at her, he'd seen that she was not quite like any other woman he had ever seen.

He had not lied to her. Her sister was too perfect to attract him. Jane might be stunning to look at, but there was nothing remotely interesting in that. Perfection offered no challenge.

Siân definitely did. She was different—in many ways. Even her name was unusual. He'd never heard it before. Perhaps because it was Welsh, like her. He'd heard it said often enough that the people from that country were savages, and as a child, he had not questioned it. Why would he have? Adults were supposed to know better. But of late, he had come to wonder. How could all the people populating a vast country be the same or even similar? He was nothing like Sir Robert, Lord Gillingham, or even his father, and yet they were all of them English. What would he think if a Scot told him that, as far as he was concerned, all his countrymen were as pig-headed as his neighbor, as entitled as the king, or as idiotic as the knight he'd met the previous day? He would be appalled.

It followed that not all Welsh people should be dismissed as savages without appeal. Siân certainly should not. She had drawn him in in a way few people had.

Perhaps because of his mismatched eyes, Christopher had always disliked physically perfect people, feeling at a disadvantage in front of them. Used to being stared at and even mocked, he instinctively sympathized with people who he imagined had experienced the same thing.

It was not hard to guess that little Siân was always compared unfavorably to her perfect sister. Her hair had a life of its own, and one of her teeth was decidedly crooked. Her manners were bold, her gaze frank. One did not think "beautiful" when one saw her but rather "endearing." One was not awed but intrigued. She was approachable, clumsy, unpredictable—everything her sister was not. You never knew what would come out of her mouth.

Her scathing assessment of his character was a good example. Not many people would have dared tell him to his face that he was not only ghastly but also positively so or that he would find it hard to seduce women. Then there had been her comment about not living in a house made of bones. That had to be the most puzzling statement he'd ever heard. As if all that was not enough, she had then asked him whether he was going to meet another woman that afternoon.

Not a man easily taken by surprise, Christopher had been piqued. A discussion with her would be sure to stimulate, and stimulation was something his life sorely lacked. No one ever challenged him, few people managed to raise his interest, and only a handful remained in his mind once he'd left their company.

He finished his cheese with decision. Today had brought a pleasant surprise, one he might explore further.

And so the next time he went back to Sheridan Manor, it was not to see Elsie or Bess but to see whether he could further his acquaintance with little Siân. He had gotten everything he was ever going to get out of the two maids. They were too fawning by far, giggling at his jests, asking questions he had already answered a dozen times, pretending not to notice that his eyes were of different colors.

Siân, by contrast, had stared at them in fascination, her own eyes darting from one side to the other as if she couldn't believe what she was seeing. As if she *liked* what she was seeing. No one had ever made him feel as if the defect could be something to be appreciated. They usually behaved as if his eyes were unremarkable, thinking he would prefer it that way.

He did not, he liked to be seen for what he was.

He rode through the gate one morning, and instead of sneaking to the kitchen like a thief, as he was wont to do, he asked for Siân like a regular, honorable visitor. But James Mortimer, the dour steward, informed him she'd gone back to Wales the day before.

Christopher left without even dismounting.

Chapter Three

A year later—England, Spring 1309

"Lord Ashton."

Siân blinked. Had she somehow been transported back through time? Last year, the day following her arrival at Sheridan Manor, she had almost walked into Christopher as he was exiting the stables. And here he was today, in the exact same place. The similarities between the two encounters were too extraordinary to be believed.

There was a crucial difference, however. This time, Christopher knew who she was. There was no mistaking the glimmer of recognition in his eyes.

"Lady Siân," he said, proving her right. The bow he gave her was elegance itself. "No puppy today?"

"No," she said, her gaze flitting to the stables behind him. She had not forgotten the reason for his visit to Sheridan Manor the previous year. In fact, she had thought about little else, wishing *she* had been the woman he'd lavished his attentions on. "Let me guess. You've come for another romp in the hay?"

He laughed as if she had said the most amusing thing. Or perhaps he was shocked she had dared suggest he had just left a woman's arms. And why not? Admittedly, she shouldn't have been so bold, but in his presence, she couldn't think straight.

"No. Someone is going to get his pleasure in the stables today, but it won't be me."

Siân blinked some more. What on earth did that mean? Did she want to know? She wasn't sure. Her conversations with Christopher always seemed to end badly. One about pleasure, even if it wasn't his own, was sure to end in disaster.

"The groom at Sheridan Manor has been asking me for months to bring my stallion to service your aunt's mare," he offered when he saw she was at a loss. "And yesterday, I finally relented."

"Angel, you mean?" She stared at the enormous animal standing behind Christopher. Muscles rippled under a sleek chestnut coat, betraying immense strength. He was magnificent, if in a slightly daunting sort of way, not unlike his master. "But ... she's the sweetest, gentlest mare you could imagine. He's going to destroy her!"

Another laugh. Why was he so amused? Other people often mocked her for her artless comments, but he seemed to enjoy hearing them.

"Worry not, my lady. Warrior knows what he's doing. It is not the first time he's been asked to perform, and it's in his nature to service the mares brought to him without damaging them. You cannot blame him for his powerful physique; it's the way he was born. As to Angel"—he made it sound as if the name was too sweet by far for any horse—"she will be just fine. It will do her good to finally be acquainted with one of the great pleasures of life."

Siân could not help but snort. "I doubt the act is as pleasurable for horses as it is for humans. Surely, it is far too quick and perfunctory to give them much satisfaction. It is, as you say, merely a call of nature."

"You really do say the most surprising things, my lady." Christopher leaned in, a dangerous flame lurking in his eyes. "You know about the pleasure that can be had in a man's arms, then? I thought ladies were raised thinking only duty and boredom awaited them in their marital bed."

She flushed. With a mother and father who plainly loved and desired one another, such a conclusion was impossible. She and Jane knew how fulfilling marriage could be for both parties, and they had long before decided that they would marry husbands who not only knew how to give a woman pleasure but also wanted to. Too many men tried to please only their mistresses, relegating the wives who'd been chosen for them to the role of breeder, saving their efforts for the women who fired their blood rather than raised their children.

A man as virile as Christopher had to know how to pleasure women, and without quite knowing why, Siân sensed he would be generous enough to want to do it. The previous year, he had hinted at the fact that Elsie needed time to recover from the attentions he had lavished on her. That seemed to suggest he had pleasured her into a puddle rather than merely used her for his own release.

All she had to do now was make him see that he wanted to make *her* benefit from his skill. Her and only her for the rest of their lives. An ambitious plan, to say the least.

"Of course Jane and I know that there is more to the act than mere procreation," she said, refusing to be daunted.

The twinkle in Christopher's eyes became an inferno. "I see. Lord and Lady Sheridan like to keep their daughters aware of the realities of life. What have they told you?"

"It's not so much what they say but what they do. It is clear that they are well matched in every sense of the word. And it is not just them. My aunt Branwen has such a marriage, as does her mother, Carys."

"Would you care to give me some example of what 'such a marriage' consists of? I'll confess to being curious to the extent of your knowledge, Little Lamb."

Oh, dear. She had been right. She should never have gotten involved in a conversation about pleasure with Christopher. If she was a lamb, he was a wolf, ready to pounce.

"I ... I can't ..."

To her relief, he didn't insist. For a moment, she had feared he would force her to reveal all she knew about what men and women did together. She was pleased to discover he had some sense of restraint. It was one of the first encouraging signs she'd seen that he might, after all, be the husband she had hoped to find. Perhaps he *had* grown out of his most scandalous phase.

He took a step back and placed a hand on Warrior's neck. "So we've established that I was here to bring him to get a foal on Angel. What about you, Lady Siân? What brings you to Sheridan Manor? You haven't been to England in almost a year, have you?"

The comment surprised and pleased Siân in equal measure. Had he kept himself abreast of her activities? She hadn't dared hope as much. Another encouraging sign.

"Jane and I accompanied my mother, who came to see my aunt. Father and the children stayed behind, as he had some business to see to. They will join us as soon as they can."

As she spoke, her gaze followed Christopher's hand, which was still stroking Warrior. The signet ring on his middle finger reminded her there was something she had always wanted to tell him.

"You know, I was surprised when I found out the heraldic animal on the coat of arms of Lord Ashton is a fish. It doesn't suit you at all."

His arched brow showed his delight at the comment. "Doesn't it? Pray tell, what would suit me in your opinion?"

She wasn't sure. Not a fish, for certain, though. Too slimy, wet, and limp by far. He needed something powerful and majestic. "I couldn't presume to say. I don't know you."

"That is true. Shall I tell you something about me to try and remedy the problem?"

Yes. Anything. Everything.

She forced herself to shrug to hide her desperation. "If you wish, my lord."

Christopher had no idea why that might be, but he was suddenly seized by the desire to tell Siân something deeply personal. Something no one else knew or even suspected. Was it because she constantly took him by surprise? Was it because she didn't know him and didn't seem to have any preconceptions about his character? Or was it because he'd always secretly wanted to admit to the truth out loud? Perhaps. He felt as if it would allow him to shed some of the burden he was carrying. He might feel better for it. At least, he would not feel worse.

"It's odd that you should mention the fish because I always thought the animal suited my father perfectly. Cold. Slippery. Utterly alien to me."

The man had belonged to another world. Almost literally. The two of them had not mixed in the same circles or even lived together. The late Lord Ashton had sent him and his mother away from his seat in Kent to live at Throckmorton, a castle that had already been a near ruin twenty years ago. Over the following sixteen years, his father had visited him merely a handful of times. Every time he'd come, he'd been more prone to criticizing his son than anything else. It had been a lonely existence because his mother had been no help. The poor woman had died a year after they'd arrived, and, as a boy of five, Christopher had been left with his grandfather, a bitter old man who'd resented having been saddled with his grandson. Indeed, the Lords Ashton had been cold fishes from father to son.

Which was why he had been so gratified to hear Siân tell him that she thought the symbol didn't suit him.

It was the best compliment anyone had ever paid him.

"You didn't get on with him, then?"

He smiled at Siân's deliberate understatement. "No. I can't say that I did. And my grandfather, who raised me, was no better." It had been a relief to see both men die and know he was finally able to live his life. Another disloyal, forbidden thought he berated himself for. People were not supposed to be relieved when their parents died.

"What about your mother?"

Her determination to find a sliver of joy in his life was endearing. Christopher would have liked nothing more than to tell her his mother's love had compensated for the two men's indifference. Unfortunately, that wasn't the case.

"She died when I was five. I barely remember her, but I do know she never loved my father, who had been forced to marry her when she swelled with his child, or me, who reminded her of the man who'd treated her so callously. Apparently, I am his spitting image even if his eyes were both brown." One final confession slipped past Christopher's lips before he could stop it. "As a child, I swore to myself that one day, I would have a big family so I would never be alone."

He shrugged. Since then, of course, he'd grown up and seen that it was not that easy. Having a family required finding a wife. And having just found his freedom as Lord Ashton, he was not ready to settle down, much less with a woman who could easily be swapped with another. He needed someone special who would make him feel special; after being neglected all his life, he would not settle for less.

"This is ... horrible."

Siân's eyes had gone as shiny as stars. Was she about to cry? Inexplicably, it tugged at his heart. The woman was nothing to him, and he was nothing to her; she should not have cared about events in his past. But she did more than care—she felt for him. And what was even more remarkable, it didn't feel like pity.

His interest in her increased another notch. Genuine compassion was rare and not a sentiment he was used to stirring in people.

"Don't fret. I'm a grown man now. I don't need anyone to look after me."

"Grown or not, no man deserves to be alone."

No, perhaps not, but it was not a question of what people deserved. Life was unfair; Christopher knew that.

"My lord!" Alfred the groom's voice called out from behind him. "There you are. Angel is ready, but we kept her at the back so as not to get that great beast of yours in a state too early. Shall we?"

Christopher nodded and handed Alfred the stallion's reins so he could start removing his saddle. Then he turned back to face Siân.

"If you'll excuse me, my lady. I need to ensure your uncle's people know what they're doing. I will not have my Warrior damaged in any way." The whole business could be dangerous for horses and humans alike. The stallion could be too rough, and the mare could kick. He would not have anything happen to his favorite mount, not when he had done such a splendid job of breaking him.

"Of course."

Siân expected Christopher to bow and take his leave, but instead, he leaned in so close that she felt his hair brush against her cheek. A clean, spicy scent filled her senses, overwhelming her. It was the first time she'd been able to enjoy her future husband's scent, and it was mouthwatering.

"Would you care to come with me and watch?" He paused, bringing his body even closer. Mercifully, they were hidden from Alfred by Warrior's bulk, because the distance between them was too small to be decent. "I wouldn't extend the invitation to all the women of my acquaintance, of course, but an unconventional, fearless, knowledgeable lady like you might find the spectacle of interest."

Siân knew she would indeed find it of interest, but she was surprised Christopher was giving her the option of coming. Not many men would agree it was fitting for a lady to see such a thing. His unexpected offer was the third encouraging sign she had seen that day. It was more than she could have hoped for, and she knew she should leave before she ruined the day's efforts with a naïve, ill-timed comment. The mating could be a daunting affair, and the last thing she wanted was to make a fool of herself.

"No, thank you. I will leave you to it."

"As you wish."

Before she could surrender to temptation, she hurried toward the solar, where she hoped to find her mother and aunt. In the women's company, away from Christopher's maddening scent and dazzling eyes, she might find the peace of mind necessary to ponder on what he had just told her.

He was not a shameless rogue but a lonely man looking for the family he had never had. Which meant that, against all odds, she was exactly the woman he needed.

It was the best news she could have heard.

"*Cariad.* Just in time. Would you help us sort out these threads?" Esyllt sighed. "The dogs upturned the embroidery basket while playing earlier, and, as you can see, we were too late to stop them from making the most of this opportunity for mischief."

"Indeed."

A litter of pups had been born to Rhwd, the late wolfhound's granddaughter, a few weeks back, and the bunch were the rowdiest yet. The stone floor was scattered with a rainbow of scarlet, azure, saffron, and emerald strands. It would have been beautiful if it didn't mean hours of work to tidy them all up. Fortunately, the warmer weather meant that the rushes had been removed from the stone floor.

The rest of the afternoon was spent repairing the damage wreaked by the pups. Siân rolled and tidied colored threads like the other two women. Inwardly, though, she was doing all she could to resist the urge to go see Warrior doing to Angel what she dreamed Christopher would do to her. Heat invaded her cheeks and then crept down her neck and her chest before settling between her thighs. When her worried aunt asked whether she was all right, she nodded and did her best to revert to more proper musings.

Like trying to identify the spice she'd smelled on Christopher earlier. Clove? No. Too strong. Cinnamon? Too sweet. Pepper? Too common. Then what? There was only one way to come up with the answer. Get near him again. She swore that this time, she wouldn't leave Sheridan Manor without having made significant progress in her seduction of her future husband. She was twenty. It was more than time.

When she finally left the room, the sun had started its descent toward the horizon.

How was Angel faring? Siân couldn't help but wonder. Had everything gone according to plan? Intent on asking Alfred if the mare had been hurt, she walked over to the stables.

The groom was patting the mare's rump affectionately and talking to young William, who'd recently become Uncle Matthew's squire, and Robert, the other groom, a man Siân had always found unsettling.

"You should have seen her. She's a natural!" Alfred sounded delighted. "I've been asking Lord Ashton to bring Warrior to service one of our mares for years, and I think I chose the right one for him. As soon as she caught sight of the mighty beast, she started to swish her tail and arch her back. By the time we brought the stud to her, she was fair panting with anticipation."

"Aye, and it being her first time as well. If only virgins of the human variety were equally desperate to be fucked! It would make our lives infinitely better, don't you think?" Siân's lips curled at Robert's comment. Was it any wonder she disliked the man when he could be so crude? "Mind you, some women are just as hot for cock as the mare was. It's not just his stallion that has this effect. Lord Bloody Ashton only has to appear, and they will spread their legs, no questions asked. Lucky bastard."

He sounded so put out that Siân was certain Christopher had bedded a maid the man was lusting after. Elsie perhaps? Or ... had he bedded all the maids at Sheridan Manor? Her heart sank, as it did every time she was reminded of his wayward reputation.

"Don't tell me you're surprised women would rather open their legs for someone like him than they would for you?" Alfred scoffed. "It's not just the way he looks, you know. It's his manners—and his title. Women will always flock to men like him. It is the way of the world. Men like us just cannot compete."

"Ah well, we should have a beautiful foal in the new year. That is all that matters," William said, ever the peacemaker.

Cheeks aflame, Siân retreated to the shadows. She could not go to the groom after what she'd heard. And all the encouraging signs she'd received that afternoon were suddenly forgotten in view of the reminder that Christopher was a rogue taking his pleasure with all the women who let him, which was to say—if Robert was to be believed—all the ones who crossed paths with him. The intimate moment they had shared earlier meant nothing. A sympathetic ear and the ability to surprise him were not what he was looking for in a woman.

When she had met him at the age of nine, she had not taken that into consideration. With the innocence of childhood, she had assumed he would fall in love with her at first sight and decide to make her his wife. But as a grown man, he was making the most of the appeal he exerted over women. Before he settled down, he would sow his wild oats and not bother about her.

It was the way of the world, as Alfred had said.

How was she going to attract him in those conditions? How could she, a naïve, inexperienced girl, convince him that a man could be happy with only one woman in his bed? Marriage was probably the last thing on his mind at the moment. He was only five and twenty. Her uncle had not gotten married until the age of thirty, when he had met the right woman. Was Siân ready to wait for so long when she wasn't even sure how—or if—she could entice him?

She suddenly wasn't sure.

"Ah, my lady. Were you looking for me?"

Siân started. Lost to her musings, she hadn't heard Alfred's approach. "I ..."

"Did you want a horse saddled?"

That was not why she had come, but she seized on the ready explanation for her presence by the stables. "Erm, yes. Perhaps Angel?"

"Oh, aye, I can get her ready for you. I know you're a bit reckless in the saddle, but she will not be opposed to a hard ride, I don't think," the groom said, rubbing the back of his neck. "It seems to be what she likes best."

Had she not overheard his conversation with the other two men, she might not have made anything of the observation. As she had overheard it, she could not help but flush. He was alluding to what had happened earlier with Warrior when the mare had let herself be ridden in a different kind of way.

"On second thoughts, I think I will wait until the morning. It's getting quite late already."

That had never stopped her before, but after the day she'd had, she didn't quite feel herself. Under the circumstances, it was probably safer not to go out alone in the dark atop a horse she had never ridden before.

Alfred bowed. "As you wish."

~

"Lord Ashton."

Christopher smiled at Siân's obvious surprise. This time, she had not almost run into him, this time *he* was the one who had gone to her.

"What brings you here today?"

"You," Christopher answered. "Today, I came to see you."

He didn't know who, Siân or himself, was the most shocked by that announcement. When he had left Throckmorton earlier that day, he'd had no intention of coming to Sheridan Manor. And yet, as soon as he'd trotted through the gate, he'd turned east, as if that were the normal thing to do. A moment later, he had reached the bottom of the hill in time to see Siân walk over the drawbridge, a basket in hand. The temptation to follow her had been so overwhelming he had not tried to resist it.

Their meeting would best be kept a secret, so it was just as well she'd left the castle.

"You came to see me? Not Elsie?" she asked with the boldness he had come to expect of her.

"No. I haven't, er, met with her, shall we say, for a year or so."

Not since that day Siân had found him sneaking out of the stables, he meant. For a reason he could not explain, the maid had lost all her appeal that day. Suddenly, he had found her tall frame unattractive, her generous bosom vulgar, her brash manners grating. And now he was ill at ease talking about his conquests in front of Siân. What had possessed him to brag about his tumble in the hay the year before? That offhand attitude was so ingrained in him it had not crossed his mind to act any differently, but for the first time in his life, he wished he didn't feel the constant need to shock people. It would no doubt make him appear crude to her, and, now that he knew her better, he didn't want that. Her opinion mattered to him.

He jumped down from Warrior and planted himself in front of her.

Siân's gaze darted from him to his stallion and back again. Was she imagining what the horse had done with Angel the other day? Was she wondering if a man could mount a woman in the same manner? Was she about to ask him whether it was possible? He wouldn't put it past her. She always came up with the most surprising comments and puzzling questions. That was what made her irresistible.

Yes ... And also why he had come, he suddenly realized. To hear more of her surprising comments and puzzling questions.

"Ask me the first question that comes to your mind," he challenged, unable to wait another moment to hear what would come out of her mouth.

She didn't even blink when the other people he knew would have stared at him before declaring they had no idea what to ask him.

"If you could choose between having two blue eyes or two brown eyes, which would you prefer?"

Perfect. Her choice was even better than what he had hoped for. His whole body surged, which was to be expected, and his heart fluttered, which was more of a surprise.

He crossed his arms over his chest before answering. "As I am not the one having to look at them, I care not. Their appearance doesn't affect me. In case you weren't aware of it, I cannot *feel* any difference. I only know I have different-colored eyes because people have told me as much." Or rather, people had mocked him because of it, taken fright because of it, asked him whether he was the spawn of the devil because of it, not dared to look him in the eye because of it ... The list was endless. Only Siân had shown genuine interest in them, and that made him feel as if they added to the appeal he exerted over her. "But *you* can see them. So tell me. What would you choose in my stead?"

"I would keep them exactly the way they are." There was no hesitation.

"Oh?" He wanted to hear more and was not going to let her get away with such a simple explanation.

"Yes. And the way you only ever arch a brow over the blue eye is just perfect."

Did he? That was interesting. What else would Siân tell him about himself? She smiled, as if he'd tried to prove her point. He hadn't. Up until that moment, he'd had no idea he could arch only his left brow.

"It suits him," she said, looking endearingly coy. "The brown one is more serious. He would never do anything so whimsical."

He?

His lips quivered. Had the little Welsh lady just gifted him with another little nugget of delight? "Tell me you haven't ..." He could scarcely credit what he was about to ask, but he forged onward. He knew the reward could be immense. "You haven't given my eyes names, have you?"

The face she made was enough to tell him that, yes, she had and she was mortified to have unintentionally revealed as much.

Something like a chuckle—a most disconcerting sound— escaped his chest. Christopher never chuckled. But how could he have helped it? The woman was wonderful. What had he done to deserve to get to know someone like her, who not only constantly took him by surprise but also accepted and liked him the way he was?

"Let me guess. You've named them Sky and Earth? Blue and brown, it would make sense."

She twisted her lips in consideration. "That's not bad, you know." Her eyes flicked to the horse standing behind him. "Did you choose your stallion's name? Warrior is such a great choice for him. Not everyone has a gift for choosing names."

"And you think I do?" That was possibly the oddest, most charming compliment he had ever received.

"I think you do."

"What else can you add to the list of qualities I possess?" Never had he been more curious to hear someone's opinion. The people in his family had never had anything positive to say about him, and his conquests only ever praised his looks or stamina, as if his body were the only thing of interest about him, while his male friends would not even think of discussing such matters. Few people were as open as Lady Siân Hunter, or as imaginative, and he found he was starving for heartfelt compliments.

"Who's to say you have other qualities?" she teased.

"You. It seems to me you are the only person who's ever tried to find what is hidden inside me instead of accepting the image you are presented." He'd not forgotten how she had told him he was nothing like a cold fish, or in other words, his father. "It's as if you were determined not to think ill of me."

Judging from the way her eyes widened, this time, it seemed *he* was the one who'd surprised her.

"Perhaps I am," she whispered. "Perhaps I want to hope there is more to you than the disreputable rogue."

"Why?"

"Do I need a reason? Don't I deserve to see the real you

instead of the 'image I am presented,' as you said? Doesn't everyone?"

That was the question. Once again, she had gone straight to the heart of the matter.

All his life, Christopher had felt undesired, unworthy of attention. His father had sent him away before the two of them had been able to forge any sort of bond, his mother had never shown him any interest, and his grandfather had never praised him or even taken him into consideration. He'd had to fight for every scrap of attention he'd gotten. He'd become the roguish seducer, the confident knight, the outrageous friend because he'd felt there was no other choice. Without that, he feared he didn't have what it took to attract people.

What if the real me is not enough? he wanted to ask Siân. *What if people don't want to accept who I am deep down, prefer-ring the character I have built to the man I am?* Who *was* he? After so long trying to make himself more likable, more notice-able, more shocking, he wasn't even sure he knew anymore.

In the end, he didn't dare say anything. He'd already said more than he should have the last time he'd seen Siân, opening up about his feelings toward his father. It wouldn't do to bare all his insecurities because he still had his pride.

"Listen, I would love to stay and talk about how likable I really am, but I fear that would be a lengthy conversation and I was actually on my way to town. I stopped here only briefly to see if you'd heard about how Angel was faring," he lied. But after their conversation, he needed to leave. A coward, was that what he was, then?

Perhaps.

"Angel?" Siân appeared surprised by the question, and no wonder. Only a moment ago, he'd told her he'd come to see her, and now he was saying he had stopped by only because he'd chanced upon her. "She is fine. By all accounts, all went well the other day. We might have a beautiful foal next year."

"You might, for the service seemed successful."

He would never tell her that he had imagined himself mounting her in that same impetuous manner only the night before as he had lain in bed, idly stroking himself. The thought, having come out of nowhere, had disconcerted him. He rarely fantasized about taking women in that primal, uncompromising manner, much less proper little ladies like Siân Hunter. What in God's name had made his desire toward such an unsuitable woman surge in such a manner?

But surged it had, and the idle caress had soon transformed into a storm of release. What would she make of it if she knew? What did *he* make of it? He didn't know.

"Goodbye then, my lady."

Christopher vaulted on top of Warrior and left the shadow of Sheridan Manor, more confused than ever.

Chapter Four

Siân came to an abrupt halt when she came face-to-face with Christopher outside the chapel door. What was he doing here? It had been only three days since his last visit to Sheridan Manor. Three days during which she had tried to find an excuse to go see him and failed. They barely knew one another. What reason could she come up with for a visit to Throckmorton Castle?

"You again."

The corner of his perfect mouth curled at the same time as his eyebrow—the left, naturally—arched. "Me again. Good afternoon."

There was a silence, during which Christopher allowed his gaze to roam over her. Siân's body grew hot wherever it landed, which was to say everywhere. Even her feet didn't escape his notice. Why was he looking at her with such intensity? Was there something wrong with her appearance ? At Branwen's request, she had just gone to replace the flowers in the vase at the foot of the altar. Had she somehow managed to stain her dress in the process? Ripped one of the sleeves? Gotten the hem wet? Did she have a smudge of dirt on her cheek? Please, Lord, no. The last thing she wanted was to appear slovenly to him.

"You know," Christopher said eventually, "you look like a bride, standing with flowers in your hand in front of the chapel."

Everything within her surged at the words. She didn't want to merely *look* like a bride; she wanted nothing more than to *be* a bride one day.

His bride.

After years spent yearning for their union, she would like nothing better than to be secure in the knowledge that she was his at last. If she looked like a bride, in his dark green tunic, he looked like the most dashing groom she had ever seen. What would he look like naked? What would he feel like?

Soft and hard at the same time, she suspected, like kid leather wrapped over steel. Was he tanned all over? Probably. Muscular? Most definitely. Hairy? If he was, judging from the color of his blond locks, his body would be adorned with hairs as finely spun and as shiny as gold strands. Would it tickle to feel them under her palms when she stroked him? Perhaps. What was certain was that she would want to run her hands over every inch of him until she felt she'd learned him by heart. A giant furry beast of her own to pet, all warm, soft, and comforting—nothing like a fish.

"No bride I know would choose to hold wilted flowers on her wedding day," she breathed, forcing herself not to dwell on how glorious it would be to lie in his arms at last.

"Of course not. Silly me. Shows how much I know about weddings." He said the word with the enthusiasm her seven-year-old sister, Seren, reserved for lessons with her Latin tutor.

"You don't like weddings, then? Why aren't I surprised?"

"Probably because I'm a man and predictable with my opinion."

"Probably. Does that mean you never want to get married?"

Her heart skipped a beat. Her breath caught in her throat. Her body tensed.

Here it was, at last, the question she'd wanted to ask him for months.

Christopher made a vague gesture with his right hand, not at all aware of what was at stake. "Eventually, I will get married, like everyone else. No need to worry about it now, though. I'm only five and twenty."

She was only twenty, and marriage—to him—was all she worried about. But she could not tell him that, not yet, not like that. Instead, she asked what she had wanted to ask since he'd appeared in front of her.

"What happened to your cheek?"

Siân had to bunch her fist around the wilted flower stems to stop herself from reaching out to touch him. There was a slight graze under his left eye, and a bruise was discoloring the skin around it. She had not forgotten what he had told her once.

I only ever take an interest in people I can either fight with or fuck.

Well, she had cut him off before he could actually say the last word, but there had been no mistaking what he'd meant. Was that what had happened? Had he gotten involved in a fight because of a woman he'd bedded? Had the blow been inflicted by a disgruntled husband? Suddenly, she wasn't sure she wanted to know.

"I had no idea it was still showing," he said, placing a tentative finger over the cut. "Is it very obvious?"

The question made something in Siân's chest tighten. What sort of a lonely life did he lead that no one had pointed out to him that his cheek was bruised? Wasn't there anyone at Throckmorton Castle who cared for him?

"It is rather obvious, yes, even if it doesn't look too serious. How did you get injured?"

A smirk. "No doubt you're hoping for a heroic tale, one where I rode to the rescue of a damsel in distress."

"I'm hoping for the truth."

"Of course you are," he mumbled. "How didn't I guess? You're not like anyone else."

"You think that people would rather hear an outrageous tale of heroism from your lips even if they knew it wasn't true?"

"If by 'people' you mean 'women,' then yes. I find they lap it up as eagerly as kittens lap at their mother's milk. I once convinced a pretty little maiden that I had fought a dragon, if you believe it."

She did believe it. The poor girl would have drunk his every word and likely gotten lightheaded with them, like someone overindulging in mead.

"How did you really get injured?" she repeated, fighting a smile. Who would have thought the mighty, forbidding, scandalous Lord Ashton could be so whimsical? "I know it was no dragon. I'm no pretty maiden you can impress so easily."

"Are you not? A maiden, I mean. Because you are certainly pretty."

All the air left her lungs at the compliment. Admittedly, it was not the first time he had called her pretty. But it had been months ago when he hadn't known her and only to highlight the contrast between her and Jane. It had not meant a thing, so she had done her best not to obsess about a passing comment thrown in a conversation meant to unsettle her, knowing he would have only wanted to be his provoking self.

"You still haven't answered my question," she breathed, choosing not to confirm that she was indeed still a maiden. He would have guessed as much already anyway, or so she hoped.

Christopher sighed and leaned a shoulder against the chapel wall. "Very well. It is a woefully uninspiring tale, but you asked for it. Don't come complaining that you would rather have heard about how I fought the dragon, which was, if I recall correctly, covered with copper-colored scales and blowing smoke."

This time, she didn't fight her smile and even gave a giggle. "I won't."

"A visitor arrived from Kent yesterday, a man who insisted on being shown the state of the castle so that he could report to my uncle. Why the man would bother himself with this, I have no idea," he added, almost to himself. "He's not set foot at Throckmorton once in all the years I've been there. Anyway, as we were going down the staircase, the man, who is rather frail and unsteady on his legs, stumbled from behind me, and I ended up going head over heels down the stairs when he fell against my back."

The flowers scattered at her feet in a shower of petals when Siân pressed her hands to her chest.

"*Arglwydd Mawr!*" He could have been killed, had almost been.

Christopher stared at her for a moment, blinked, and then burst out laughing. It was not a sound many people would have heard from his mouth, she suspected, and utterly intoxicating.

"Now, what does that mean, I wonder? 'You silly man' perhaps?"

"No. It only means 'Dear Lord,' I'm afraid."

"Disappointing. But then again, it would have been cruel to mock me when, in reality, I probably saved the old man's life."

She kept staring at his bruised face in dismay. He was making light of it, but she had heard of more than one person breaking their necks on stairs. His fall could have had serious consequences. He might have saved the man, but he could have died.

"Ah, poor little Welsh lamb, are you disturbed by the gruesome sight?"

"Yes." She was. Not in the way he meant, but she was disturbed. Not because it was gruesome but because it made her think of what could have happened.

"Don't worry. I'll live."

He gave a crooked smile, and she had to avert her eyes because every time he smiled that special smile, she wanted to kiss him. The fault did not lie with the impish curl of his lip, though, but with her and her growing feelings for him. She fought a constant battle with her need to kiss him when they were together.

"What are you doing here, then?" she croaked, kneeling to retrieve the flowers she had dropped on the floor. Better to do that than reach out to him.

"The decision to come had nothing to do with me this time," Christopher said, kneeling in turn to help her gather the scattered stems. The spontaneous gesture delighted her. The much-reviled Lord Ashton was not only whimsical but also gallant and helpful. That was unexpected.

Or was it?

The more she saw of him, the more convinced she was that he was not the man everyone thought him and would indeed make a perfect husband for her. He seemed interested in what she had to say, he never made her feel clumsy, and with him, she could fool herself into believing she was as elegant and beautiful as Jane. All she had to do now was convince her family that he could make her happy. The rest of the world didn't matter. They could think what they wanted. She knew the truth.

"What do you mean, you didn't decide to come?" she asked, reaching out to a yarrow stem that had landed by the chapel door.

"Your uncle bade me come. He sent a message to Throckmorton this morning."

"Did he?" Siân's heartbeat picked up. Why did Matthew

want to see him? That didn't bode well. Had he noticed them talking over the last few days? Did he disapprove of the connection? "Do you know what he wants? Did he say in his message?"

Christopher's blinding smile took her breath away. He, at least, was not worried. "I have absolutely no idea. But if you'll excuse me, I'd better not keep him waiting for longer than necessary."

When he handed her the flowers he'd collected for her, their fingers touched. She held her breath and stared into his amazing eyes. Would their children's eyes share their unusual coloring? Would they have a little girl or a little boy first? She cared not, as long as they were—

Stop, Siân chided herself, knowing she was getting ahead of herself as usual. Now was not the time to start thinking of the children they would have once they were married, as they would have to get married first. Which meant she had to make him see he wanted no other wife than her, something she still had no idea how to achieve.

Once all the flowers had been gathered, Christopher stood up with easy grace and held out his hand to her. "My lady. Please allow me."

Arglwydd Mawr, indeed. Had Siân not been in love with Christopher Harrison already, she would have tumbled head over heels there and then.

"You'll never guess who visited Sheridan Manor this afternoon."

Siân focused her attention on the flowers she was preparing to replace the ones in the vase by the chapel altar. It was best to avoid looking at Jane because she already knew who that mysterious visitor had been.

"Who?" she asked, doing her best to sound natural.

"Lord Ashton."

As she'd suspected. Except he'd not come for a visit as much as been summoned by Uncle Matthew for some unknown reason, of course. She cut a cornflower stem and waited, certain Jane was about to tell her what that reason was. It had worried her all afternoon.

"I knew he was an unprincipled rogue, so I guess I shouldn't be surprised, but I can scarcely credit it ..."

Siân selected an oxeye daisy from the pile and narrowly missed cutting her finger when she snipped the stem at the right length. Her patience was starting to wear thin, but she forced herself not to turn around. Jane was pacing the room, unaware of the turmoil agitating her.

"Listen to this, he got Elsie, the maid, with child, and he's now refusing to acknowledge the paternity or offer her his support. Can you believe it?"

"*No.*"

The word was not an answer to Jane's question but a reaction to what she'd heard. Siân placed both hands on the table to stop herself from falling to the floor. It was a good thing she still had her back to Jane because she suspected all the blood had drained from her face.

"Fortunately, Uncle Matthew said he would force him to do the right thing by Elsie and the child, one way or another," her sister carried on, not stopping her prowling for a moment. "She is not due until the end of the year, from what I understand, so I hope he will prevail by then. Lord Ashton's disregard for the woman's predicament is really quite shocking."

The babe was due at the end of the year?

The fog in Siân's mind dissipated in the blink of an eye. It was only spring. If Elsie was no more than two or three months along, then Christopher could not be the babe's father. He had told her himself only the other day that he had not bedded the maid in the last year, which meant that even if she had fallen with child from their encounters, she would have given birth months ago.

The dates just didn't correspond.

Hope surged through her. Perhaps what Jane had called disregard on Christopher's part was nothing like it. Perhaps he didn't want to have anything to do with the babe because he knew he was not the father, could not be.

She shoved the flowers in the vase haphazardly and rushed to the door.

"Where are you going?" Jane called out.

"I need to speak to Uncle Matthew."

And warn him something was not right.

It took her a while to locate him, which only increased her agitation. For a long moment, she erred around the castle, asking everyone she met whether they had seen their master. At long last, James, the steward, told her he'd seen him go to the rose garden with his wife earlier. Even better. Branwen was a woman, and being highly sensible, she might agree with her that something was off. If not, she could at least soothe her husband when the discussion inevitably raised his ire. If anyone could manage an angry Matthew, it was his beloved wife.

Siân walked through the arched gate and into the garden.

"Can I have a word?"

Matthew still looked tense from the confrontation with Christopher, or so she imagined, but he gave her a smile. "Of course."

"Jane told me Lord Ashton came to Sheridan Manor." No point in prevaricating. That was why she was here.

"Yes." Matthew cleared his throat and exchanged a glance with his wife. He was obviously wondering whether to reveal the reason for his visit to her. Once again, she decided to be blunt.

"I know you asked him to come and why. But he cannot be the father of Elsie's babe."

A stunned silence followed the declaration. Then her uncle spoke, his voice gruff. "I'm sorry, but we know he can all too easily be."

Siân bunched her fists because, yes, unfortunately, she knew Christopher had bedded Elsie, probably repeatedly. But not in the last year. Which made it impossible for the maid to be carrying his child now. She stood her ground. "Ask her for more details and how she can be sure it's him."

"Are you suggesting she has other lovers?" Branwen asked when Matthew stared at her in incredulity.

Siân shrugged. Was that so hard to believe? The maid wouldn't be the first woman to indulge in such affairs, and why would she not? She was widowed, and her life was her own. "I just feel that something is not right."

"How would you know that?"

There, she hesitated. As far as everyone was concerned, she barely knew Christopher. How could she explain that she knew things about him no one else knew? The other day, he'd told her he'd not "met," to use his own word, Elsie in a year. He would have had no reason to volunteer the information if it wasn't the truth. At the time, he had not known he would be accused of anything. He had not used the declaration to preempt any accusations.

Though their acquaintance was brief, she felt as if she had a good understanding of his character. She'd seen the pain in his eyes when he'd talked about his father and his hopes for a family of his own. That was not something he could or would have wanted to feign. Rather, she suspected he would be horrified to know she had seen the hurt and the yearning. But she had seen it, and considering how alone he was and how unloved he'd been as a child, she was convinced he would never deny a baby he'd fathered.

Something was definitely amiss.

"I just know. We talked the day he came to bring Warrior." And the time before that. And the day he'd come to see her at the bottom of the hill. And earlier today, by the chapel.

She knew him.

"I'm sorry to say that Lord Ashton would not be the first man to shirk his responsibility." Branwen sounded both disapproving and angry. Matthew, who seemed all too relieved to let his wife take the lead in the discussion, had started to pace around the garden in agitation. It was clear the conversation was painful to him, and she regretted having to stir bad memories. But it had to be done.

"I know. But if Elsie were really with child, why would she come to you instead of confronting him about it?"

"Because she did confront him and he refused to listen to her!" was the cutting answer Matthew gave her. "So it is now up to me to sort out this bloody mess."

This sharpness was out of character, but Siân knew why her uncle would be more affected by that story than most people. His mother had been a maid just like Elsie, and for years, he had believed himself abandoned by the unprincipled nobleman who had burdened her with his child. That he had been reunited with his real father later on did not change the facts. Matthew would want to see men forced to face their responsibilities and do the right thing by the women they had bedded and the children resulting from the encounters.

He wanted to right a wrong, and unfortunately, Christopher's reputation made it too easy to believe the worst of him.

"Did he tell you he was not the father?"

"He did. But what else could we expect? Now that he's

taken his pleasure, he only means to wash his hands of the whole affair."

"Did he tell you why he thought he could not be the father?" she insisted.

Matthew waved a hand in a dismissive gesture. "Predictably, he said the dates didn't coincide."

Yes. As she'd thought. "Then why don't you believe him?"

"Because it's too bloody convenient, that's why!" Matthew roared, goaded beyond endurance. "And it's his word against Elsie's. Why should I believe him over her?"

Indeed. He was a rogue—everyone knew that—and he didn't deserve the chance to prove his innocence, whereas Elsie had worked here for years.

Siân bunched her fists. It was getting dark already, but tomorrow, she would ride to Throckmorton Castle. She had to get to the bottom of the situation.

Chapter Five

In the morning, it rained so much that Siân had no choice but to wait and hope the weather would clear in the afternoon. It did, but then there was another unexpected delay. As her horse was being readied for her, her father and younger siblings arrived with their retinue of men-at-arms. Suddenly, there could be no question of leaving.

"Siân!" Seren and Rhys threw themselves into her arms at the same time while Gwenllian hugged Jane and their parents exchanged a passionate kiss.

"I've missed you, my love," she heard her father murmur in her mother's ear.

"It's been little over a week, you know."

"I know. An eternity."

"Yes. An eternity. I've missed you too."

Siân's heart constricted. Growing up with such parents, how could she not aspire to have her own happy marriage someday? Christopher, who had not known love and security as a child, was understandably in no hurry to wed. But she, who had seen how fulfilled a loving union could make a person, could not wait.

"Is everything all right here?" Connor asked, straightening up to look around.

"Yes," Esyllt answered. "Come. You must all be in need of a drink."

The rest of the afternoon was spent in a boisterous reunion. Though they had been apart for only ten days, there seemed to be a number of things the members of the family wanted to tell one another. Looking around the table where more than a dozen people were chattering happily, Siân did her best not to picture Christopher at Throckmorton, staring at an empty hall, a glass of ale in his hand, alone, as always. Did he even have a dog to keep him company? She gave the puppy settled on her lap a rub behind the ears and sighed. It was high time he had the family he craved, the family she wanted to give him.

Shortly after the sweetmeats had been consumed, their father pretexted his fatigue from the travel to retire to his bed early. She and Jane exchanged an amused glance when their mother followed him without a word of apology. Who were they trying to fool? Riding in the company of children would have taxed Connor as much as lacing his shoes did. He was not tired; he simply wanted the warmth of his wife's arms, and who could blame him?

The next morning, shortly after dawn, Siân set off for Throckmorton. Heavy clouds threatened, but she did not let that deter her. She would not be denied a conversation with Christopher a second time.

As she drew close to the castle, she saw a familiar shape in the distance. Christopher on Warrior. He was trotting back home, looking as relaxed as always. For a moment, she enjoyed watching him move as one with his horse, then she waved her arm to signal her presence. As she was wearing white, it didn't take him long to spot her. In the next heartbeat, he launched his mount into a full gallop to reach her.

A moment later, he was by her side.

"Little Lamb. What brings you here?"

Angel was tall for a mare and Warrior had been bred more for strength than height, which meant that, for once, she was able to look Christopher in the eye. It made the encounter more thrilling—and even more daunting.

"I ..."

"Is aught amiss?" Christopher asked when Siân's words dried on her lips. She had gone the color of her cream dress, a most unusual attitude for her, and worry spiked through him. She had never come to see him before, which was no wonder, as they barely knew one another. So why was she here? Was she in trouble? "Please, tell me how I can help."

"I came to say ... Well, I just wanted to say that I believe you. About Elsie. About you n-not being the father of her child, I mean ..." She was stammering dreadfully, something that was quite unusual for her, and from pale a moment ago, her cheeks had gone a bright shade of pink. "Even if no one else believes you, I do. If you say you cannot be the babe's father, then you arc not, and that's all there is to it."

For a long moment, Christopher simply stared at her.

This declaration would have been unexpected had it not come from her. But by now, he knew the little Welsh woman was capable of the most surprising reactions. And ... undeniably, her support was welcome. All the more so because she had every reason to doubt him, as she knew he had bedded the maid last summer. He had told her as much himself. Christopher's insides roiled at the thought. Dear God, had he really boasted to her about having left Elsie to recover from his lovemaking alone in the hay?

Yes, he had, because it had amused him to shock Perfect Little Jane Hunter's sister, who he had assumed to be a proper, naïve, predictable lady. Was it any wonder people thought him the worst kind of rogue when he behaved in that way? No, it was not.

And yet little Siân had come all the way to Throckmorton, presumably behind her family's back, to tell him she did not believe him to be as callous as to abandon a child he had fathered. She could not know he always took care to spill outside his lover's body, and she had no reason to trust his word that he had not bedded the maid in over a year, but, despite all that, she believed him.

Her trust touched him.

"Thank you." To hide the extent of his emotion, he nudged Warrior into a walk. "You believing me means a lot. People are not usually prepared to give me the benefit of the doubt."

It had never been an issue before. He was used to dealing with people's indifference or contempt. He had never, however, been considered an honorable man who had been wronged and could feel hurt as a consequence.

"Is it any wonder people distrust you when you behave the way you do?"

Well, damn him if the little lamb wasn't blunt under all her feminine loveliness. She had dared call him out on his behavior. He was amazed and delighted in equal measure. "No. Perhaps not. But I'll tell you a secret. The 'way I behave,' as you call it, is only an unfortunate consequence of my family's neglect. Had I been raised in a more loving home, I think I would have ended up a very different man."

"How do you mean?"

"I told you that, growing up, no one paid attention to me." She nodded, unusually earnest. He could see that the notion if him being neglected bothered her. "Well, once I was old enough to do something about their indifference, I made sure the people I met noticed me. Being quiet and unassuming is not the way to do it, though there are some notable exceptions."

Would she guess he was talking about her? He wasn't sure, but in her own quiet, unassuming way, the little lamb was the most intriguing person he'd ever met. Admittedly, if what she had told him was true, he had not noticed her the first two times they had spoken, but he'd soon rectified the mistake, so much so that he was starting to wonder if he was not a little bit obsessed with her. What was certain was that he spent more time thinking about her than all his other acquaintances combined.

The frown on her face cleared up, as if she'd just understood something. "And when you saw women were taking an interest in you, you could not resist the temptation of seducing them because you felt you had been seen at last."

She sounded relieved to hear there had been a reason other than lust for his going from conquest to conquest. Christopher could have been his usual shocking self and pointed out that he was like any young man, in need of physical release and keen to get pleasure in women's arms, but she was right. He was not governed only by his urges. What he could not resist was the notion that he'd been seen, been noticed—and wanted.

"I suppose."

"It is lucky you grew up to be so tall and handsome, then. It would have been a lot more difficult to be noticed otherwise."

A smile tugged at his lips. Did she realize what she had just said? Perhaps not. She was just being her usual honest self.

"You think me handsome, Little Lamb?" That was good to know. So far, she had seemed interested in what he had to say, and it had been a welcome change. But he could not deny he liked to hear she was not immune to his charm. Christopher was not such a worthy man that he did not have a penchant for vanity, and he knew he was better-looking than most. It was time she had noticed.

"Of course. I would be mad not to think so." The flush on her cheeks was highly becoming.

"Oh, you're anything but mad. We both know that."

With those words, he jumped down from the saddle and went to her. To his delight, Siân obeyed his silent command to lean into him so he could lift her off her horse. His hands closed about her waist, and her scent wrapped around him. A moment later, she was in his arms.

"So tell me," he said, keeping her close, with her toes barely touching the ground.

He was enjoying their closeness a little too much, if truth be told. But how could he not? The feel of her petite body so tight against his was surprisingly erotic. Usually, when he got so close to a woman, it was because he was about to make love to her. This time, it was different. It would lead nowhere, so he was able to enjoy the intimate embrace for what it was, as he knew it was all he would be allowed to have.

"What would you like me to tell you?" Siân's voice was hoarse. He guessed that she'd rarely, if ever, been held so intimately, and she'd just told him she thought him handsome. It thrilled him to be the first man to unsettle her so.

"I know you like my mismatched eyes." Of all things, she liked the one aspect of him that was not perfect. It seemed very significant somehow. "What else do you like about me?"

Siân reddened all the way to her toes. How could Christopher ask her such a direct question while he was holding her? And how could she answer?

I like everything about you. Your hair, your mouth, your eyes, your arms, of course, but even the parts I'm sure no one has noticed before, you included. The bones on your wrists, the three little blond hairs between your collarbones, the scar under your right ear, the vein running down the side of your neck, the shape of your nails. Everything.

She could not say any of that. So she decided to focus on what she liked about his personality instead. It was far safer. "I like that you listen to me and never balk at my questions or comments."

He never made her feel like an oddity. In fact, he usually asked for more. To prove it, he smiled. "That's because your questions and comments are the most stimulating I've ever heard. You constantly outdo yourself. I dread the day you won't have anything odd or shocking left to tell me."

Siân knew a challenge when she saw one, and she was only too happy to rise to it. Straightening her spine, she delivered what she knew would be a blow. "I was abducted once."

The satisfaction she felt at seeing his eyes bug out of his head was ample reward for her efforts. It wasn't hard to guess Christopher Harrison was not a man easily shocked, but she had managed to do just that. What had he said? That she constantly outdid herself? It seemed he hadn't been lying.

"Ab— Who dared?" His left hand actually went to the hilt of his sword, while his right arm tightened its hold around her.

"An enemy of my father, a Welshman called Gruffydd ap Hywel. He blackmailed my mother into handing him over to a group of rebels by abducting me. I was seven at the time, and my father had just arrived in Wales."

"Dear God."

Siân stared at Christopher in amazement. His reaction was far stronger than she had imagined it would be. She had only wanted to play along with his game, tease him, but he seemed horrified and ready to skewer the man.

"It's not as bad as it sounds," she couldn't help but soothe. "He never hurt me. I didn't even realize I had been abducted at the time. He took me to his house and left me in his niece's care for the night, leaving my mother to imagine the worst. It was only years later she told me what had actually happened."

"That is no excuse. The bastard should be throttled for what he did." He sounded as if he would be only too glad to do the honors.

"He's dead now," she said in a low voice, regretting having raised the subject. "My parents never told me exactly what happened, but I know he went into hiding after Uncle Matthew rescued my father from his clutches. A couple of years later, he was found and … punished."

"Good. I hope they made him suffer."

My … He sounded so fierce that Siân actually recoiled. Here was a side of the charming, carefree rogue she had never seen before. Her resolve to marry him only strengthened. With a husband like that, she would be well protected.

"I'm sorry I upset you. I should never have talked about this."

"Ah, Little Lamb, you are too—"

"Stop calling me that," she snapped, extracting herself from his too-dangerous embrace. It wasn't the first or even the second time he'd called her that, and suddenly, she couldn't bear it. It made her sound meek and helpless when, in his presence, she felt strong and determined. Christopher was the last person she wanted to consider her a harmless little creature.

"Why should I stop?"

"Because that's not what I am!"

A brow arched over his mischievous blue eye. Did he have any idea what it did to her when he did that? Probably. And he loved unsettling her, that much she knew by now.

"You mean you've been lying all this time?" he asked, his tone provocative. "You aren't truly Welsh? What is that language I have heard you use with Jane then?"

Oh, the infuriating man! He knew very well that the Welsh was not the part she objected to. She did not bother answering, not wanting to give him the satisfaction. "How would you like it if I called you a small English ... goat?" she finished, seizing on the first word that crossed her mind.

How had she thought for a moment that Christopher would feel contrite? He gave her such a devastating smile that her insides started to sizzle.

"I would tell you that I *am* English and that, while I just might look like a goat in a certain light, there is nothing small about me."

Oh.

She had better put an end to this conversation before it turned into an utter disaster. Christopher would never relent. To ward off any ill-advised impulses to throw herself into his arms, she asked what she had always wanted to know.

"Why were you so nasty to my sister growing up?"

He stilled. The change of topic had thrown him.

"Never have I met anyone like you. You constantly surprise me."

It could have been a way to avoid giving her the answer she wanted, but she knew he had paid her a heartfelt compliment. She did not allow the pleasure of knowing that her unpredictability delighted him to distract her, however. The question had not been merely a way of steering the conversation away from dangerous paths; she genuinely wanted to know, *needed* to know, why he had behaved so appallingly toward Jane. By now, she'd seen he was not just a monstrous rogue, so there had to be an explanation, and she dearly wanted to hear what he had to say.

"Would you mind answering the question?"

Stalling, Christopher ran a hand through his hair. It was longer than it had been the year before, she noticed. Was he too lazy to see it cut, or did he think it suited him better that way? If that were the case, she could only agree. He looked more handsome than ever.

"I guess I was jealous," he finally said. "And it pleased me to see that I could not easily rile her. She was tougher than most people I knew, and it made me twice as determined to try and twice as delighted when I did manage to upset her."

Siân had not expected such an honest answer. "Jealous? How?"

He shrugged. "It was hard not to be envious. She was so obviously her father's sweetheart, whereas mine cared nothing about me. He had sent me to my grandfather as a boy because he could not muster the will to raise me. I didn't want much, I don't think. I didn't go as far as expecting him to love me, but I would have liked him to show some interest in me and my achievements—keep me with him in Kent at the very least. But he never cared, never wrote, and barely visited. When he died four years ago, he did not think it necessary to send me a last message."

Siân was appalled. "How is that possible?"

Raised by Connor Hunter, a man who, despite not being her real father, had given her all the love and support a child needed, she could not imagine being ignored by one's real parent.

"He never loved my mother, so I imagine it was enough for him to know he had his all-important heir. There was no need to actually live with me. My existence meant he had fulfilled his duty to his family. He did not have any interest in knowing me, caring only that there would be another Lord Ashton after him. I grew up with no children my age and a cold old man for sole company. And every time I went out of Throckmorton Castle, desperate to escape the gloom, I saw Jane running in the fields with her beloved twin sister, Jane sat astride her father's big stallion and him looking on with pride, Jane laughing at something he'd said, Jane, Jane, Jane. I took my revenge on her, and, sad as it is, it did make me feel better—for a little while at least—to know that for once, all was not perfect in her life." Christopher looked at her from under his lashes, looking as shamefaced as she imagined he could look. "She told you about it, I suppose?"

"Yes." There was no point denying it.

"Did she suffer much?" Her hesitation was too long for him not to understand what her answer would be. "So she did." He nodded. "I'm sorry. I see now it was pathetic, but you asked."

"I did." A silence. "I think I had better go."

Her absence would have been noticed at the noon meal, and the longer she stayed away, the more difficult it would be to make anyone believe she had simply forgotten the time. Uncomfortable questions would be asked.

"Thank you for coming," Christopher told her as she led Angel to a fallen log that could act as a mounting block.

"'Tis nothing. And I promise we will find a way to prove Elsie is lying about the babe."

He simply nodded. A moment later, she was galloping back to Sheridan Manor.

With her discussion with Christopher preying on her mind, Siân found it hard to fall asleep. She had wanted to hear his reasons for tormenting Jane, but his answer had horrified her. Because now she knew *he* was the one to be pitied. Her sister had been harassed, admittedly, but each time he had mocked her, she had gone back to her family and forgotten all about the cruel boy's taunts, safe in the knowledge that she was loved.

Whereas he had gone back to an empty home, a dead mother, an absent father, and an indifferent grandfather. Was it any wonder he'd become the man he was after growing up in such a home? Even his womanizing was not the proof of a debauched nature but that he was lonely and desperate to be seen and appreciated.

When she married him, he would be seen and appreciated —nay, loved. Perhaps with such an assurance, she might manage to lure him in. Yes. If she made him understand that once she was his wife he would never again feel ignored, she could—

"What's the matter?" Jane's voice sliced through the silence of the night. Damnation, she had thought her asleep.

"What do you mean?"

In the darkness, there was no way of knowing what her sister's reaction was, but it was not hard to guess she had arched her brow as if to say, "Are we really going to pretend nothing is weighing on your mind?"

From the moment they'd met, Siân had never kept anything from her sister. It felt disloyal to keep a secret, especially when it concerned something—someone—that was so important to her. And yet, in all these years, she had never allowed her feelings for Christopher to shine through. She had kept silent about their recent meetings and been careful not to betray undue interest whenever he was mentioned in her presence. It was becoming too taxing.

It was time she confided in someone. Her secret was burning her from the inside, and after his confession that afternoon, she found herself hoping Jane would see he was no longer the boy she had hated, understand the reasons behind his behavior, and forgive him.

She braced herself and opened her mouth. "I'm in love with Christopher."

There. It could not have been clearer.

The body next to her tensed up, as if its owner were afraid to understand what had been said. "Christopher?"

"Harrison. Lord Ashton to you."

This time, Jane bolted upright. "You ... But you can't be!"

"I can, and I am. I've been in love with him from the moment I saw him all those years ago when we came here for Iorwerth's christening."

"Siân, he's always been horrible to me! I told you, and you've seen it yourself. It was almost as if he went out of his way to make me cry every time we met."

"That is precisely what he did," Siân whispered. "To make himself feel better."

Jane didn't sound sympathetic. "What do you mean?"

"I saw him this morning during my ride, and he explained it all to me." Keeping very still, she relayed their intimate conversation, his pain and loneliness as a child, his jealousy of Jane and her family. It could have felt disloyal to reveal his secret, but she had the impression he would have approved. "He said he regretted it."

"Oh, he does?" A scoff. "I suppose that makes it all right, then."

Siân's stomach fell. "Please don't be like that. I hate the idea of you disapproving, but I can't help what I feel. I love him. And I think if you got to know him, you would see that he really is sorry for what he made you endure."

Her sister was a forgiving, gentle soul. Had she seen the look in Christopher's eyes when he'd confided in her, she would have known he was telling the truth.

"I'm sorry. I just ..."

Siân wasn't sure what Jane wanted to say. Was she disappointed in her sister's choice? Did she fear it would be impossible for her to forgive the boy who had caused her so much pain? It was not impossible.

What would it mean for them, who had never had a moment's disagreement since the moment they'd met?

Because as much as she hated the idea of a rift between her and her beloved sister, Siân knew she could never stop loving

Christopher. It had been impossible to do so when she had thought him an insufferable rogue, so what chance did she have now that she knew what was hidden behind the façade? She didn't want to forget about him. Her feelings for him were like sunshine. Even if she'd tried to block them out, she would still have felt them bringing light and warmth to her whole being. They were intangible but there all the same. And she didn't want to get rid of them, any more than she wanted to live without sunshine. These feelings were what made her life more beautiful. Nobody wanted to languish in the cold and rain when they could be luxuriating in the sun.

She didn't want to be without Christopher, imperfect as he was, infuriating as he could be, because she wasn't perfect either and could be just as maddening. Unlike other people, he did not ignore her; unlike other men, he thought her pretty. He teased her, admittedly, but that was only proof of his interest. He listened to her, asked her opinion. In his presence, she was not the shy girl she was too often reduced to. When he looked at her, she didn't feel insignificant but intriguing, even ... beautiful.

Yes. The man everyone took for a rogue brought out the best in her.

"You heard what I told you the other day?" Jane started hesitantly. "He's fathered a child onto Elsie and refuses to—"

"He has not!" Siân cut in, feeling close to tears. She had never imagined she would have to work so hard at convincing her sister, the person she loved the most in the world, of the suitability of the man she had chosen for herself, and it was painful. "The child is not his and cannot be. I asked him, and he confirmed it."

"You—"

"We have seen one another quite a few times since I arrived. I have gained a better understanding of him. And I trust him. Elsie is lying about the babe."

A silence.

"I promise to try and think on everything you've said." Jane's tone made it clear it was the most she would be able to do for the moment. It would have to suffice. At least, she had not left the bed in outrage.

"*Diolch.*"

It was only when she thanked her that Siân realized they had conversed in Welsh. They always seemed to revert to her language when discussing intimate matters. From the start, it had been their secret, private language. It was fitting they would discuss the man she loved in Welsh.

A moment later, with her sister's hand tucked inside hers, Siân finally fell asleep.

Chapter Six

In the morning, the chance to finally vindicate Christopher presented itself. Even better, Siân didn't even have to do anything.

While looking for his youngest daughter, Eirlys, during a game of hide and seek, Matthew caught Elsie kissing George, the farrier's son, at the back of the stables. During the interrogation that followed, the girl admitted that he, not Christopher, was the father of her unborn child. The two of them had been seeing one another for a while and had thought to ensure themselves a comfortable future by naming a wealthy nobleman as the baby's father, knowing the master of Sheridan Manor was too honorable to allow anyone to shirk his responsibility.

Lord Ashton would have been made to provide for the babe, thereby making them rich beyond their wildest dreams.

Siân was enraged at the couple's perfidy. They had taken advantage of her uncle's good nature and gambled on Christopher's reputation, hoping his past actions would make it impossible for anyone not to believe the worst of him, and unfortunately, they had been proved right. No one had believed him when he'd claimed not to be the father. No one had wanted to listen to her when she had taken his defense. No one had even thought to question Elsie's claim. Well, now, they had no choice but to accept that Christopher was not quite the scoundrel they took him for and that he'd been telling the truth.

"I hope you are going to apologize to him?" she asked her uncle.

Matthew looked at his brother, as if to confirm that they were in agreement over what to do. Connor nodded, indicating that they were.

"I will send him a note explaining we have discovered we've been misled, but I will not apologize," he ruled. "He might not have made the girl with child, but he did undoubtedly bed her, so I hardly think there is cause to congratulate him on his actions."

"I said apologize to him, not congratulate him," she retorted. It was not quite the same thing. One was justified, the other ludicrous. He was deliberately misunderstanding her. "And he bedded Elsie with her full consent, perhaps even at her instigation. When two people, er ... get intimate, the blame for it—if blame there is—is shared. And surely, him making sure she would not have to bear the consequences of their affair proves he's not quite as debauched as you seem to think?"

"Not quite as debauched as that doesn't mean not debauched at all, far from it!" her father snapped, clearly not impressed by the argument. "And what do you know about people getting intimate, as you say? About what Ashton does or doesn't do to ensure his conquests do not fall with child?"

Oh no. It seemed that in her vehemence, she had unwittingly led Connor to wonder if the man he took for a shameless rogue had not waylaid her, his own daughter. He had not, unfortunately, and she regretted it every moment of every day.

"Have you ever heard of anyone claiming to have birthed his bastard?" she threw back, hoping her faith in Christopher was justified. "If he is as debauched as you say and yet still has no child to show for it, surely, it means he is careful not to—"

"Enough! We are not here to discuss his dubious morals but Elsie's scheming. That she lied about the paternity of the child does not make him a saint. She is not the only maid here he's bedded."

"Indeed. He had better not show his face at Sheridan Manor ever again," her uncle added, putting an end to the discussion.

Siân's whole body sagged.

Although Christopher had been found innocent of the crime he'd been accused of, her family still considered him unsuitable company.

~

Wasn't the murmur of the water supposed to be soothing? It was, and Siân had hoped an outing to the river would help distract her, but so far, it had failed to do that. She played with the hem of her dress, wondering what she could do.

"Are you all right?" Jane asked once Gwenllian and Seren had left them to run toward the water like two excitable puppies. "I've never seen you so despondent."

An unladylike snort escaped Siân's lips. "How could I not be? The man I love is your enemy. Father despises him, and Uncle Matthew has forbidden him access to Sheridan Manor. Christopher has no idea what I feel or what my intentions are with regard to him, and I cannot see how this is going to change. Half the women in the county have bedded him, and the other half probably dream of doing so. Shall I continue?"

"No." Her sister sighed. "And he's not my enemy exactly."

"But he was once. And you're only trying to change your opinion about him for my sake. It's not going to work because it is the wrong way to go about it. Remember when I tried to force myself to like mutton when you arrived at Castell Esgyrn because I knew it was your favorite? I could never manage it. Years later, it still tastes foul to me."

Jane let out a tinkling laugh. Had she been anyone else than her beloved sister, Siân would have resented her for that innate elegance. Only a moment ago, she had deplored her own lack of grace. She didn't giggle; she snorted. She blurted out her inner thoughts, she said words she shouldn't even know, and she could barely keep her clothes clean. To her dismay, at that moment, she understood what Christopher had meant. Jane was always so poised, so graceful, so perfect, one could not help but feel inadequate in front of her. The thought didn't help her feel better.

"Come, that is hardly the same, and you know it," Jane said, taking her hand. "Lord Ashton is nothing like a sheep to be cut into chops."

"No, perhaps not. But you know what I mean," Siân mumbled. The attempt at levity had failed.

"I do. And I promise I will try to understand what you see in him. I trust you. If you love him, he must be worthy of it."

This answer earned Jane a squeeze to the hand. "Thank you."

Siân let out a sigh. Even if she won Jane over, she would still have the rest of her family to contend with. She had no idea how she would convince her father and uncle, in particular, to see that Christopher was not quite the rogue they took him for.

"I think I'd better go and see what Seren and Gwenllian are doing," Jane said, glancing over to where the two girls were splashing water at one another by the riverbank. The giggles from earlier had become veritable shrieks, heralding a possible mishap.

Siân knew her sister was only trying to give her a moment's

privacy, but it was probably a good idea to go and prevent a catastrophe. They had been able to sneak a dripping-wet Seren into Castell Esgyrn and avoid a scolding once last year; she could not imagine how they would be so lucky a second time.

Left alone, Siân took another swig of the flask of ale Avice had placed in the basket of food she'd prepared for the outing and watched the wind play in the tree branches overhead. She had been so full of hope only days ago, thinking she was making good progress with Christopher, but she was no longer certain. It was not just that her family was hostile toward him even if that was a problem. It was also that he still had no idea of her feelings for him. He probably saw her as a friend. It was no small achievement, considering that not so long before, he could not remember who she was, but she was still a long way from expecting a proposal.

"That is quite a feast for one person. Mind if I join you?"

Siân let out a little squeak when the voice sliced through her thoughts. Where had Christopher come from? And how had she not heard his approach? You would not credit such a large man with the ability to move with the stealthiness of a cat.

He sat next to her before she could tell him he could join her and reached for a slice of hare pie as if he had every right to it. Someone else might have bristled at his arrogance, but she found it endearing because it proved he was at ease with her, as he should have been.

"This is most propitious," he said once he'd swallowed a few mouthfuls of pie. "Here I was, famished and wondering how long it would take me to walk home, and here you are with more food than you can possibly consume in two days, like a wood nymph waiting to see to my needs."

To see to my needs.

He had no idea that was exactly what she wanted to do for the rest of her life.

"There's a simple explanation for all the food," Siân said quietly, not dwelling on the thought. "I am not here on my own. My sisters are over there by the river."

Or rather, they had been. Right now, they were out of sight, having no doubt found the perfect spot to dip their toes in the water. Siân's heartbeat increased another notch at the realization. She was alone with Christopher, and they were side by side on the blanket, half-lying down already. It was a situation rife with possibilities, each more licentious than the last.

"Why did you think you would have to walk home?" she asked before her mind could start imagining some of those possibilities. Warrior, she had noticed, was tethered at the edge of the clearing. Why could he not ride him? "Is your stallion injured?"

"No," he said, taking another bite of pie. "But *I* very well could have been. The billets on my saddle broke while I was galloping through the field yonder. Thankfully, I fell on soft ground and managed to roll out of the way of Warrior's hooves, but ..."

Yes.

But.

Feeling sick, Siân placed the sweet she'd been about to bring to her mouth back in the basket. For the second time in as many weeks, Christopher could have died. Dear God, that was not something she had imagined would happen before long. But of course, he was only a man and therefore not immune to accidents and diseases. What if he died before they could get married? Before she could spend a night in his arms? It did not bear thinking about.

"You could have died," she said in a horrified whisper.

"Yes. Easily." Though he was agreeing with her, he seemed completely undisturbed by the notion. "I will have a word with my squire about the state of my saddle when I get back home. You would have thought he'd take better care of me."

"Yes. You would have thought so." Had the man appeared in front of her, she might have struck him.

"Anyway, these tartlets are delicious," Christopher observed. After devouring his second slice of pie, he had moved on to the sweets, selecting the biggest without hesitation.

"Yes," Siân answered, deciding it was better to discuss the food than his brush with death. "Avice has always been the best of cooks. Whenever we visited from Wales when I was younger, I would look forward to what I would find here at Sheridan Manor."

Avice's tarts had been only the second-best thing about their visits to England, of course, but she would not admit to that, least of all to Christopher, even if the words were straining to get out.

Worry spiked through her. How long would it be before her secret leaked out of her? Or rather, exploded? After having held on to it for so long, it was bound to erupt when she least expected it, when neither was prepared or able to deal with the revelation. Perhaps she should tell him what she felt at the first suitable opportunity. Would it be such a bad thing? Even if he rejected her, at least she would know where she stood.

It was time anyway.

They were both of marriageable age, and she feared it wouldn't be long before Christopher found someone he wanted to marry. That someone had better be her because she would go mad otherwise. She could not afford to wait at the risk of seeing him captured by one of his numerous lovers. Though she hated the fact that he'd had more women than she could count, she reasoned that it was better he went from one meaningless conquest to another than become enamored with a sweetheart with whom she could not compete.

As far as she could tell, women came and went. But she was a constant in his life, had been for years even if he'd not realized it. Hadn't he just said he was glad to see her? Granted, it might have been because she happened to have food with her, but if eating was all he'd been concerned with, he would have taken a few tarts with him and gone on to Throckmorton Castle. Instead, he had sat down and started to talk to her.

Even more pointedly, he seemed happy to share a moment with her.

This was good, but there was still a big obstacle to her plan. After what had happened with Elsie, she dreaded having to announce to her family who she had chosen as a groom. Uncle Matthew had said only the day before that he did not want to see Christopher ever again, her father had called him a debauched seducer of women, and, of course, Jane might never be able to offer her wholehearted support.

"You seem lost in thought. What's on your mind, Little Lamb?"

Unwilling to be honest, she seized upon the first thing she could think of.

"You see that tree over there?" She pointed to a young oak behind him with branches covered in vibrant green leaves. "I planted it myself."

Christopher's face softened. "You never disappoint, do you? You always come up with the most surprising statements, and this in the blink of an eye, when other people, me included, would be at pains to think of a single intriguing thing to say when pressed. Tell me more about this tree of yours."

She blinked, both disconcerted and delighted by the order. What was it with him wanting—nay, *liking*—to be surprised? As to his wanting to know more about the tree, it was not the first time he'd asked her to expand on something other people would have found tedious.

"I was nine when I planted an acorn in the meadow, hoping

it would grow into a mighty tree," she started. "I thought ... I had come for a visit, and I wanted to remember that day."

The day she had found her future husband. She had wanted to be able to sit in the shade of that tree once they were married, and maybe later, Christopher would bring the children he had given her to play in a tree house he'd made for them. The fanciful, naïve dreams of a child.

Growing up, Siân had liked to visit the tree every time she'd come and see that it was going strong, just like her feelings for him were.

"Why an oak?" he asked, taking her by surprise for once.

She stared, not sure what to answer. She had never thought about it. "I suppose because I knew they grew from acorns, whereas I had no idea what to plant to get, say, a birch or a willow."

"And why did you decide to plant a tree that day in particular?"

There was no choice but to lie. Siân was not about to admit to the truth while Christopher was waiting and looking her in the eye. Fortunately, she'd always had a quick mind. "That day, I had met our cousin, Iorwerth. He was my first-ever cousin, and I was elated to meet him. I think I imagined I would plant a tree for each of the others."

"And did you?"

"No." Of course not. There would only ever be one tree, like there was only one Christopher.

He helped himself to another tart. Lord, but the man had the appetite of an ogre ... How did he not have a paunch like so many rich noblemen she knew? But he was just perfect, all lean limbs and taut muscles. With such a physique, he would feel—

"How many do you have?"

"How m-many w-what?"

"Cousins?"

Oh. She had been so lost in contemplation she'd had no idea what he was talking about, and she was relieved to see that he had not realized it. "Three, so far."

"So far?" He arched a brow.

"I suspect my aunt Branwen might be with child again."

Her heart leaped at the thought of welcoming another cousin to the family, of having another chubby little baby to cherish soon. Since that day more than ten years ago when she had fallen in love with Iorwerth, her craving for children had only grown—as had her impatience. When would she have her own? Heat crept up her cheeks because, of course, she imagined the man next to her as the father, and, no longer a nine-year-old girl, she had a good idea of what the act of getting with child involved.

She couldn't wait.

"Look at you blushing." Christopher beamed. Fortunately, he had no idea she was blushing because she was imagining him naked and poised over her, doing what was required to make her with child. "I would have thought that a woman as knowledge-able as you seem to be would not be coy about the notion of a couple—"

"I'm not!"

"Clearly not." Chuckling, he wiped his hands on the piece of cloth nearest to him.

Siân glanced nervously toward the river, not sure whether she wanted her sisters to come back or not. On the one hand, it would put an end to the embarrassing moment, but on the other, she wasn't sure she wanted to be seen alone with Christopher. What Jane would think if she saw them together, the despised Lord Ashton smirking and her with her cheeks flaming red, didn't bear thinking about.

His appetite finally sated, Christopher settled himself on

one elbow. "You know, you never told me what you named my eyes."

She knew she had not. And, in all honesty, she had hoped he'd forgotten about it because she had regretted admitting to something so embarrassing. But it was clear he would not be distracted this time, so she decided to answer. He would only insist if she did not.

"The blue one is Ellyll and the brown one Blaidd."

"I see." A corner of his mouth quivered. "That doesn't help me much."

"You asked what I named them, not what the names mean."

"True, as I thought it went without saying. So. What will I have to do to get that information out of you?" He leaned over to her. "Fair warning, my lady, I can be very, very persuasive."

Oh. Lord.

This she didn't doubt for a moment. And surely, he knew he had reduced her insides to a puddle with his husky voice?

"There will be no need for any extreme measures," she started, tripping over her own tongue. She had to tell him what the words meant before he decided she had to be persuaded. "Ellyll is a sort of mischievous elf, and 'blaidd' means 'wolf.'" She shrugged. "I could have done better, I think, but I was only nine when I named them."

"Nine?" Christopher sounded shocked, as well he might. She had just inadvertently revealed she had been obsessed with him from a very young age.

"Or ten—or eleven—I don't remember. And I did tell you we had met a few times before you started remembering me. Or have you forgotten that as well?"

"I was once a fool, but believe me, I will not forget that, according to you, one of my eyes is a wolf." The purr he gave was worthy of the animal itself, and she knew then that she could not have chosen a better name for Blaidd. "Do you know what wolves do to little lambs such as you? They devour them whole."

He'd thought to shock her, possibly even frighten her, but it took all Siân's inner strength not to throw herself at him and beg him to do just that. She was old enough and more than ready to be devoured at last. Should she tell him as much? No. Such an admission required some planning. Instead, she reached out for a tart. If her mouth was occupied, then she would be unable to blurt out anything she would regret later.

"I think you enjoyed that," Christopher said once she had swallowed the last mouthful. The mischievous blue Ellyll winked at her. "At least as much as wolves like to eat little lambs. But look, now your fingers are dripping in honey." Before she could do anything, he took her hand in his. It was so big it almost engulfed hers. She did not protest, did not even look at it. If she saw their fingers entwined, she would be lost. "Let me."

Could she do anything other than agree? No. She nodded. Slowly, keeping his eyes on her, Christopher licked first her index finger, then her middle finger. The ring finger, the one where he would place a wedding band soon if she had her say, was next. Finally, he sucked her little finger straight into his mouth. So hot, so wet, so delicious. A moan built in her throat, a shiver rippled down her spine, and she closed her eyes, overwhelmed by sensations.

What was happening?

When he'd said he would deal with the honey, she'd thought he would use the cloth he'd just discarded to wipe her hand clean, not ... not make love to her fingers and reduce her to a puddle of need.

"Delicious. Give Mistress Avice my compliments when you get back to Sheridan Manor. I've never eaten anything like that."

With those words, he released her hand and stood back up.

Siân's eyes were still closed. If she opened them and saw him towering over her, his lips shiny from sucking her fingers, she would either swoon or launch herself at him. Neither option would be wise. She had decided only moments earlier that she had to think carefully about the way she would reveal her feelings and her plans regarding him. She opened her eyes only when she heard his footsteps in the distance.

After one last scorching glance in her direction, Christopher led Warrior away.

It was only when silence fell back in the clearing that Siân remembered that the tarts Avice had given her were walnut and fig—not honey.

Chapter Seven

Let me.

Dear Lord, how many times would Siân relive the delicious, decadent moment when Christopher had licked her fingers clean? It seemed she had done little else the night before and this morning. She could still feel the heat of his mouth, the ripples of pleasure he'd stirred within her. Would it feel the same to have him suck on other parts of her? She hadn't guessed fingers could be treated in that way, but she knew that breasts and nipples could be. Perhaps Christopher knew of other places—

A voice cut through her lewd wonderings.

"Have you seen Seren and Gwenllian?"

"No." Siân instantly picked up on Jane's agitation. Her sister was not easily ruffled. If she was worried, there was probably just cause. "Why are you looking for them?"

"I have a bad feeling. Rhys just came to say they were playing hide and seek together and he cannot find them anywhere. And after yesterday ..."

This time, her heart skipped a beat. "What about yesterday?"

She could think of only one thing that had happened the day before. Her meeting with Christopher, when he had acted as if he wanted to entice her into his bed. Had Jane seen the scandalous way he had licked at her fingers? No, she would have mentioned something if she had. And it could have nothing to do with their two young sisters' disappearance. Supposing they had disappeared, that was. But everything was possible. Hadn't she been abducted once by one of her father's enemies, as she'd told Christopher the other day?

She forced herself to stay calm. For one, she was still not sure anything *had* happened. For all she knew, Gwenllian and Seren had found the perfect hiding place and Rhys, too lazy to keep looking for them, had come to Jane for help.

"They loved our outing to the river yesterday," Jane explained. "While you stayed in the clearing, we found an enchanting little spot with a gravel beach from which we could easily paddle in the water."

"So?" She still didn't see what that had to do with anything even if she was reassured to hear that her sister did not suspect what had come to pass between her and Christopher.

"This morning, it being a nice day, they asked me if we could go back there again, but I was busy helping Mam and Branwen sort out the linen, so I said no, adding that we would go later on in the afternoon, once I had finished. I fear they might have gone unaccompanied, unable to wait."

Oh no. That, unfortunately, sounded too much like something the girls might do. It was only a short walk to the river, one even a child like Seren could manage, especially if she was determined. Now, Siân was truly worried.

"Let us ride there, just in case. If they are, as I hope, huddled together in a corner of the castle waiting for Rhys to find them, they will soon get bored when they see he is not coming for them. And if they *have* decided to go to the river, then the sooner we reach them, the better."

Seren and Gwenllian both knew how to swim, but the rapid river was nothing like the lake near Castell Esgyrn they were used to going to. Even a strong swimmer would find it hard not to get swept away, and they were only slight girls.

The two sisters ran to the stables, desperate to prevent a disaster but skidded to a halt when they saw that Connor and Matthew were already there, each with a white stallion in hand. Bought in Wales some ten years ago, Raven and Snowball were still the brothers' favorite mounts. Siân cursed her luck. Her uncle and father rarely went out riding together these days. Why did they have to choose today of all days to do it?

"Where are you two going in such a hurry?" Connor asked, instantly on his guard. He could always tell when his children were up to no good.

Siân and Jane exchanged a look, loath to voice their suspicions. If Gwenllian and Seren had not gone to the river, they shouldn't get into trouble for nothing. If they had, then there would be time enough to see them punished for their recklessness later on.

Before they could say anything, a horse was heard approaching in the distance. A moment later, a stallion rounded the bend at the bottom of the path. Warrior. On his back was Christopher, holding a wet and trembling Seren against his equally wet body. Though his back was too broad to allow her to identify the owner of the two arms wrapped around his middle, Siân guessed it was none other than Gwenllian. As the horse came to a halt, the girl's face, crowned with dripping wet hair, peeked from behind his shoulder.

Siân and Jane let out sighs of relief. The sisters were safe even if it was clear they had indeed taken a tumble into the water.

"Ashton. What the *devil* are you doing with my daughters? And why are they soaked to the bone?"

To say that Connor's voice was icy would have been like calling a hailstorm a gentle April shower. By his side, Matthew was also glaring. Despite Elsie's confession that he was not the one to get her with child, the two men still regarded Christopher as a scoundrel of the worst kind.

"Didn't I tell you only the other day not to come here again?" her uncle snarled.

Christopher did not let the animosity impress him, as could have been predicted. He straightened his spine and tightened his hold around Seren, who showed no sign of wanting to escape the warmth of his embrace. Siân sympathized. She would like nothing more than to nestle into his arms herself.

"Father, please do not scold Lord Ashton. I don't know what we would have done without him," Gwenllian exclaimed, jumping down from the stallion's rump. "He rescued us from the river."

"Did he now? And just what were you doing there alone, may I ask?" His face like thunder, Connor held his arms out to Seren, who did not dare refuse to let him lift her off the horse.

While the two sisters gave their confused explanations as to how they had ended up at the river on their own, Christopher jumped down from the saddle and waited. His wet clothes were molded to his body, and Siân could not have taken her eyes from the sight if her life had depended on it. It was a wonder Jane had not spared him as much as a glance. Couldn't she see he was the most gorgeously sculpted man who had ever lived? Those arms ... those legs ... that ...

Her throat went dry because she could all too easily guess what caused the bulge at the front of his skin-tight hose.

"Jane, Siân, see to your sisters," Connor ordered, pushing the two girls in their direction. "Get them warm and comfortable as quickly as possible. Don't tell your mother what happened. I'll speak to her myself once I've dealt with the girls."

His tone made it clear they would get a thorough scolding for their imprudence. Siân could only agree they needed to understand the danger they had escaped. The only problem was that she did not want to leave Christopher alone with the two brothers, who seemed to have forgotten that they owed him the girls' lives. Anyone else would have thanked him effusively by now, but they were scowling at him.

She threw a glance at Christopher, hoping to convey her thanks for saving her sisters, and the wretched man actually winked at her. Fortunately, he'd made sure to choose the moment when her father and uncle handed their horses back to the groom. There would be no riding today.

Taking Seren by the hand while Jane wrapped an arm around Gwenllian's shoulders, Siân walked to the main hall.

"So. Care to tell us what happened out there in the forest?"

Despite the abrupt question, Christopher noticed that the two brothers were looking at him with marginally less venom than when he had ridden through the gate. They would have calmed down by now and understood they owed the two little girls' rescue, and possibly their lives, to him. *Nothing like relief and gratitude to soften a man up*, he thought wryly.

"I was actually on my way to see my friend, Sir Alexander Rathbone," he started, taking pleasure in elaborating on a part of the story they would not be interested in. "He lives just beyond the valley, and it being such a nice day, I thought I would—"

"Who cares about the weather!" Lord Sheridan cut in. "Just tell me what happened to my daughters."

Christopher did not have the heart to tease him further. It was not hard to guess that he'd been scared witless at the idea that he could have lost his children, which was all too understandable.

"As I was crossing the bridge over the river, I heard cries for help. Some distance away, I saw Gwenllian trying to haul little Seren out of the water with a branch. Before I could do anything, she fell into the water herself, being too slight to lift her sister out. As luck would have it, I was downstream from them, so the current swept them toward me. I jumped down from the saddle, then off the bridge and thus was able to intercept them as they floated next to me a moment later. I brought them to the bank and then back here to you after they explained who they were."

He kept his voice level, his explanation simple. There was no need to insist. The men would guess it had required a herculean effort on his part to keep the two little girls afloat in the churning waters and bring them back to the shore. The last thing he wanted was for them to think he was using the incident to ingratiate himself back into their good graces. He was not. He had simply been lucky enough to be in the right place at the right moment and strong enough to do what needed to be done. Up until Gwenllian had revealed their identities, he hadn't even known who the girls were. His shock at being told they were none other than Siân's younger sisters had stunned him.

As he'd lain on the grass, panting from exhaustion, all he had been able to think about was how she would have been devastated by the loss of her beloved sisters and how relieved he was to have spared her that awful pain. Christopher was not a selfish man, but he could not claim to be entirely selfless either. Yet he had jumped into that river without thought for his own safety or expectation of a reward. It had seemed like the right thing to do.

The two brothers glanced at one another, as if trying to decide what to make of his tale, then nodded.

"You have my gratitude for what you did." Lord Sheridan said eventually.

"Please." Christopher waved the words away. "I did what anyone in my place would have done."

"You know very well that not everyone would have been willing to put themselves in danger for two girls they didn't know, much less able to actually save not only one but both of them. On behalf of my wife, Esyllt, who would never have borne the loss of her daughters, I thank you. For my part, I thank you for having spared me the worst heartache a man can endure. I'm not sure how I would have lived with the knowledge I had lost another two of my children."

The man's voice had become slightly hoarse, betraying a depth of emotion that twisted at Christopher's guts. He'd heard how Connor had lost a wife and two daughters before marrying the Welsh woman the king had selected for him.

"Please," he repeated. No one should have to go through that pain. He, who had never had what anyone would call a family, understood it better than most. "I'm glad to have been of help."

"I, too, would like to thank you for what you did. My nieces are very dear to me," Matthew Hunter said, coming forward, as if to allow his brother a moment to recover. The two men had always been very close, Christopher knew. The proof of their bond caused his chest to tighten. What wouldn't he have given to have such a loyal brother by his side ...

He cleared his throat, determined not to let his emotion show. "As I said. Think nothing of it." Having genuinely not meant to use the incident to his benefit, he was getting uncomfortable.

Matthew nodded, as if to signify the subject was closed. "Do you need to go to the main hall to get warm before you leave? A fire is blazing in there. I can ask for spiced wine to be brought to you."

So much for not being allowed to put a foot inside Sheridan

Manor. Christopher smiled. Mere days after the threat had been issued, there he was, being offered refreshments like any prestigious guest.

"No, I thank you. Sir Alexander will be waiting for me. The day is warm enough. I'll dry off in no time riding on Warrior. He goes like the wind." He patted his faithful horse's neck. "Go and see to the girls."

Without waiting for his dismissal, he hoisted himself back onto the saddle and trotted off toward Audley Castle.

∾

Later that day, as he was galloping back toward Throckmorton, Christopher's heart started to beat in the same rhythm as his horse's hooves. That shape in the distance, white against the green backdrop of the trees ... Could it be what he thought it might be, who he hoped it was ... Yes, it *was* a woman sitting on a log. And not just any woman. The slight figure crowned with a riot of curls could belong to only one person.

The one he wanted to see.

The sight brought a welcome warmth to his chest. Though his clothes had dried long before, as predicted, he'd not quite managed to shake off the cold of the river, and he'd just been wishing for the tenth time that he'd asked Alexander to lend him a cloak for the ride back home. In the blink of an eye, thanks to the woman waiting for him, he forgot about the cold wrapping around his bones and smiled.

Warrior was brought to a halt next to Angel and tethered before he went to Siân, who'd stood up from the log at his approach. His heart leaped anew at the sight of her. He had guessed she would come to him, but he had not expected it to be today. It was late already. Had she waited on that log all day for him to appear? Damnation, why had he stayed so long at Audley Castle?

"Little Lamb, what are you doing here?" he asked, making his way toward her. He expected her to offer her tearful thanks for saving her sisters.

Instead, she threw herself into his arms.

"Oh, Christopher!" she cried out, her mouth pressed against his chest.

It was the first time she had called him by his name, and the warmth in his body became an inferno. What the hell? That was absurd! Christopher was his name. Why should hearing it provoke such a reaction? It was not as if she had just dropped to her knees in front of him and started to unlace his braies.

"It's all right," he said awkwardly, not knowing what to make of the situation.

"'Tis not all right ... The girls ... My sisters ... Little Seren ... Dear God, Christopher, you saved them, both of them, you realize that? I don't know what to say. I don't know how I, how *we* all would have borne it if they had—"

"Hush," he told her, placing a hand at her nape. She was getting frantic, and he had to calm her down. His head bowed of its own accord, and before he knew what he was doing, he'd placed a kiss on her soft hair.

It felt good to have her against him. From the start, that woman had been like no one else. She seemed determined to see only the good in him, to trust that the bad was only a façade, to believe that he could be trusted, no matter what others thought. And perhaps because of it, he felt almost worthy in her presence.

"I thank you for coming, but you shouldn't be here on your own, especially at this time of day. It's too dangerous," he chided, looking over at the horizon. Dusk was slowly descending, stealing all the pink in the sky and replacing it with velvety purple. Even if she had wanted to see him, she should have set off for home long ago. By the time she reached Sheridan Manor again, it would be pitch black.

"I had to see you. I had to thank you for what you did. You no doubt think you did nothing worthy of note, but I—and everyone in my family—know different," she murmured, her mouth still against his chest. Against his heart. "You saved more than the girls today. My father has lost two daughters already. It would have been unbearable for him to lose two others in such tragic circumstances."

"I know, but he didn't lose Gwenllian or Seren, so there is little point lingering over what could have been. How are they now?" He hoped they weren't feeling the worse for their bath in the cold water. He, a grown man, had found it hard to shake off the cold, so he could not begin to imagine how two slender children would fare. But he knew they had been well taken care of. With luck, they were feeling better than he was.

"They are mortified to have caused everyone such worry," Siân said with a sigh. "They were so appalled at their folly that Father didn't even have the heart to scold them, thinking —quite rightly—that they had learned their lesson the hard way. I am certain they will never go to the river unaccompanied again. Which brings me to my second message of thanks."

With those words, she drew away from him. Her eyes were glinting in the fading sunlight, almost as clear as crystals or even diamonds. It suddenly occurred to Christopher that she was very beautiful. Not just pretty or intriguing or easy to be with but beautiful.

This was quite a shocking discovery to make after so many days spent in her company. Little Siân Hunter was a beautiful woman, one he might have wanted to bed had he met her in other circumstances.

Unsettled by the thought, he asked, "What is this second message?"

"Jane asked me to thank you. She feels responsible for the girls' misadventure, and, having already lost two sisters, one of which was her own twin, she could not have borne another such loss."

Siân waited while Christopher seemed to absorb the information. What would he tell her?

Please, do not make any scathing comment about Perfect Little Jane Hunter having finally faltered, she prayed silently. *Please, let me see the proof you are not the rogue everyone thinks you are but a good man.*

"Tell Jane she doesn't need to thank me. As I told your father and uncle, I'm just glad to have been there. It is not so often I get to do something right." He rubbed the back of his neck. Had he been anyone else, she might have thought he was embarrassed. "And she is not to feel responsible for the girls' mishap. They told me as we were riding back that they had wilfully disregarded her instructions to wait for her before going to the river. She could not have known they would be so reckless. She has nothing to blame herself for."

It was then that Siân knew for sure Christopher was the husband she wanted, the man she loved, and the person she had hoped he would be.

He *was* a good man, the only one she wanted.

"Thank you."

He tapped a finger on the end of her nose in a surprisingly playful gesture. "Think nothing of it. Come now, I will ride with you back to Sheridan Manor before people start to wonder where you are."

He was right. After the fright her parents had suffered earlier that day, it would not do to make them think a third daughter had gone missing. Before she could hoist herself onto her saddle, she turned to Christopher, who had already vaulted onto Warrior's back.

"Christopher?"

"Mm?"

What did she want to tell him? She had no idea. Perhaps she had wanted only to say his name out loud again. It felt intimate. Right. She shook her head and placed her foot in the stirrup.

"Nothing. Let's ride."

Chapter Eight

That night, Siân dreamed Christopher was rescuing her from a churning river instead of Seren and Gwenllian. After diving in to fish her out of the icy waters, he lifted her into his arms, carried her to the riverbank, and deposited her onto the mossy ground, where he proceeded to cover her in kisses. His lips were cold, his tongue hot, and his breath smelled of that elusive spice.

Even in her dream, she could not place which one that might be.

She spent the whole day trying to shake the sensations created by his kisses, imaginary as they had been. Instinct told her he would be just as skilled, taste just as good, feel just as hot in real life. Because she knew Christopher was the man she wanted to marry, Siân had never taken any interest in anyone else, never tried to attract any suitor, never paid attention to the few boys who had tried to impress her. It would have only been a waste of time because it would never have led anywhere. As a consequence, she had never been kissed. She had no way of knowing whether a real kiss would feel as wonderful as the ones she and Christopher had shared in her dream, but she had a strong suspicion it would.

That night, she went to bed hoping for more decadent moments in Christopher's arms.

The following day, after a disappointing night spent dreaming of being chased by a giant hound with teeth made of iron, she climbed onto the north battlements. An idea had suddenly struck her. Could she see Throckmorton Castle from the high vantage point? As she peered into the distance, hoping for a glimpse of the whitewashed walls, women's voices reached her from down below. Siân leaned in and saw Maggie, the scullion, and one of the laundresses talking together while enjoying a spot of sunshine.

"Judging from the looks we've been exchanging, I think he knows I'm ripe for the taking," Mildred, a small, buxom woman, said. "Next time he comes, I'll pretend to twist my ankle, step on a sharp nail, or anything else that ensures I fall to my knees in front of him. Then, once I'm there, I'll make sure he understands he can make the most of the opportunity whenever he wants."

"What do you mean?"

"Lord, Maggie, what do you think I mean? Don't tell me you've never sucked a man's cock?"

"I ... No, of course not!" the scullion, who was only a young girl, exclaimed in shock. "Why would I want to do that?"

Mildred chuckled. "Heed my words, girl, for they will serve you well. Men, be they high- or lowborn, will agree to almost anything to get their cocks between a woman's lips. They love it even more than they like sticking it between a woman's legs. It is the one thing we women can use to get what we want. And what I want is him. Once I've sucked him dry, I will tell him he can use me again but only if he fucks me first. I can tell you he's not going to refuse the offer, and that way, I will get what I crave."

Siân's mind was whirring. She had the awful impression she knew who they were talking about. And unlike Maggie, she knew what the laundress was referring to even if, of course, she had never performed the act herself. In truth, she was disgusted by Mildred's advice, which reduced women to scheming whores and men to malleable fools. Up until that moment, she had never considered taking a man into her mouth for any other reason than to give him—and herself—pleasure. Inexperienced as she was, she was certain it could be a beautiful moment, nothing like the cold bargaining tool the laundress had described. She would make sure to tell Maggie she should not heed her friend's words.

It would be shocking, of course, but the girl needed to know that her body was not to be used by anyone, herself included, for any purpose other than to give and receive pleasure. Siân and Jane were lucky enough to have been raised by women who had made love matches, and between them, their mother and aunt had kept them informed of what went on between men and women. Of course, their advice had been nothing as crude as Mildred's. On the contrary, it had emphasized the connection two lovers could share. While too many husbands were selfish and treated their wives as commodities, others, they had assured them, were generous and respectful in and out of bed.

Could Christopher be such a husband? A selfless and considerate lover as well as an ally in life? She didn't doubt he would be passionate in his lovemaking, but would he be willing to bring her pleasure as well as take his own?

That decided her.

The next woman he would make love to would be none other than herself. It would be the best way to find out what kind of lover he was—and let him know of her intentions with regard to having a future together. Making love to him would also have the added advantage of putting an end to the torturous desire she felt for him.

Leaving the two women to their conversation, Siân started to descend the wooden ladder. As soon as she touched the ground, she went to the stables and surprised the grooms by saddling Angel herself and thundering out of the gate.

Her patience had finally come to an end; she had to see Christopher without delay.

She found him in the lists with a man she assumed to be his squire. The two of them were exercising their horses, putting the animals through their paces. The young man was riding an enormous black destrier that almost made Warrior appear fragile. He seemed just as skilled in the saddle as his master, and for a moment, she watched them, enjoying the display of strength and agility. Then Christopher asked Warrior to rear up. Though she could see he was in complete control of the maneuver, Siân could not help but gasp. Such power ... The woman in her quivered. As he patted his mount, he spotted her. Wiping his brow, he trotted over to her, leaving his companion to make his way back to the barbican.

"Lady Siân. Good morning."

He seemed surprised to see her, and no wonder. It was the first time she had come to Throckmorton for no discernible reason.

"Good morning. Who was that enormous beast?"

Christopher barked a laugh at the question. "That was Harry, my new squire. And he will be gratified to hear you think him enormous. He's forever complaining he has not yet grown into a man."

She stared. Indeed, the young squire was as slender as a damsel, if evidently stronger. "I ... I meant the black horse, and you know it!"

His eyes twinkled. "This is where you're wrong. I *never* know what you're going to say next, my lady, which is why I like talking to you. It is not everyone who shares your talent for the unpredictable. And the horse's name is Lucifer."

"Good choice. Did you say Harry is your new squire?"

"Yes. The previous one disappeared after I had words with him about the maintenance of my saddle billets. Mind you, I don't bemoan the loss. The man had been sent from Kent by my uncle as a favor to his friend, but he was useless."

More than useless if he had allowed his master to take such a tumble. Siân shivered. Indeed, Christopher was well rid of the man.

"Now. What brings you here, Little Lamb?"

"Nothing, only Mildred, one of Sheridan Manor's laundresses, overheard me asking for Angel to be saddled. She asked if, by any chance, I intended to ride past Throckmorton, seeing as she had a message to deliver to you. It was just as easy for me to come here as go the other way to the coast, so I agreed." Siân was careful to make it appear as if the favor had been a spur-of-the-moment thing, as, of course, a laundress would never use a noblewoman to deliver her personal messages. "But now I'm wondering if the message was intended for you, after all. Perhaps I misunderstood and she actually meant your squire," she added as inspiration struck. "It would make more sense because ... Well. Yes. It would make more sense."

Christopher smiled, as if enjoying her feigned confusion. Perhaps being seen as clumsy and unconventional had its advantages. People didn't suspect you of deliberate scheming. "What did she say?"

"She wanted you—or Harry, now I'm not sure—to go meet her in the meadow tonight after dusk. You know the one, in the river bend, with the oak in the middle?"

Where only the other day, he had licked her fingers until she'd thought she would pass out.

"Aye, I know the one." Christopher's eyes glittered. Was he remembering the moment or getting aroused at the idea of a woman waiting for him? "Thank you. I will talk to Harry, and between us, we'll see what this is about. Tell Mildred someone will definitely meet her tonight."

Siân nodded. The die had been cast. She had no doubt the man who would go to the meadow would be Christopher himself. If, like the laundress had said, he really knew she was "ripe for the taking," he would not miss the opportunity for a tumble with a willing woman. Well, if she had her say, it would be the last time he answered such an assignation. Soon they would be married and the only woman who enjoyed his touch would be her. He wouldn't need to go to other women to repair the hurt his family had caused him. It would be her pleasure and privilege to do that.

"Now. Shall I race you back home?" Christopher offered. "After all his hard work, Warrior has earned a good gallop."

"You can try. But only if you're prepared to lose."

He arched a brow at the unusually confident answer on her part. But Siân knew herself to be a reckless rider, one who could best almost anyone she knew. Why not him? She would have no chance to outrun him on foot, of course, but on horseback, everything was possible.

"I *never* lose, Little La—"

Siân had kicked her horse before he could finish his boast.

There she was, a dark shape barely distinguishable amongst the saplings. Christopher saw the woman only because he knew she was here, waiting. He moved forward, stealthy as a cat. At first, he had been surprised by the bold invitation, but perhaps he shouldn't have been. The laundress was not the first woman who'd made her desire for him plain. No, the surprising element was rather that the assignation had come through Siân. Did his little lamb have any idea what kind of licentious message she had delivered? Of course she would. She had already hinted at the fact that she was not as innocent as he might think. Rather surprising for someone of her rank, but wasn't she full of surprises? Wasn't it what he liked about her?

Yes, what he liked too much, if truth be told.

Which brought him to the most surprising thing of all. He had almost not come tonight; instead, he'd considered asking Harry to take his place.

In the end, he had decided he might as well make the most of the woman's willingness. It had been too long since he'd been with a woman—weeks, if not months. That must account for his unusual mood, he decided. He wasn't sure if he was restless, despondent, or plain bored with a life that seemed to be sorely lacking in excitement. It was time to shake it off, whatever it was.

Perhaps a tryst in the woods would help. He had rarely taken his conquests outside in the open, but he had to admit that the forbidden, unusual element added a certain thrill to the idea. An adventurous lover himself, he liked an imaginative partner, and the place of the meeting had convinced him to go himself instead of sending Harry.

In any case, here he was, about to pounce on the waiting, brazen laundress.

Thanks to her hood, she wouldn't see him approach, and he was confident in his ability to move silently. Mildred would be surprised when he swept her into his arms and deposited her onto the mossy ground. Or ... should he pin her against the tree and lift her skirts? Pleasure her first, then bend her over and take her from behind? Aye, perhaps he should do that, as, for some reason he could not fathom, he didn't want to see her face.

As soon as he had put a foot in the clearing, his mind had been assaulted by memories of little Siân sitting on her blanket, eating her simple tart like other ladies might eat an exotic, expensive delicacy. His groin tightened when he remembered the way she had moaned when he had licked her dainty little fingers. It hadn't been the most wicked thing he had ever done to a woman, not by a long shot, but it had fired his blood in a most unexpected manner. Damn and blast, he'd gone hard just thinking about it.

Oh well, Mildred was just out there, waiting. The discomfort would not last long.

He wrapped an arm about her waist and drew her to him, murmuring soothing words in her ear when she gasped in shock. Though he had wanted to surprise her, he hadn't meant to frighten her.

"It's only me, sweetheart. Have you been waiting long?"

She nodded and whispered her answer, almost too low for him to hear. "Too long," he thought he heard her say.

"Well, I'm here now. Let me give you what you've been waiting for."

Keeping her back to his chest, he took her earlobe between his teeth.

The moan escaping her mouth was the most provocative he had ever heard. It seemed wrenched from her very soul, unrestrained, betraying a wild, sensual nature he wasn't even sure she was aware of that inflamed his blood further. As soon as he cupped her breasts, she reached back to place a hand over his straining groin, the message clear.

She needed more.

Only too happy to comply, he slipped a hand under her bodice and felt a petal-soft nipple. He growled his satisfaction when it peaked under his caresses. Desperate to hear more of her moans, he tugged at the hardened nub at the same time as he suckled her earlobe and lifted the hem of her dress. Suddenly, she was not just moaning; she was talking.

In Welsh, as far as he could tell.

Well, what of it? It would hardly be surprising if someone employed at Sheridan Manor had been brought over from Esgyrn Castle. It didn't matter what language she spoke or where she came from, not when her hand was pressing down on his hardness and his fingers were inching their way up her silken thigh. When he reached her most intimate place, he could not help but groan. She was so wet and so hot he knew it would take only a few moments to bring about the release her body was desperate for.

A finger slipped inside her sheath easily. Christopher groaned. He'd always liked pleasuring women, and the one in his arms seemed made for his caresses. There was nothing like a willing, daring partner, and she was like living fire, exquisitely responsive.

It was not long before she flooded his fingers with her release, gripping his wrist so tight he already knew he would wear the imprint of her nails for days. Oddly, the thought pleased him. He would wear the marks with pride.

"Beautiful," he rasped in her ear. "Now give me your mouth before I take my turn."

Though he had elected not to see her face only moments earlier, after what they had just shared, he felt the irresistible need to kiss her. She turned her head, and her hood fell. A mass of unruly curls tumbled down to her shoulders. He frowned. From what he'd seen at Sheridan Manor, Mildred's hair was as dark as night and nowhere near as thick. It was really a wild profusion of hair. He knew of only one person with such a mane of hair.

"*Siân!*" He took his hands from her as quickly as if he'd been burned. Shock made him swear out loud. "What the fuck are you doing here?"

"I ... I was ..." She didn't seem able to talk; her breath was coming in short pants, and her eyes were glazed. And no wonder. She was recovering from a very intense release. Christopher could still feel the heat of her desire on his palm, the proof of her pleasure was still coating his fingers. Christ on the cross, what had she made him do? He'd thought to tup an experienced woman, and he'd almost deflowered Lord Sheridan's daughter in the middle of the woods. If he hadn't felt the urge to kiss her before possessing her, he would even now be bending her over and ramming himself inside her with all the strength of his need. It didn't bear thinking about.

Thank God he'd seen who she was before it was too late.

Christopher muttered another curse. He had not felt any intimate barrier while his fingers had been inside her, but that didn't mean she had ever been possessed by a man. He had heard from some of his less honorable friends, who—unlike him—didn't balk at the idea of bedding virgins, that not all of them bled, contrary to what one might hear. He had concluded that not all women had a maidenhead to breach.

It mattered not. Maidenhead or not, Siân was an innocent. Willing or not, she was a virgin—and a lady. He shouldn't have done what he had done. He shouldn't want to do more. He shouldn't still be hard as rock.

For more safety, he took a step backward. If he touched her, there was no telling what he might do.

"Where is Mildred?" A silence. Christopher crossed his arms over his chest, doing his best to control his rising temper. He'd been played for a fool, he was painfully hard, and he'd had to put an abrupt stop to the one thing that would bring him relief. He was in no mood to be patient. "In case you hadn't real-ized it, this is the point where you explain what is going on."

Siân swallowed at the anger in Christopher's voice. Instead of answering, she looked at her hands kneading the cuff of her dress, at the pebbles at her feet, at the crack in the tree bark opposite her. She looked anywhere but at the man standing in front of her, waiting for her to explain what was happening.

How could she do it? How could she tell him that she wanted him to make love to her? It was the last thing he would expect to hear.

Well, perhaps she could show him what she wanted.

Bracing herself for his reaction, she allowed the cloak to drop at her feet. Underneath, she was wearing only a shift. She'd made the most of the warmth of the evening, hoping the sight would make it impossible for Christopher to resist her. If the tensing in his body was any indication, it had been an inspired idea.

"Bloody hell. Didn't I say that you constantly surprise me?" he said through gritted teeth. "I didn't know the half of it."

But there was nothing surprising in her going to him. Siân had known in her heart she would marry that man for years. As young as she had been when she'd first set eyes on him, she had known. And her childish admiration had grown into something very much like lust as her body—and his—had developed. And now ... Now she was in love with him.

It was inexplicable, and she wasn't sure anyone would understand how it had happened, but it was a fact.

And so tonight, she was not doing anything scandalous; she was only giving herself to a man she had been in love with for ten years, the man she had chosen to be her husband, the only man she had ever wanted.

And he wanted her. She had felt his desire earlier when

he'd pressed himself against her and given her pleasure such as she had never dreamed possible. It was time he took her.

"I'm a virgin." The words passed her lips easily.

"Yes, I know. That is why I cannot believe what you made me—"

Her hand landing on his hardness cut off him midsentence. Before he could protest or slap her hand away, Siân started to stroke him, her intent clear. Her gestures would be clumsy, betraying her lack of experience, but with luck, he would understand she was willing and ready.

"I'm a virgin, but I want you all the same," she whispered. "That is why I'm here. I want you to be the first man I welcome inside my body, the only man. Make love to me, Christopher. Here. Now."

Each shocking word was punctuated with a stroke. It was not long before she felt him go from stone to granite. Hope swelled in her chest. Perhaps she would be able to make him overcome his scruples. She had been honest about her inexperience because she didn't want him to think she was in the habit of going to men to be pleasured, but she would not allow it to deter him.

"Jesus, woman, I swear, you'll make a man lose his mind!" He imprisoned her wrist with his fingers. The gesture only caused her heartbeat to go faster, her resolve to strengthen. She had held him thus while he'd pleasured her earlier. "I can't ... We can't—"

"We can because we are going to get married."

"We are?"

"Yes. I am old enough that my parents cannot stop me, and I will do what I know is right for me."

When they were done, she would tell him about her plans for the future, make him see that it was not a passing fancy. She had it all decided. For once in her life, she was not going to be shy. For once, she would do what she wanted. But for the moment, she had something other than their wedding to focus on; there was a throbbing in her body that would leave her no peace.

With determined gestures, she freed Christopher's rigid member. The groan he gave when she closed her hand over him, skin on skin, was the most beautiful sound she had ever heard. She reached up to him, desperate for a kiss. Though he had touched her with shocking deliberation earlier, she had yet to feel his lips on hers, and she needed to taste him at last, like she had in her dream.

"Siân, please don't do this."

Instead of lowering his mouth to her, he straightened to his full height, making it impossible for her to reach him. He was just too tall. Siân tilted her head, not defeated. He refused to offer her his mouth? Very well. She would just have to kiss another part of him. And she knew just which one. She would do to the member straining toward her what he had done to her fingers the other day. Judging from the reaction it had provoked in her, it would send his bones to a liquid mess, making it impossible for him to resist her.

Without further ado, she dropped to her knees.

Christopher could not speak, could not move, could barely breathe. But at the back of his mind, he knew it was all wrong. Siân had allowed him to pleasure her with his fingers, had stroked him as intimately as a lover would, was even now gifting him with a caress he'd thought only whores would dare perform. And that was not all. She wanted him to dishonor her, to plunge inside her untried body. She was talking about *marriage*, for Christ's sake. He should flee. He should be horrified.

Instead, he was more aroused than he had ever been.

The way she had moaned and writhed in his arms earlier, spasmed around his fingers, then, most scandalously of all, dropped to her knees and taken him into her mouth made it impossible to think rationally. His bones had become a liquid mess.

Before he could stop them, his hands came up to cradle her head, his fingers enmeshed themselves into her wild, oh-so-soft hair. That was what her beautiful mane was made for, he decided, to anchor her in place while he thrust into her willing mouth. How had he not thought so before? It was just perfect. A single word escaped his lips.

"Yes."

When he heard his voice slice through the darkness, he realized he had meant to say the exact opposite. "Stop" would have been preferable—or "no." "Wait," at the very least. The last thing he should have done was encourage her, damn it all!

Siân didn't stop for a moment, barely gave him time to breathe. Jesus, how long did she intend to suckle him? How would he withstand the assault?

With a mighty curse, he wrenched himself away from the warmth enveloping him. "Enough! Do you want me to spill in your mouth? Force you to swallow my seed?" he snarled, hoping to shock her into more proper behavior. "I swear you're making it impossible for a man to do the right thing."

As he could have expected, the little minx was not shocked or deterred in the least. The caresses over his shaft didn't stop even if, with her mouth freed, she was able to answer his questions.

"The right thing in this instance is doing what I'm begging you to do." A kiss landed on the tip of his cock, sending sparks all the way to his skull. "I want you, and I can see you want me too." Her tongue, slow and torturous, licked a fiery path along his length. Dear God, where had she learned to do that? He closed his eyes. "I'll do anything to convince you this is meant to happen."

Two lips wrapped around him, and he felt the delicious suckling again, stronger than before. It was too much. Bloody hell, he'd never been so desperate for release.

"You ... are ..."

What did he want to say? He had no idea. Nevertheless, Siân answered, proving she'd understood anyway. "I am. Take me."

As if to leave him no choice, she engulfed him in her mouth completely, licking, teasing, moaning, showing him what she wanted him to do to another part of her—then abruptly stopped.

The loss of her heat was too much to bear. Drunk with need, Christopher tumbled her to the ground and raised the hem of her shift all the way to her waist. She surprised him by taking it off altogether, revealing her gorgeous body to his gaze. Was she trying to kill him? No. She was trying to make him take her and then marry her. She had just said as much.

Marry her?

He would have to worry about that part later because, right now, his brain had been reduced to fire. If he was to think straight, he had to allow his seed to shoot out of him first. With her naked and spread open under him, he was unable to do anything; the only part of him able to function at the moment was the swollen member straining between his thighs.

"It will hurt at first."

He had to warn her. He could not prevent the pain, but he could at least ensure she was not surprised by it—and then make her forget about the discomfort when he made her come once more.

"I know," she rasped, her voice as hoarse as his had been. "But I also know that no woman has ever died from it."

No, not as far as he knew. Christopher groaned. How did she always know the right thing to say?

"Are you still wet?" He hoped to God she was ready

because he feared he would not have the patience to prepare her if she wasn't. A quick brush against her folds told him all he needed to know. She was slick and hot, just like before. It would seem that sucking on him had inflamed her as much as it had inflamed him. The thought was enough to send his rigid shaft leaking.

Damn it! He had to take her without delay, or he would spill like an untried lad. That ignominy had never befallen him, thank the Lord, and he would be damned if it happened with the first woman he actually wanted to keep seeing once he'd taken his pleasure with her. With anyone else, he would simply have made sure never to cross paths with her again. But he could not imagine never seeing Siân again.

"Christopher, please, take me. I'm dying."

So was he.

He pushed in as slowly as his raging desire allowed him. Feeling no resistance, he slid in deeper. Of course she was tight, her body having never welcomed a man inside before, but his instinct had been right. There didn't seem to be any barriers to breach. Even better, as it meant the possession would hurt her less than it might another woman. Only when he was fully seated inside her heat did he pause to give her a moment to adjust.

"Ah!" Her cry was one of awe and triumph combined. She knew she had won, but Christopher was only too glad to let her enjoy her victory. He would benefit from it as well.

"Yes. You asked for this, you infuriating little minx. So take it."

Heedless of what she might think of his forceful behavior, he lifted her left leg up and hooked it over his arm, opening her as far as she would go and plunging into her with renewed vigor. He was past reasoning, past caution, past everything that was not the feminine heat keeping him captive.

In that moment, what was happening felt meant to be. It was the oddest sensation, but he allowed himself to revel in it because it was also intensely satisfying. Siân was matching him thrust for thrust, displaying a sensual nature that had him completely enraptured. She cried her pleasure a moment later, allowing him to at last let go of his control.

At the last moment, he pulled out. He'd been driven so close to madness that he erupted before he had time to take himself in hand, before he could aim anywhere in particular. His seed shot out of him in great spurts, coating her stomach all the way from her navel to her breasts. It was iridescent in the moonlight, almost pretty, as if he'd adorned her with pearls instead of being unforgivably crude.

Panting hard, feeling slightly disorientated, Christopher stared at the vision in front of him. With a faint trace of blood on her thighs and his seed cooling on her skin, Siân was marked as his in a way no other woman had ever been.

He knew then that she was right. They were going to get married. Because no matter how much of a selfish bastard he could be—and had been at times he would not leave her to face her family's disapproval on her own or let her deal with the humiliation of having to explain to her future husband why she was no virgin on her wedding night.

Even more to the point, there was no way in hell he was going to let any other man touch her now.

Chapter Nine

Lying on her bed, Siân concentrated on staying still so as not to awaken her sister. It was a miracle she had managed to slip into bed without disturbing Jane. As a matter of fact, she had barely any recollection of how she had made it back to Sheridan Manor.

After Christopher had withdrawn from her sated body, she had been too dazed, too happy to do anything but breathe and let him wipe her stomach clean. Her guess was that he had taken her home on Warrior's back and then carried her to her bedchamber door, half asleep already. As soon as she'd collapsed on her bed, sleep had claimed her. As a result, she had been unable to tell him what she had meant to tell him. He still had no idea she was in love with him and had been for years, he still didn't know she had given herself to him because she could not imagine a life where she was not his wife, and he had still not agreed to get married.

Yes. That was the biggest problem.

"Is that you?" Jane asked, her voice disembodied in the darkness. Though dawn was not far away, no light pervaded into the room yet. "Is everything all right? You didn't come to bed at the usual time last night. And I could not find you anywhere in the afternoon. Where were you?"

"I ... I ..." What could she say?

Her sister stilled, alerted by her hesitation. Siân imagined her eyes had grown as wide as cart wheels. "You went to him, didn't you? He took advantage of you, didn't he, like the rogue he is? He—"

"He did not."

Jane's body relaxed. "Thank God. Forgive me. For a moment, I thought he'd touched you."

Oh, he *had* touched her—rather thoroughly. And she had touched him just as thoroughly. The whole thing had been spectacular. "I mean ..."

The silence in the room became as dense as smoke. "You mean ...?"

"We lay together," she blurted out. After that admission, the rest of the confession came tumbling out. "It's not what you think. He didn't force me into anything. We made love on the forest floor, and it was at my request. You know what I feel for him. I told him tonight I want to marry him, and I ... I forced his hand most shamefully. Please don't hate him, Jane. Don't hate me. Please. What was the harm in us lying together? We are going to be husband and wife anyway."

For a long moment, there was nothing.

Then, when Siân was bracing herself for a torrent of reproach, Jane asked, her voice low and tentative, "How was it?"

Relief flooded Siân's veins. Her sister wasn't angry; she didn't think her unforgivably wanton. As long as that was the case, she could face anything. Then she shook her head, unsure how to answer the question. There were no words to describe what she had experienced, but at the risk of worrying Jane, who would think she didn't dare tell her she'd been hurt, she had to try.

"I always knew I would love being in his arms, but the reality surpassed my imagination."

"Did it hurt?"

A pause while Siân thought. "No. I cannot say it did. It was odd, that's all."

They had often heard it said that it would hurt, and Christopher had warned her about it before he'd taken her, but Siân could not describe what she had felt when he had surged inside her as pain. Perhaps she had been too desperate to notice; perhaps it was because he had stroked her beforehand and made her erupt in pleasure. She had felt how wet and slick she was when he'd stroked her just beforehand, and instinct told her it had eased his penetration.

"It was wonderful, indescribable, like crying and laughing at the same time. I always thought he was the right man for me, and this proved it." She paused. "You will see when your time comes."

It was light enough by then for Siân to see Jane make a face. She didn't seem convinced, either because she couldn't credit Christopher with being the right man for anyone or because she imagined him behaving roughly in bed. Siân should have reassured her, but she was ill at ease. How could she tell her sister what they had done together? If Jane knew she had taken a man into her mouth and enjoyed every decadent moment of it, she would think of her differently.

"I will ask for a bath to be drawn for you," Jane declared, putting an end to the discussion.

A bath. Yes. How had Siân not thought of that? It would do her good. Remembering the way Christopher's seed had coated her stomach, she started to blush. She should have washed herself before going to bed, but she had been too tired. Could Jane smell the unusual scent? Was that why she had suggested she take a bath? The heat spread further, reaching the roots of her hair, but she refused to be embarrassed. The whole encounter had been wonderful, and she had loved every moment.

"Thank you. A bath would be good."

"And I promise I will not tell Father where you went."

All the blood drained from Siân's veins. All of a sudden, she wasn't hot anymore but icy cold. Of a certainty, her father would object to what had happened last night, every single moment of it. He would be appalled at the deception she had played on Christopher by dragging him to the meadow under false pretenses and then pretending to be Mildred, as well as shocked by her wantonness. He would also condemn Christopher's inability to resist her advances and disapprove of the manner of his possession.

At the idea of confronting her parents and telling them she had finally found a husband, her whole body tensed. What would they think of her choice? Esyllt would have no reason to question her decision as she didn't really know Christopher, but Connor did. The two men had lived side by side for years before he'd gone to live in Wales. He might well have known about what Christopher had made Jane go through, and later, he would have heard all about his exploits with the womenfolk. As if that were not enough, Matthew had told him about the incident with Elsie. Even if the maid's lie had since then been exposed, the fact remained. He had bedded her, along with many others.

Would Connor give his blessing to a union with such a man? She had no idea.

Perhaps it would be best to go and see Christopher before she did anything—to confirm his intentions toward her. That way, she could face her parents with a clearer conscience. They could even go together, make it look as if the decision had been made of a common accord.

Yes, she decided as she plunged her aching body into the water a moment later. That was what she would do. Go to Throckmorton Castle and see Christopher.

~

Luck was with her. As she rode into the bailey, the first person she saw was Christopher himself. He'd been talking to one of his men by the barbican, but he dismissed him as soon as he saw her. He was at her side before she could dismount.

"We need to talk," he said before running a hand through his hair. "About last night."

"Yes," Siân agreed. That was why she was here. Not to talk about last night but rather the future.

She jumped down from the saddle, expecting him to lead her to the main hall. But instead of steering her that way, he took her back through the gate and into the lists. She fought the unease invading her. It was as if he didn't want to be seen in her company. Why? When they married, she would be mistress of Throckmorton Castle. There was no shame in having her around.

"You haven't changed your mind about us marrying, have you?" she asked as soon as he'd come to a halt. Was that the reason for the secrecy? He didn't want his people to see him with a woman who, ultimately, was to play no role in his life?

Christopher gave her a strange look, one that made his dark eye swirl and her insides ripple in response. "I wasn't aware I had made up my mind to marry in the first place."

Her stomach fell to her feet.

Indeed, up until last night, he'd had no intention of marrying her or, indeed, anyone, at least not yet. She'd suspected as much, but she had forced his hand most shame-fully. And now that her mind was not cloudy with desire, she realized he had never actually said he would marry her. She had simply taken his lack of refusal for an agreement because it was what she'd been desperate to believe.

What if she'd gotten it completely wrong and he had simply made the most of her willingness to be taken, ignoring her ridiculous statement that they would marry afterward? His senses had been stirred; he'd been ready for a woman, having come to the meadow expecting to bed Mildred. And fool that she was, she had pleasured him and then lain naked under him. Had he just slaked his lust, knowing she would have no way of pressuring him into anything once it was over? There certainly had been no formal betrothal, no announcement, no courtship even. As far as everyone was concerned, they barely knew each other. True, his reputation made it likely people would believe her if she claimed he had deflowered her, but if she added that they had agreed to get married afterward, they would dismiss her claim as wishful thinking or, worse, an outright lie. It would be her word against his, and no one would believe Christopher Harrison had promised marriage to a woman like her.

"I ... I don't—"

"Siân." Christopher interrupted her and gave a sigh. "Of course I will marry you. I am not such a despicable rogue that I could deflower a lady and leave her to deal with the consequences alone. Surely, you must know that?"

She didn't exactly know it, even if she had hoped it would be the case. "I left you no choice," she mumbled. Considering what had happened the night before, he had every right to feel trapped. She had tricked him into pleasuring her and then licked him into surrender.

The laugh he gave was somewhat shaky. He, too, was remembering what she had done. "You certainly made it impossible for me to think straight. But the blame is shared. I could have refused to take you and instead made use of your mouth to reach my release. It seems to me you wouldn't have minded."

Made use of your mouth.

The place between her legs started to throb at the crude statement. Christopher seemed as affected as she was. He had stiffened, and the light in his eyes had changed from teasing to stormy.

He cleared his throat, as if regretting putting such a lewd image in both their heads. "In any case, what I'm saying is, I did make love to you, I did take your maidenhead. You are the first virgin I've ever bedded, and I will do my duty by you."

"Duty." The word sat ill with Siân, who would marry him for love, but she did not let it worry her. The important thing was to secure his agreement. The rest would come in time.

"Shall we go speak to my father, then? When do you want to get married?"

Her heart skipped a beat. That was it. Finally. After spending so long hoping, plotting, fearing a disaster, she and Christopher were about to become husband and wife. Dare she ask him if they could get married on the morrow? As far as she was concerned, the sooner they could have the ceremony that bound them one to the other, the better. Before the end of the month, she fully intended to be Lady Ashton. Christopher would then belong to her.

As for her, she had always belonged to him.

"Not immediately, my impatient little lamb," The smile he gave made it clear he had read her thoughts. "Before we wed, I need to go to Kent to see my uncle."

Siân recoiled. That was the last thing she had expected him to say. He wanted to go to the other end of the country to see an uncle he only ever talked about in scathing terms? Why? It was not as if he needed the man's permission to get married. Why on earth did he have to go now, when his presence was needed at Sheridan Manor? She couldn't get married without her groom.

"Can't it wait?" She hated herself for asking the question, but the idea of him walking away when she was so close to fulfilling her lifelong ambition was too dire to contemplate.

"I'm afraid not. I received a letter this morning informing me he is at death's door. This is most unexpected, as he is still a man in his prime and has not yet reached his fifth decade, but last month, he was struck down by a mysterious chill. He now fears he will not see the end of the month. As it is, I am not certain I will be in time to see him. There isn't a moment to lose. When you arrived, I was giving the order to saddle my horse. I was about to ask Harry to ride to Sheridan Manor to inform you of my departure."

"Oh, Christopher." Siân placed a hand over his forearm, her disappointment melting in view of his announcement. Here she was, complaining about a little delay when he was about to lose the only family member he had left. Even if he and the man were not close, it would be hard for him. "I'm so sorry."

He shook his head slowly. "Don't be. I cannot pretend to be sad. The man means nothing to me, and, in truth, I have no idea why he wants to see me. I would say we never got on, but we never met enough times for me to make that claim. He's as good as a stranger."

"That's ..."

That was even worse. She had known his childhood had been unhappy, but that was simply heartbreaking. Having been raised in a loving family, Siân could not begin to imagine how he had felt, shunned by his father, ignored by his grandfather, without any siblings to turn to. He'd always been alone in the world, never knowing she wanted to give him everything he needed.

She didn't know what to say. So instead, she kissed him.

Making use of a block of stone at her feet, she put her face level with his and gave Christopher the kiss he had refused her the night before.

It was their first kiss—*her* first kiss as well—but because she had imagined it countless times in her mind and had even dreamed of it, it almost didn't feel new. What she hadn't expected was that he would lift her into his arms or that the feel of his tongue inside her mouth would make her think of what other part of him she had welcomed between her lips.

They were kissing, but it felt as if they were making love. She could feel his hardness poking at the place between her thighs, searching, demanding entry. Siân wanted nothing more than to give her permission, but she could not. Not here, not like that, in full view of everyone. So she kissed him again and again, using her tongue, rubbing her body against his, bathing in his wonderful scent. Was it ginger perhaps?

Before she could decide, he drew away.

"God on the cross, but you drive me mad, woman," he rasped, grinding his hips to illustrate the point. The message was clear. He wanted to be inside her as much as she wanted to welcome him in. "Why is that? Will you tell me?"

Because we are meant to be together. I've always known it. Nothing of what's happening is a surprise to me. Because I love you.

Could she tell him as much? They had just agreed to get married, but he still had no idea of the depth of her feelings. He thought she wanted to marry to save her reputation; he had no idea her heart was engaged. Should she—

One look at him made it clear the moment was ill chosen. He was about to leave to go on a difficult mission. He was not ready to hear such a momentous declaration. Though he had agreed to marry her, Siân could not fool herself into thinking that he loved her. Not yet, at least. He had called marriage to her his duty only a moment ago. He felt desire for her, and affection. For now, she had to accept it was enough.

In time, he would fall in love with his wife; she was sure of it.

"Come back to me, Christopher," she said, speaking against his lips. "With me as your wife, with the children I will give you, you'll have the family you never had growing up."

His eyes sparkled. It seemed to Siân that his hold tightened and he was about to say something, but she couldn't be sure because the gleam disappeared as quickly as it had come. A moment later, she felt him lift her off the stone and place her gently on the ground.

"I need to go."

His stallion was already saddled when they entered the bailey together. Christopher vaulted on top, turned to her, nodded once, and then left in a thunder of hooves.

~

"Lord Ashton? Really? Of all men, you had to choose him?"

The lack of warmth in her father's voice was not promising, but Siân stood her ground. Unfortunately, she knew what he thought of Christopher, but she hoped he would change his mind in due time. No one could get to know the man she loved and hold on to their prejudice.

"Yes. We agreed last night to get married."

"Last *night*?" This time, his tone was distinctively icy.

"I m-mean yesterday, late in the afternoon," she stammered, stealing a glance toward her mother, who had placed a hand over her husband's arm in an appeasing gesture. "I can't remember what time exactly."

Of course she remembered the exact moment she had informed Christopher that they were going to be married. He had been braced over her on muscular arms, ready to plunge inside her, and she had been lying under him on her cloak, naked as the day she was born.

"You mean that, after all these years, you have finally found a man to whom you can imagine being married, *cariad?*" Esyllt asked in an evident effort at conciliation.

Siân threw her a grateful smile. "Yes."

She had found him a decade ago, which was precisely why she had refused to get married before now or even look at other men. Her parents had been led to believe she had exacting standards and was waiting for the right man to come along. It was not the case. She had simply been waiting for the right moment to ensnare Christopher.

"Then we're going to have to trust your judgment." Her mother threw her husband a meaningful look, one that warned him not to pass any comment. He did not. "Feminine intuition is a powerful thing, and I'm sure this Lord Ashton isn't half as disreputable as some people make out. He did save two of our daughters, after all."

"Yes, but he made a third one utterly miserable as a child!" Connor snapped, not so easily appeased.

So he knew. Siân did not let it defeat her. Her parents would soon see she was right to trust him. She raised her chin defiantly. "I love him, Father."

The air in the solar stilled. Then her father's shoulders sagged.

"If you love him, and he has agreed to marry you, then there is nothing else to say."

There wasn't.

And so the long wait started.

Chapter Ten

"Did you know Lord Ashton was back? I heard the people in the village say they spotted his retinue entering Throckmorton Castle three days ago."

Siân blinked at Jane's declaration. No, she didn't know Christopher was back. And he'd brought back a retinue with him? That was a surprise. He had left alone and had no family. Who in Kent had decided to accompany him up north? Her heart leaped and then sank in rapid succession as a dozen questions assaulted her mind. Christopher had been back for three days and not sent word of his return? She refused to let her dismay show and allow Jane the satisfaction of criticizing her future brother-in-law's behavior even if she could not deny being uneasy.

Why had he not called for her or at least sent word of his arrival? A day's delay to put his affairs in order was perhaps understandable, but three?

"Of course, I knew," she lied. "But do you think you could stop calling him Lord Ashton? We're about to be married. Call him Christopher." There. Much better to steer the focus away from her.

Jane made a grimace. "You really are going through with this wedding, then?"

"Yes." Never had she been more determined. "Now that he's back, we can finally start planning for the ceremony. Not that it needs to be a lavish affair." She cared not about impressing the local lords or anyone else. All she wanted was to be Christopher's wife and fulfill her life's destiny. "Come. It's time to eat. I'm famished."

The whole family was already in the main hall when the two sisters entered. As soon as he saw her, her father walked over to her.

"Matthew tells me Lord Ashton is back."

Siân barely contained her irritation. Was she the only one unaware of her betrothed's comings and goings? Apparently. Still, just like with Jane, she thought it best to pretend she knew that already. "He is."

Connor arched a brow. "Does that mean his uncle died, then?"

Once again, she was at a loss as to what to say. Because if Christopher was back, it meant his uncle had either indeed died in the last month or recovered from his chill, making his nephew's presence in Kent no longer necessary. Somehow, she didn't think a miraculous recovery was the explanation.

"This I do not know," she finally admitted.

Mercifully, her father didn't ask any questions and put an end to her torment. "Well, if he's back, we'll be able to start preparations for your wedding."

"Yes!" Seren shouted, standing up in her excitement. "I like weddings! And I like Lord Ashton."

This show of support amidst the barely concealed disapproval warmed Siân even if, considering he had saved her life, it was hardly surprising the little girl would approve of Christopher.

"So do I." It was Gwenllian's turn to speak.

It warmed Siân further to see that no one hushed the two girls and told them they had no idea what they were talking about. Perhaps they were finally coming round to the idea of her becoming Lady Ashton.

She beamed at her sisters. "Thank you. And he likes you too."

Her father nodded and decreed, "We'll go to see him in the morning."

"We have come to see Lord Ashton."

It was very early for a visit, but Siân had been up before dawn, and mercifully, her father was an early riser as well. They had broken their fast together in the hall and, of a common accord, gone to the stables as soon as they had finished their meal. A moment later, they had been galloping in the direction of Throckmorton Castle.

To her relief, he had not once asked her if she was certain that was what she wanted. He seemed to have accepted that her instinct could be trusted.

Despite the early hour, no one in the bailey seemed surprised to see them. Her shoulders relaxed. Of course, knowing her, Christopher would have told his people to expect a visit.

"Let me go get his squire," a young man Siân had never seen before told them. Then again, it was no wonder she didn't recognize him, as she had never set eyes on anyone at Throckmorton Castle save Harry. She had not ventured past the gate or seen anything other than the bailey during her visit the previous month.

Well, that would soon be remedied.

A moment later, the groom was back with a tall man who nodded at them. "This way, my lord, my lady. Lord Ashton has just finished breaking his fast and will receive you."

Who was that? Where was Harry? Siân frowned as she followed the man. Had Christopher's uncle forced him to replace his squire with another of his own men? She dearly hoped not.

"Here you are."

With a bow, the squire opened the door to the solar. It was a spacious room well lit by three bay windows facing south, but in spite of the large openings, it lacked warmth. Siân found herself rearranging the furniture in her mind. When she was Lady Ashton, she would place the chest farther away from the hearth, cover the stone benches with soft cushions, and replace the heavy armchairs with more comfortable folding stools. New tapestries would have to be hung, as the ones facing her were faded and moth eaten. Throckmorton Castle was in sore need of repair and a woman's touch.

No matter. Once she lived there, it would all change.

"Good morning," the man in the middle of the room greeted them.

"Good morning. Apologies, we are here to see Lord Ashton," Connor repeated, looking to the door where the squire had just disappeared after taking them to the wrong man. Siân could see he was getting irritated by the delay. Oh dear, their visit was not going well.

"Yes. I am he."

Father and daughter looked at one another, confusion etched on their faces. Was the man mad? Had he just said—

"There must be a mistake. I have known Lord Ashton for years, and you are definitely not him."

The man chuckled. "You haven't known the real Lord Ashton, my lord, merely the usurper."

Usurper?

Siân's whole body felt suddenly encased in ice. Nothing was making any sense. Where was Christopher? And who was this man acting as if he'd always belonged here? Tall and blond, he looked uncomfortably similar to the man she loved. Of course, both his eyes were the same color and he was nowhere near as handsome, but she supposed the two of them could be related. Christopher didn't have any family, however, since his grandfather, his father, and probably his uncle were dead.

So what was going on?

"Christopher, I believe his name is. I'm afraid he never had any right to call himself Lord Ashton. The title was mine all along and will be my son's when I die," the man continued. He sounded delighted by their reaction, as if he'd waited for years to expose the man who'd been impersonating him. He gestured at the chest by the hearth. "Should you require proof of my claim, I will be only too happy to provide it."

There was too much conviction in the man's voice for anyone to doubt he was speaking the absolute truth. Was she dreaming? If so, she prayed she would wake up soon, before the dream turned into a veritable nightmare.

"So he—" Connor started, only to be interrupted.

"My advice to you is to forget the man. I doubt he will dare show his face round these parts ever again now that I'm back."

Forget?

Forget the man she loved? The man she was supposed to marry?

Siân did not dare look at her father, not wanting to see the condemnation in his eyes. She already knew what he would be thinking. That he'd been right from the start and Christopher was nothing more than a despicable liar who had never been worthy of her, had meant to desert her all along, and she didn't know how she could bear to face his disapproval when her heart was breaking.

"Please," she whispered. "Let's just go."

~

"You should eat something."

Siân glanced at the pottage getting cold in its wooden bowl and shook her head. She could tell all her favorite ingredients were in it, but the idea of swallowing even one mouthful of food was too much to bear. "I'm not hungry."

Jane placed a hand on her arm. "Shall I ask Avice to make some of her famous tarts if you—"

"No!" Not the honey tarts, not the walnut and fig tarts, not any tart whatsoever, which would only make her think of Christopher and the way he had licked imaginary honey from her fingers that day in the clearing. *What had possessed him to do such a thing?* she asked herself for the hundredth time.

She scoffed. What was she doing trying to understand the workings of the mind of a man who had posed as Lord Ashton and fooled everyone in the process!

Last year, she had heard James, the castle steward, tell her and Jane that in the right context and in the absence of contradictors, the most outrageous lies could be swallowed. He had been talking from experience, she'd realized, when he'd explained how his sister-in-law had once tried to trick him into marriage by making him believe she was carrying his child.

Well, she could see the truth of his claim now. Christopher's lie had been even more outrageous and yet he had gotten away with it for years. It was no consolation to know that she had not been the only one to be tricked because she suspected she was the one who had suffered from the deception the most.

Unless ...

Unless she was not the only woman he'd promised marriage to before abandoning her. The thought had never crossed her mind before, but why would it not be the case? Who knew what the man was capable of? Had he tricked dozens of naïve little virgins in the same way, knowing that if their fathers came to demand retribution, they would only end up being brought to the real Lord Ashton down in Kent?

She pushed the thought out of her mind. It would serve no purpose to think like that except to torture her further. He had hurt *her*, made a fool out of *her*, and that was all that mattered.

After a week spent languishing in her room and avoiding her family, Siân grew restless and decided to go for a ride. Perhaps having to focus on managing a horse instead of her bitterness would help her shake some of her despondency. Once in the saddle, one could not allow their feelings to control them for fear of making their mount nervous.

She refused to take Angel, who reminded her too much of Christopher, and instead chose a gelding in his twilight years, as reliable as any horse she had ever seen. No sense in taking risks just because Christopher had been exposed as an even worse rogue than everyone thought. On Clover's back, she would be safe.

The gallop did help, as did the fresh air rushing through her hair, wiping her tears, and blowing away some of her pain. Then, just as she was dismounting to allow the gelding a drink in the river, movement in the distance caught her eye. Copper sparks appeared through the undergrowth.

Was she dreaming?

Of course she was not. She would have known that tall, forbidding shape anywhere. Hadn't she spent years looking for it on the horizon? Hadn't it become more familiar than her own shadow?

Christopher.

The usurper.

The deserter.

At any other time, she would have gone—perhaps even run —to him. Today, all she could do was remain rooted to the spot and wait for him to come near if he dared. He did dare, first jumping from the saddle and then eating the distance between them with long, graceful strides she couldn't help but admire. He stopped in front of her, both eyes equally bright. Even the brown one seemed piercing for once. What was he doing there? It had been a week since she and her father had gone to Throckmorton Castle to be told the man she was supposed to marry was not who everyone thought he was and would never come back, a week since she'd been told that her life as she knew it was over.

Siân had not thought to see him again. His deception unveiled, he had vanished, abandoned her without a second thought. During the week she'd spent in bed, reliving her conversation with the real Lord Ashton, there had been no word of Christopher. She had no idea whether he was still in Kent. Would he ever come back? Lord Ashton had hinted that he would not.

Well, apparently, he'd been wrong because Christopher was most definitely here.

What did it mean? Dare she hope she'd been wrong and it was all a misunderstanding? Had he come back to beg her forgiveness and assure her he still intended to honor his promise to her? Her heart started to beat unbearably fast in her chest because if he did, she suspected she would forgive him. The usurpation of identity didn't worry her.

As long as he wanted to be with her, it didn't matter who he was, what he had done, or why.

And perhaps there was a good reason for him to have impersonated the man. He'd been accused of the worst villainy once, of forsaking his unborn child and its mother, and the accusation had been proved to be a lie fabricated to take advantage of him and his status. Could there be an explanation for his posing as Lord Ashton? It was not impossible.

She should not have left Throckmorton Castle so hastily the other day; she should have demanded to be told what was going on. After the shocking revelation that Christopher was gone and had lied about his real identity, she had been so upset, so unable to carry out any semblance of conversation that her father had had no other choice but to take her home.

But now, she was regretting it. The man—Lord Ashton—had offered no explanation.

Let Christopher do it then.

"Siân." He allowed his gaze to wander over her, taking in her disheveled state and the look in her eyes, which she assumed reflected her state of confusion. "You've heard, then."

This opening did not impress her. Was that the best he could do? A flat statement, certainly no denial, and no apology either. She was incredulous. Did he really think his deception mattered little as long as he had come back for her? That she was not owed an explanation?

She could manage only a nod, followed by a single word. "Yes." She knew who he was, or rather who he was not.

"Then you know why I cannot marry you."

Siân felt as if a crossbow bolt had hit her square in the chest. He could not marry her? She knew no such thing! She'd been told by the real Lord Ashton that Christopher had lied about his identity for years, but that was quite a different thing, as anyone would agree.

"You ..." she started, not quite knowing what to say or *how* to say it. Her whole body, including her tongue, seemed to have gone liquid at the realization that he had *not* come back for her, that he *had* abandoned her even if he was here in front of her. She could barely stand or speak for shock.

"I am not Lord Ashton, never have been, so it—"

"I don't care if you're Lord Ashton or not!"

That was true, even if the deception had hurt her. But, ultimately, she cared not who Christopher was. All she cared about was that he was hers.

"Well, *I* care. And I cannot marry you now. Surely, you understand."

"Understand?" she roared. "No, I do not understand why you would agree that we should get married and then go back on your promise a few weeks later. I do not understand why you would not trust me with your secret, why it amused you to play me for a fool! I understand nothing!"

Christopher stilled under the onslaught.

The little Welsh lamb had gotten her claws out—or whatever other fearsome weapon lambs possessed. Only a few months ago, he would not have credited her with so much impetuosity. But he had since then seen how wild she could be when making love. It made sense she would be as fierce in anger.

It only made his situation more difficult. Not that he had dared hope she would accept his decision easily, but that ... that was something else altogether.

"Siân, I cannot marry you. Surely, you must see—"

"Cannot or will not?" she interrupted, hitting at his chest with surprising force. "And I 'must' nothing. How can you do this to me? I almost fell out with my sister when I tried to justify your behavior toward her, all the while knowing how much you had hurt her in the past! Everyone in my family sees you as the worst kind of rogue, but I stood up to them, took your defense when Elsie accused you, then told them you were the man I wanted to marry and assured them you were not the person they thought. But you made a fool out of me because you did go back on your promise and are just a despicable, untrustworthy, lying schemer who took advantage of my—"

She stopped, and he wasn't sure whether she thought she had revealed too much of her feelings for him or whether she could not talk for sheer anger. Both were possible. He had never seen her in such a state.

"I did not intend to make a fool out of you," Christopher said through gritted teeth, fighting his own mounting anger.

Was that all she had to say, that he had made her appear ridiculous in front of her family? In other words, loving, perfect people who would support her no matter what? Was he supposed to pity her? Did she think he was happy about the situation? Did she think it was easy for him? Where was the understanding, sympathetic woman he'd started to fall for? Had she been an illusion all along?

He'd thought she might have started to develop feelings for him, but he was no longer sure.

In view of her reaction, he was forced to reconsider everything. The daughter of a man as prestigious as Lord Sheridan might have the right to expect a good marriage, but she would also be aware that her being Welsh might be an issue for most English families. He, on the other hand, had not let it bother him. So was her ire caused by the realization that all her ploys to ensnare an English nobleman had failed?

He knew she had been desperate in her bid to extract a proposal out of him. She had, after all, gone to him *before* marriage had been mentioned, impersonating Mildred, rendering him incapable of thinking, making him take her. She had given herself to him fully, relying on his sense of honor to trap him into a union with the highborn virgin he had deflowered.

And now that she had found out he was not a lord, she was playing the victim.

Far from considering how he might feel, she saw only that she would never be a lady if she married him. As his wife, she would be a nobody. She had worked to entice him, surrendered her maidenhead, and played the whore for nothing. No wonder she felt cheated and bitter.

"But you did make a fool out of me," she carried on. "You said you would marry me. You took my maidenhead!"

Her voice had reached an alarming volume, but she did not seem to care. He didn't particularly either, as they were in the middle of nowhere and no one could hear them. But he cared that she was still thinking about herself and unwilling to see his predicament. Enough was enough.

Christopher trapped both her wrists in his hand before she could hit him again. He did not intend to have her inflict real damage on him and it was going that way.

"As to that, I took your maidenhead because you left me no choice, and we both know it. But I was careful not to make you with child," he rasped against her ear, remembering the effort it had taken him to withdraw in time. It usually wasn't that hard to stay in control, but with her, he had been lost in the moment and the pleasure of their joining. "I spilled outside your body, so there is little damage done."

For her at least. She could still make a good marriage since no child would ruin her reputation. No one needed to know she was not a virgin anymore. She had not bled on her first time, and he could not be the only man who knew it could happen that way. Her husband would just accept her word that she was untouched. Yes, she would be all right.

As for him, his prospects had never appeared more dire.

There is little damage done.

Was that what Christopher really thought?

Horror invaded Siân. It was even worse than she had feared. Christopher had planned his escape all along. That night in the clearing, while she had lost her mind to pleasure, he'd been thinking ahead. At the time, she had assumed he'd withdrawn because he wanted to protect her, make sure no one questioned her virtue if she happened to give birth to a child too soon after their wedding. In fact, he had only ensured he could not be made accountable for his actions, like he had done with the other women he'd seduced, Elsie and his countless other lovers. How had she thought he'd felt any different with her?

Oh, his betrayal was a hard blow to deal with. Would she ever recover from it?

"I hate you!"

Siân would have pushed at him, but with both her wrists imprisoned in his big hand, she could not move. Being so close to Christopher physically when they had never been so far apart emotionally was tearing at her heart. Hadn't he hurt her enough? Why had he come back? To torture her further, make her see what she had lost? It made no sense, but she was past trying to understand the workings of his mind. In the last week, she had dealt with enough disillusion, enough pain, enough humiliation to last her a lifetime. All she knew was that his decision was made and it was over between them.

He would never marry her.

Eventually, she stilled and he let go of her wrists.

"I hate you," she repeated more weakly.

But even as she hoisted herself up on Clover's back, she knew that was a lie. She didn't hate Christopher; she loved him. She had wanted him from the moment she'd set eyes on him all those years ago, and she feared she would love him till her dying day, betrayal or not.

Chapter Eleven

A third glass of mead. Or was it his fourth? Christopher wasn't sure. Still, it wasn't enough to forget the pain that had sliced through his chest when he'd told Siân he was forced to renounce their plans and seen her selfish reaction. He would need at least another three glasses of mead to make that particular pain disappear.

Or four.

The fire crackled, making one last effort at a flare before going completely out. How apt. Everything within him was slowly dying as well.

Christopher stared at the hearth, not seeing the struggling flames or the glowing coals. Despite the heat emanating from it, he felt chilled to the bone. This afternoon, Siân had made him feel every bit like the careless, scandalous, insensitive rogue people likened him to. And it had made him realize that, deep down, he wasn't like that. Because he cared. At least, he cared about *her*, say what she might. She might not be the first woman he had hurt with his actions, but she was the first virgin he had deflowered. That alone should ensure he was not indifferent to her fate. She was also the first woman he had agreed to marry.

And, as unexpected as it might be, as he'd ridden closer to Kent and farther away from her, he had realized that he was actually looking forward to their union.

It was not just the pleasure he'd felt in her arms and her brazenness as a lover that appealed to him and made him see marriage in a new light. It was everything else as well. He *had* been falling for the intriguing little lamb. With such a woman by his side, he would never be bored. And once he was married, he would have what he had never had, what he had always wanted—a family.

But he'd been forced to give up the dream as soon as it had formed. He could no longer marry Siân, and judging from what he'd seen today, her supposed attraction to him had only been an act destined to make him overlook her Welsh origins and a spontaneous nature that would make most men balk. As soon as the truth about his identity had been revealed, she'd lashed out, posing as the victim, conveniently forgetting that he was the injured party.

What would he do now? Where would he go?

By the time the fire had dwindled to embers, he still didn't have the answer to those questions.

The door opened, and the light of a candle fluttered on the wall behind him. Silent as a shadow, Sir Alexander Rathbone entered. Upon his return from Kent, in the impossibility of returning to Throckmorton Castle, Christopher had turned to his oldest friend, who had welcomed him in, asking no questions and pretending not to notice anything was amiss.

Well, it seemed his patience had finally come to an end. Nevertheless, Christopher stayed silent. A confrontation was sure to come.

"What the hell is wrong with you?" Alexander finally exploded. "I don't mind having you here at Audley, you're my friend, but I'd like to know what has turned you so glum. And I say glum for want of a better word. You've not been yourself since you came back from Kent."

Christopher almost laughed out loud at the choice of words. His friend had expressed the situation better than he himself could have done. That was precisely the problem. He *wasn't* himself anymore, or at least not who he'd thought he was his whole life.

"What's wrong with me? Nothing, as far as I can tell," he said with a sigh. That was the irony of it. He had done nothing wrong. And yet, he was being punished in the cruelest way. "I am the same man as I was last month. Except that I am not Lord Ashton now."

A scoff. "Come, what nonsense is this?"

"I wish it were nonsense. Unfortunately, it's the sad truth. When I went to Kent, I was told I had never had any right to the title and everything that goes with it. I am not Lord Ashton. Thomas Harrison is."

His half brother.

On his deathbed, Christopher's uncle had revealed the truth. The man had not summoned him because he'd wanted to see him one last time and make his peace with a nephew he'd never bothered to get to know but because he'd wanted to inform him of the situation he was in. Christopher was not, contrary to what he had believed all his life, his father's eldest son and therefore heir. The man had been married before, and his son by his first wife was the real Lord Ashton. That son, Thomas, had been summoned to Kent to be informed of the fact and take his rightful place at last.

A fit of coughing had interrupted the shocking declaration before any questions could be asked. In the morning, the old man had been unable to talk and could only point to the chest where Christopher had found a letter confirming what he'd been told. Stunned, he had read about his father's secret, and by noon, his uncle had been dead, having not uttered another word.

The following day, a blond man in his thirties had arrived from Norfolk with his wife and son and been welcomed as Lord Ashton. From then on, it had been a whirlwind of actions. Letters of proof had been produced, legal documents signed, deeds handed over, people made aware of the new situation, and Christopher had been left alone to deal with the change and loss on his own.

On his own as usual.

His friend stared at him. "What do you mean? Who is this Thomas?"

"As it turns out, my father had another son. Another, *older* son we never knew about. That was what my uncle wanted to tell me, why he called me to his deathbed."

Alexander waved the words away and resumed his pacing. "So what? Plenty of men have sired illegitimate bastards, and I can't say I'm surprised your father was one of them. It doesn't mean you should—"

"Thomas is not illegitimate."

That stopped him in his tracks. "But he cannot— *What?*"

Christopher sighed, seeing there would be no avoiding the telling of the whole sordid tale.

"My father had a first wife, a woman he had married for love as a young man and who died birthing a son a year after their wedding. Broken with grief, he sent the baby away to a distant cousin of his mother's, not wanting to have anything to do with the person responsible for killing his beloved wife, or so he saw Thomas," he started to explain in a flat voice. "A few years later, he married a lady he'd gotten with child—my mother —when her father forced him into doing the honorable thing. Neither of them knew this would not be his first marriage. Unsurprisingly, my father quickly found out he couldn't bear having us around any more than he could bear to think of Thomas, who grew up not knowing who or what he was. My mother and I were soon sent away to Throckmorton, the crumbling family estate inhabited by the ailing Lord Ashton. And that, as far as my father was concerned, was the end of the matter. He was free to live his life as he wished, unencumbered by people he didn't want, much less love, and wait for the title to be his."

"So then what happened? How did everyone find out the truth?"

"My father's confessor, having heard the whole story during his last rites, urged him to make peace with his maker and call his real heir back. He dictated a long letter to his mother's cousin to explain everything and asked him to send his son to Kent so that he could be restored to the title that belonged to him by right."

Christopher did not feel any resentment toward the meddling priest, even if his zeal had ended up ruining his life. The late Lord Ashton was the real culprit. Had he been less vainglorious, more honorable, and honest from the start, none of this would have happened. His two sons would have known about each other's existence and who was to inherit everything.

There would have been no confusion.

"Too feeble to see to it himself, he asked his brother, my uncle, to send the letter to Norfolk, informing him of the contents. For a reason I'm ignorant of, the man didn't do what he'd been instructed to do, and my father died without word of him having reached Thomas."

Perhaps it was not so hard to guess what his uncle's intent had been. An unscrupulous man himself, he'd thought to use the information to his advantage. With only a childless Christopher standing between him and the title, had he hoped to inherit it himself one day?

Whatever the reason, he'd kept the letter and the confession in it a secret for three years.

"On his death bed, like his brother, he was seized by fear for his immortal soul and called me to inform me of the situation. The original letter had been long burned, but he had enough proof to produce, having done his own research in the years since he'd been told the truth. So you see, Thomas, not me, is the heir," Christopher concluded, pouring himself another drink. "Thomas, not me, was Lord Ashton all along. I am no one. I have nothing."

"You don't—"

"I have nothing," he repeated more forcefully. "Because I have lost the woman I was to marry. She is a lord's daughter and had thought, understandably, to marry according to her rank. With no title, no fortune, nowhere to live, no family support, and a reputation in tatters, what kind of life can I offer her? A pitiful one. It is better for both of us if she finds herself another man, a man who can give her the status she was after."

A man who would not be hurt by her scheming.

When he had set off that afternoon to speak to Siân, it had been with a heavy heart because he'd known it would cost him every ounce of resolve he possessed to free her from their promise to marry. The prospect of losing her had been a frightful one. What had given him courage was the knowledge that he was doing the right thing by her. Marrying the man he was now would have condemned her to a life of misery. And it was not just the lack of funds since perhaps her family could have helped with that. The Hunters were both rich and generous, he knew, and they loved her. They would have seen to the couple's comfort if that was what Siân had wanted. But how would she have dealt with the mockery and scorn? It would have been hard enough to be Lady Ashton and endure jests about being married to a man who had bedded all the women who had thrown themselves at him for years. But everyone would have also pitied her for having been trapped by a usurper with no scruples, as people were bound to see him. They would have made her feel her comedown in the world and looked at her with pity, concern, or ill-concealed glee.

He'd wanted to spare her all that pain and give her a chance to be with a man who could offer her the life she deserved because he'd thought she was a good woman.

But today, he'd seen her true colors, and he wasn't sure anymore.

She'd not cared to console him after the bewildering turn of events or even asked how he felt. Instead, she had made it sound as if he had deliberately set out to trick her and complained that he had made her look a fool in front of her precious family. She had even dared accuse him of deflowering her and leaving her to deal with the consequences. As if she didn't have a huge part of responsibility in the whole affair.

As if she'd not knelt at his feet and—

"You were about to marry? You?" A stunned silence followed the question. Alexander was shocked, understandably. The two friends had often talked about their female conquests and how neither was ready to marry just yet.

"I was."

But not anymore. And because of his current lack of prospects, perhaps never.

Christopher emptied half his glass in one gulp. Even years after his death, his father could still ruin his life. An impressive feat, he had to admit.

Alexander slammed the flat of his hand on the table, causing the candle to fall and extinguish itself, plunging the room into darkness. Neither man moved to light it again. "By all the saints, how could the old man do this to you? And your uncle? They are nothing more than weasels."

Weasels, aye. Or slimy fish.

A smile curled the corner of Christopher's lips. He'd known all his life that the men in his family were worthless, cold individuals interested only in themselves and their pleasure, so, unlike his friend, he could not claim to be surprised. His father had not thought of what it would do to him—or indeed Thomas—to be told what the reality was so late in life, and his uncle had hoped to see him die before his time and inherit in his stead. With no one knowing of the existence of another, older son, the title and fortune would have gone to Lord Ashton's only brother. Had he made plans to have Christopher killed?

It was not impossible, he realized.

Hadn't he jested with Siân that he'd been particularly prone to accidents and mishaps of late? The broken saddle billets, the fall down the stairs ... Had there been more than met the eye in those events? In light of what he'd learned in Kent, he was reassessing what had happened to him in the last few years. As a child or even a youth, he had not been as clumsy. It was only in the last three years or so that strange accidents had started to plague him.

In other words, since his father's death.

Had his uncle decided to aid fate? Had he sent some of his men to Throckmorton Castle, charging them with the disposal of the supposed Lord Ashton? The old man who'd visited from Kent a few weeks earlier could easily have pushed him down the stairs instead of simply tumbling. The squire who had disappeared so suddenly might have been paid to cut the billets of his saddle. It was all too possible. Until he'd been struck down by his sudden chill, his uncle had had every reason to believe he could reach a ripe old age. If his nephew, the sole surviving family member, had died in a tragic accident, he could well have enjoyed the title for another two or three decades.

Should he ask Siân what she thought? She was bound to have some useful insight.

The thought was a punch to the gut. Of course now he would not get to ask her that or anything else. In all likelihood, they would never meet again. Their encounter that afternoon had been a disaster. Would he see her angry face every time he thought of her? Probably. The prospect was a frightening one because he already knew he would think of her often. Far too often.

She, however, might well forget about him and start her search for a more suitable husband without delay.

"They could do it because the two vile men never considered anyone other than themselves," Christopher said with finality. That, at least, was true and made him see that for all his supposed wicked ways, he was no true rogue. He had never done anything half so treacherous as what his father and uncle had done.

Alexander was silent for a moment. Then he went to light the candle on the fire embers and sighed. "I'm sorry. I don't know what to say."

Christopher emptied his cup in one gulp—the fifth one. Another three to go, and he would be well on his way to oblivion. "That's because there is nothing to say," he concluded.

∼

"Are you happy now?" Siân lifted a tear-stained face to her sister.

"Happy?" Jane cried out, tightening her hold around her. "Of course I'm not *happy*! Not when you're feeling so wretched. What do you take me for?"

The two sisters were holding on to one another desperately. After her encounter with Christopher by the river, Siân had hoped to sneak into her bedchamber unnoticed. But fate had decided she had not suffered enough for one day. Her sister had been in the room, and one look at Jane's face had been enough to make it clear she had better tell her what was amiss.

Unable to contain herself any longer, Siân had thrown herself into Jane's arms and burst into tears. Little by little, through her fits of sobs, she had told her everything. The meeting with Lord Ashton—the real Lord Ashton—the week before, her father's lack of reproach—which somehow made her feel more wretched than anything else—her encounter with Christopher, and his refusal to get married.

This, of course, was what had broken her heart. She suspected she could have forgiven the deception if he'd given her his reasons for doing such a thing, but his betrayal was too much to swallow.

I cannot marry you now. Surely, you understand.

Oh, she understood all too well that he had never meant for her to be his wife but only to make the most of the pleasure she'd been offering.

"You warned me he was a rogue, didn't you?" she said once the whole story had been wrenched out of her. "You must at least be satisfied to have been proved right."

"I'm not." Jane made a face, betraying both confusion and anger. "And, if you must know, I thought ... I really thought he could make you happy. Because from what you told me, with you, he was nothing like he was with me or even with anyone else."

Well, Siân had thought the same thing. With her, Christopher was not quite the scathing man he could be with others. She had hoped that it meant something, that he allowed himself to be who he really was with her because she made him feel at ease. But she'd been wrong. He had seduced her like the callous lover he was and found an excuse to disappear before they could speak to her parents to formalize a betrothal. Had his uncle really called him to Kent? Did he even have an uncle? It was far from certain. Then, a month later, he had reappeared out of nowhere, only to announce he could not marry her, without offering any explanation as to why he had impersonated a nobleman and making it appear as if he was doing it for her benefit.

Her sister was right. The way he had behaved toward Jane had nothing in common with how he had been with her. He had not lied to Jane, he had not made her fall in love with him, he had not taken her maidenhead, he had not made her believe they would marry and then broken her heart into a thousand pieces.

Old Myfanwy's predictions suddenly flashed through her mind.

You will fall in love with a man with two identities.

So *that* was what she had meant then. He indeed had two identities. The usurped one and the real one. The title he'd had no claim to and the man underneath. Lord Ashton and plain Christopher Harrison.

The old woman had been right as usual. Siân *had* fallen in love with a man who had two identities. A liar, fornicator, and disreputable rogue on the one hand and a whimsical, protective, passionate lover who'd made her feel worthy of attention, interesting, beautiful even, on the other.

Of course, she now knew it had only been part of his seduction plan. How satisfying for the great seducer to see that he had brought her to her knees in a matter of days. Literally.

He would have enjoyed the time spent posing as Lord Ashton and fooling everyone.

The irony was not lost on her. Hadn't she remarked a few weeks ago that his family's coat of arms didn't suit him? Of course it did not since he had never had any right to it. The scoundrel! How could she have been so blind? But there had been so much sincerity in his voice when he had told her the animal reminded him of his estranged father, when he'd shared his story of loneliness ... Surely, that hadn't been feigned? And he did look remarkably like the man who had welcomed them at Throckmorton Castle. So *was* he the late Lord Ashton's son? Only a bastard one who'd decided to act as if he were legitimate and give himself a title he had no right to, knowing the people down in Kent might never get to hear of the deceit? Had it been his way of making himself feel better, of pretending he could be someone? She could almost feel sorry for him if it had been.

Why, oh why was she torturing herself thus? It didn't matter what his thinking had been, it didn't matter how happy he had made her feel, since it had been for naught. Who he was or wasn't was of no import if he didn't want her.

"I don't want to hear about or see Christopher Harrison ever again," she said, bunching her fists.

It did not take her long, however, to see that that was not true. What she truly wanted was revenge. She wanted to make him pay, to humiliate him, to show him he had not hurt her even if he had.

Siân wiped her cheeks clean. She had shed her last tear over the man.

Christopher didn't want her? Well, she would find others who did—and then she would show him.

Chapter Twelve

A week later, a visitor came to Sheridan Manor.

Lord Cantle's father had been a good friend of the late Lord Sheridan, and he'd been a regular visitor since. He was a few years older than Connor and tall, with neatly cropped hair that had gone almost completely white and blue eyes that betrayed a propensity to smile. Siân liked him immediately, which was a good thing because she was not in the mood to meet new people right now. Since her encounter with Christopher, each moment had been more difficult than the last.

But over the next few days, she found herself often alone in the kind lord's company and even managed to enjoy herself. He was one of those rare Englishmen who did not see Welsh people as inferior, and his conversation gave her something other than Christopher's betrayal to focus on. He had been part of the late Edward I's army in 1277, and he was curious to know how the country was faring more than thirty years after the invasion. His questions revealed a sensible nature that delighted her even if it was far from enough to make her forget the constant pain in her heart.

Was that what the rest of her life would be like? Trying to

find distractions to stop herself from thinking of all she had lost and the man she still loved?

It was not a cheerful prospect, to say the least.

One morning, Lord Cantle found her in the rose garden, where she had gone in search of solitude. Jane had taken Gwenllian, Bethan and Seren to the market in town, but Siân had declined the offer to accompany them. Instead, she had spent the morning alone, crying. After so many days spent pretending she was doing all right for her family's sake, she needed to let her feelings out. Otherwise, she feared she might well shatter. Though it had not been hard to keep to her resolve never to see Christopher again since she didn't even know where he might be, she had found it impossible to stop thinking about him and stick to her resolution not to shed a single tear over him.

When her mood was dark, which was most of the time, she thought back to his betrayal and the way he had pretended to agree to get married before disappearing. When she lay in her bed at night, she relived their tryst in the meadow in all its lewd, excruciatingly vivid details. When she ate honey, she remembered how he had licked her fingers clean in the meadow. The color of the sky, reminiscent of his blue eye, the hue of the wood on her bed frame, as dark as his other eye, the puppies that had overturned the basket the day he'd brought Warrior to service Angel, Angel herself—everything made her think of him.

It was torture.

She had once compared her love for him to sunshine warming every little corner of her soul. She was now convinced it was more like rot pervading everything little by little with implacable thoroughness. There was no stopping it. Soon there would be nothing good left of her; it would all have been consumed by her doomed feelings for him.

To add to her dismay, that morning, she'd heard the grooms congratulate themselves. Warrior had indeed gotten Angel with foal, and they were waiting for a birth in the spring, the finest horse they had ever bred.

"Lady Siân. May I?"

"Of course."

When Lord Cantle sat down next to her, she didn't move or shy away from her chagrin. He would have seen her tears already, and there was something about him that made it easy not to be embarrassed.

"Are you all right? Forgive me. That was a ludicrous question to ask. It is obvious you're not."

Siân could not help a small smile and replied with equal frankness. "No. But I suspect I will be, eventually." At least, that was the hope. Surely, when she was in her old age, the pain of Christopher's desertion would have faded away? No one could suffer with the same intensity for half a century.

"A young man broke your heart?" he ventured. Though that was a startlingly bold assertion to make, she didn't even think of pretending it was not the case.

"Yes."

A silence followed. Then another odd question.

"How old are you, if I may ask?"

"Almost one and t-twenty," she stammered. What did that have to do with anything?

"Just like Constance was," he murmured to himself. Siân waited. Who was Constance? His late wife? No, it couldn't be. She'd heard that the woman had died recently, and she couldn't have been her age if she had been married for three decades. Lord Cantle provided her with the answer before she could ask. "I had a daughter who must have been born the same year as you. She died a few weeks ago. You remind me of her. She had the same eyes as you and the same spontaneous nature. I suppose that is why I enjoy talking to you so much."

"I'm so sorry." Siân did not have to force herself to feel

sympathy. She could all too well imagine the horror of losing someone you loved. Everyone in her family had done so. Her mother had lost her first husband, Connor a wife and two daughters, and Jane had lost two sisters, including her twin, Elspeth. Siân alone had been spared that awful pain.

"She died ... by her own hand."

Siân was frozen in place. What could she say to that? Nothing. Taking one's own life was considered one of the worst sins a person could commit. What had pushed the poor girl to do such a thing? Having heard Lord Cantle's confession, she felt she owed him a more complete explanation as to the reason for her tears.

"The man who broke my heart ..." She stopped before she could say his name. Not only did she have no right to call Christopher by the title he had usurped, but she wanted to preserve his anonymity even if she wasn't sure he deserved it. "I've wanted to marry him all my life. Or at least since I was able to understand what being married meant. Finally, earlier in the summer, we decided to be married." Heat invaded her cheeks at her tame choice of words because they had not exactly *decided* to get married.

I forced his hand by making him take my maidenhead. At first, he tried to do the right thing and refuse, but then he surrendered when I took him into my mouth.

"What happened?" Lord Cantle asked when she went silent.

Siân cleared her throat, chasing the shocking image from her mind. "He left before we could speak to my parents, and I discovered afterward that he'd been lying about his identity and, most likely, his intentions all along. He made me believe he'd agreed to marry me, but he told me last week he would not make me his wife, after all. And so now I fear I will end up all alone."

A hand landed on her knee, the gesture paternal. "I don't

think that's a concern, my dear. You're a charming, beautiful young woman. I dare say plenty of men would be happy to take you to wife."

Not when they found out she was no longer a maid. Though *how* they would find that out, she wasn't sure exactly. She did not think Christopher would spread the word of what they had done together, but she couldn't be sure. Many people considered him a rogue, he had just been exposed as a liar, and she knew that he liked to boast about his conquests. She had heard him do so herself. Wouldn't he tell his friends how daringly Lord Sheridan's respectable daughter had pleasured him? Would these men not delight in spreading the word? It was all too possible. But she didn't even mind.

"No one will want me when they know I have lain with him. So certain was I that we were meant to be together that I allowed him every liberty. Which only goes to show I am a fool because now I know he never wanted me."

Lord Cantle gave a cough, as if surprised that she should want to share such intimate details. And perhaps she should have kept silent. But suddenly, she needed to confide in someone who didn't know Christopher, who wouldn't judge him, or her, but simply listen. Perhaps hearing the whole story out loud would make her realize how pathetic it was and help her to move on. It could not make her situation worse, at least.

"You must think me terribly brazen, but you see, it's not just that I wanted to marry him. I've been in love with him all my life." She didn't add that she suspected she would be in love with him until her dying day. There was a limit to the humiliation she was prepared to endure. "I didn't think I was taking any risks because I never imagined I would marry anyone else. And now, because of a moment of folly, I fear that I never will. I will be left behind, a burden on my parents, an embarrassment to my family, a broken-hearted old woman."

And what a frightening prospect that was. For a long moment, Lord Cantle stared ahead, as if lost in contemplation. He didn't offer empty words of comfort. Instead, he said the last thing she had expected him to say.

"Do you think you could consider marrying me?"

"I ... I b-beg your pardon?"

Had he just offered her marriage? Surely, she had misheard.

"You seem to fear no one will ever marry you. I'm saying that I would. That way, you won't end up alone or be a burden to anyone."

Siân wasn't sure what to think, much less what to say. "I—"

"I know I am not exactly an enviable party for someone like you. I'm an old man, widowed twice over." She kept her face impassive, but that information was new to her. She'd had no idea that he had lost not one but two wives. "I have four sons and two daughters left. There is no need for me to have any more children or, indeed, remarry again. But I like the company of a good woman, and I confess I am moved by your story. I would like to help."

This time, Siân could not prevent her eyes from widening in bewilderment. She had confessed to wanton behavior and the man was *moved*?

"You heard what I said?" The conversation was embarrassing, but she had to be sure. "You realize I'm not a virgin anymore?"

And will likely never fall in love with you.

His blue eyes crinkled. "Believe it or not, virginity is not the sole quality a man worthy of the name looks for in a wife. I'm sure that having been raised by men like Connor and Matthew Hunter will have made that clear to you," he answered wryly. "Like them, I am intelligent enough to believe that an untouched body is not the most important attribute a woman can possess."

This extraordinary answer took Siân by surprise. Indeed, her father and uncle had always respected women and praised them for their intelligence and wisdom, but she did not think many men shared that opinion. For many, virginity *was* a woman's most prized possession.

"I'm impressed by your generosity of spirit, my lord."

"Don't be. I'm doing for you what I couldn't do for Constance." He was still staring into the distance. "I couldn't save her from despair, but I could save you. It could be a way of appeasing my conscience. She killed herself, you see, after a man she loved used her and she thought that, because of it, her life was over."

The blood froze in Siân's veins. Was he saying ... Was he afraid she would end up killing herself? She didn't know whether to be moved or horrified because despite her heartbreak, the idea of ending her own life had never crossed her mind. Would she one day wake up and think it was her only solution?

"I thank you and I promise to take your offer into consideration." Anything to avoid such a dreadful outcome.

"Wait. There is something I have to say before you decide anything."

Lord Cantle paused. Evidently, the confession would not be easy for him. This really was the most unlikely marriage proposal Siân could have imagined.

"If we marry, I fear I will not be able to be a true husband to you."

Siân adjusted her position on the bench, ill at ease at the turn the conversation had taken. She'd heard that men over a certain age or weight could sometimes find it difficult to perform in bed. Was that what Lord Cantle was trying to tell her? That he would not be able to fulfill his marital duty? She could not imagine he suffered from any shortcomings. He was only a few years older than her father, who was at the height of his virility, and he appeared just as lean.

"May I ask why that may be?" Despite the delicate nature of the question, she needed to know. They were being honest with one another, and she desperately wanted to hear the problem did not lie with her. After Christopher's rejection, she could not bear to hear that another man found her lacking or unable to stir his desire in bed. If that were the case, she would not even consider marrying him.

"My daughter looked so much like you that I know it would be impossible for me to be with you … in that way. In view of this, I would understand if you refused my offer."

The air stilled around Siân. The man who'd just offered to marry her to save her from ruin and a life of solitude was telling her he would not put a finger on her because it would feel wrong. Her relief was so acute that she sagged on the bench. Undoubtedly, the bedding had been the one aspect of marriage to Lord Cantle she had viewed with apprehension. But now, he was telling her he would not touch her. It was too good to be true because it meant she could accept his offer. Still, she felt guilty because, say what he might, she had the impression she would be the sole one benefiting from a union between them.

He saw her avert her gaze and mistook her guilt for disappointment—or offense.

"I will be a good husband, I will care and provide for you, but I will never consummate our union or give you children. I'm sorry. I know it is not fair to you, so I'll understand if you would rather—"

"No," she said hastily. She could guess how much that confession had cost him, and a rush of pity swept through her. "I understand. And I think your scruples honor you, my lord."

Indeed, it was the mark of an honorable man that he had been honest instead of trapping her into a marriage that would be in name only. And his refusal to possess someone who looked like his daughter was reassuring. Too many men she'd met seemed governed by their baser needs. As Lady Cantle, she would be protected and get the companionship she needed. She would not end up alone and a burden.

Even more to the point, she would do what she had hoped to do, show Christopher that someone wanted her even if he did not.

The thought caused her to straighten her spine. She'd been looking for a way of taking her revenge and making herself feel better, of proving to him and herself that she could be chosen for the qualities she possessed. That could be it. Married to a good man who valued her company by day and did not press his advances on her at night, she would have a normal life. No one would pity or mock her. In time, she might learn to be happy.

The prospect of Lord Cantle not touching her did not frighten her—quite the contrary. Because she could not imagine another man doing to her what Christopher had done. A lifetime of chastity was preferable to feeling another man's hands on her, another man's heat inside her. This union was the perfect solution.

Except ... except it meant she would never have children, which had been the whole reason she, at the age of nine, had decided to get married.

She shook her head, fighting a fresh wave of tears. It mattered not. She had understood the moment Christopher had refused her that she would not have the life she had dreamed of. And at least Lord Cantle was offering her a chance at respectability and contentment.

It was the best she could hope for. With three sisters and a brother, she would likely have a dozen nephews and nieces. She would have to be content with that.

"No one will know that our marriage was never consummated. I swear, it will be our secret," she told Lord Cantle.

"Does that mean you accept my offer?" He sounded half hopeful and half dismayed on her behalf, as if he could not believe what she was sacrificing.

Siân hesitated only for a heartbeat. "Yes, I do."

"Are you really going to marry Lord Cantle?"

Though Jane's voice did not betray any condemnation, Siân knew all too well she was disapproving. The stiffening in her spine made that clear.

"Yes. He's a good man."

"He is. That doesn't mean he's the husband for—"

"The husband I want and thought to marry," Siân cut in with an uncharacteristic snarl, "doesn't want me. He told me so in no uncertain terms only a few days ago, and there was no mistaking his meaning. So what am I supposed to do? Pine after him like I have done all my life? Wait for him to change his mind like a pathetic creature? Forever be the unmarried daughter of Lord Sheridan while I watch my sisters and brother leave one by one? Forego all chance at dignity and contentment?"

She had never sounded so bitter. Perhaps because she had never *felt* so bitter.

So dejected.

Jane placed a hand on her shoulder. "I understand. But it's only been a fortnight since you found out about Lord Ash—about his treachery. Should you not take the time to absorb the shock you've endured before making such a drastic decision as to marry a stranger?"

Yes, it had been a fortnight since her confrontation with

Christopher. In other words, an eternity. Siân didn't see how she was going to survive another fortnight like it, much less a lifetime. Marrying a kind man intent on helping her, a man who would not make demands on her and save her from the indignity of being rejected, was not a drastic solution. It was exactly what she needed not to drown in despair.

"I've had all the time I'm ever going to need," Siân said with decision. "My situation is not going to change. This is the best, fairest offer I'm ever going to get, considering ..."

Considering I'm not a virgin anymore.

Jane bit her bottom lip. She'd understood all too well what Siân hadn't said.

"Now, come. I need to go tell Mam and Father we have a wedding to organize."

Understandably, the news of Lord Cantle's proposal—and her agreement—was received with a fair amount of disbelief. To their credit, however, her parents did not overwhelm her with questions and unnecessary comments. They seemed to understand she was doing the only thing she could do to protect her sanity.

"Lord Cantle is a good man," her mother said in a low voice. "I'm sure he will make a good husband."

But perhaps not for you.

Though the words were not spoken out loud, Siân heard them all the same. It was what Jane thought as well, what everyone thought.

What could she say? She knew her mother's reticence had nothing to do with her future groom's age. She had been married to an older man before she'd become Lady Sheridan. Siân's real father, Gwyn, had been one of her father's best friends and some thirty years her mother's senior. Esyllt knew such a marriage could bring a woman a measure of contentment.

If, of course, she was not in love with another man and they could enjoy a true marriage.

Siân did not let such considerations bother her. Lord Cantle was the perfect husband for her precisely *because* their marriage would not be a true one.

As promised, she hadn't told anyone about their secret arrangement, but her parents seemed to know what the situation was anyway. Her mother had just alluded to it, and her father's green gaze was even more piercing than usual. He might have met the blonde, blue-eyed Constance and guessed his friend would find it impossible to bed his new wife because of the resemblance between the two of them. It was not impossible. Connor Hunter was a very astute man.

In any case, it made no difference. She would become Lady Cantle. There was no other path for her.

"Come then, we will go see him," her father finally said.

Chapter Thirteen

The wedding was celebrated two days later. Given the circumstances, no one saw any point in waiting any longer.

In the lavishly decorated chapel, only the family was present. There had been no time to assemble guests, and Siân had preferred to keep things simple.

All throughout the ceremony, she could not help staring at the vase at the foot of the altar, remembering the day not so long ago when Christopher had told her she looked like a bride with her wilted flowers. Here she was now, a bride in truth even if her attire was as simple as it had been that day. A dress of pale green linen, a veil held in place by a gold band, and a single ring on her finger. A few weeks earlier, at her demand, Branwen's mother, Carys, had started to embroider a cream velvet gown with tiny yellow flowers in preparation for her wedding to Christopher. Of course, no one had dared suggest she wear the precious garment for her wedding with Lord Cantle.

She'd been told she looked lovely, which was all that mattered. It would not do to cause her groom to regret his generous impulse. Judging from the smile he'd thrown her when she had entered the chapel, he did not.

"Do you, Siân Alys Hunter, take this man to be your lawfully wedded husband?"

"I do."

The two little words she'd often imagined saying in front of Christopher could barely pass her lips. Lord Cantle had already done his part, which meant they were husband and wife. It was done. She was a married woman—and she wasn't sure what to feel. Only that summer, she had been certain her wedding to Christopher was finally going to happen, and she had just become Lady Cantle.

She exited the chapel in a daze and, arm in arm with her new husband, led the way to the main hall, where a small feast had been laid out. The atmosphere was joyous, but Siân could not help but feel that her family was making an effort on her behalf, only pretending it was what she had wanted all along.

How painfully ironic.

They had been reluctant to see her married to Christopher because of his appalling reputation, but they didn't seem happier to see her wed to Lord Cantle, who was unanimously considered a good man. Across the table, Jane gave her a smile she returned as best as she could.

Once the sweetmeats had been consumed, Lord Cantle lifted her hand to his lips in a gallant gesture. Siân's chest constricted. This would be the most daring physical contact she would experience with a man from now on. He would likely come to her bed tonight to give the impression their union was being consummated, but he would not touch her, as promised. Never again would she feel kisses on her lips, caresses on her skin, pleasure deep in her body. Never again would she even feel desire. Was she ready for such a life?

She stiffened because that was not the question.

There was no other choice. If she couldn't have Christopher's kisses on her lips, Christopher's caresses on her skin, Christopher's heat inside her, then she wanted no other.

"We shall leave for Clearfield Hall soon, Lady Cantle."

The announcement caused panic to flare inside Siân. Leave? She was not ready to leave her family yet and remain in England permanently. Quite stupidly, considering she had wanted to marry Christopher, who was an Englishman himself, she had always imagined she would end her life in her native country. Dear, oh dear, her family was right; she hadn't thought this through.

She disentangled her hand from her husband's as calmly as she could. "Could we wait a week or two? I think I would like some time to get used to the idea that I am a married woman before we leave."

"I understand." His smile was kindness itself. Siân's insides withered. She should never have accepted that man's offer of marriage. It was not fair to him. She would never make him happy. "However, I'm afraid we will have to leave at the end of the month. I have business at Clearfield that cannot wait any longer."

"Of course."

Two weeks. Siân swallowed hard. She had two weeks to get used to her new life.

~

"May I offer my congratulations, Lady Cantle?"

The dark voice made Siân shiver in delight, a reaction she had no control over. She would have preferred not to feel anything, but it was hard to do otherwise, considering that for years, her body had responded that way to Christopher's proximity. In that moment, even if the image was hardly a flattering one, she felt like a dog responding to its beloved master's call, and she feared her body would always react in that way no matter what her mind was telling her. Then the words registered. He had called her by her new title.

So he knew.

She'd been married only for a few days —and in a very private ceremony—and yet he knew about it. That meant he had either been keeping a close eye on what was happening at Sheridan Manor—and her—or he was staying somewhere so close he'd heard it through one of the few local lords who'd been invited. She straightened up. It mattered not how he knew. This was what she had been waiting for.

Revenge.

Bracing herself, she turned around.

Arglywdd Mawr.

Siân's insides collapsed in dismay. Why did he have to be so handsome? She hadn't seen him since that awful day he had told her he wasn't going to marry her, and despite the anguish on his face, he had never looked better. In the golden evening light, he appeared like an angel fallen down from Heaven. The tension in his jaw and the spark in his eyes made his masculinity more glaring, not that he would have looked less than stunning otherwise.

Her bones crumbled at the same time as her blood caught ablaze.

A vengeful angel, indeed, come to torment her.

"You may." Two words. A pathetic effort at conversation, but at least her voice hadn't wobbled.

"You didn't waste any time getting married, I see."

No. But why would she have? The last time she had chosen a husband, it had taken her more than ten years to get him to agree to marry her. And it had ended in a disaster.

"Should I have waited? I don't see why. It is not as if another man wanted me for himself, after all. I was free to marry whoever I chose."

The pique fell flat, like a lance thrown by a child falling pitifully short of the knight it was supposed to hit. Dear Lord, she had woefully overestimated her abilities in this revenge affair. Or perhaps she was fighting a too-formidable adversary. Christopher was the embodiment of icy indifference. Well what had she expected? For him to fall at her knees and beg her to reconsider her decision? For him to sweep her into his arms and say he could not bear to live without her before taking her mouth in a fiery kiss? Of course, he did neither.

He only stared at her, as impassible as the stone wall behind him. What was he even doing in the rose garden with her? Had the decision to come been a sudden, uncontrollable urge, or had he been spying on the comings and goings at Sheridan Manor, waiting for the best moment to find her alone? Dare she read anything into it? Should she? The only thing she knew was that she would never manage to exert any sort of revenge on him.

If one of them left the encounter crushed beyond repair, it would be her.

"Tell me, do you want this Lord Cantle like you wanted me?"

No, not like that, I will never want another man like that.

"I married him, didn't I?"

Not quite a clear affirmation, but it was the best she could do when she was on the verge of collapse. Resisting the urge to sit down, she clasped her hands together. She had to at least *appear* as if she was not defeated.

"Yes. You definitely married him."

Christopher bunched his fists. Here was the definitive proof that Siân had wanted him only for his title. Less than a month after finding out who he was, she was married to another man. He'd suspected she'd been after a prestigious husband, but to hear it so clearly confirmed was a blow nonetheless.

From the start, she had planned to make an advantageous marriage, trap herself a lord. Then, when he'd been exposed as a younger son with no prospects, little more than a nobody, she'd reverted to ensnaring a good-natured old man who, he imagined, couldn't believe his luck at having found himself such a vibrant young wife. The speed with which she had replaced him, her choice of husband even, made it obvious she had been after only one thing, standing. No beautiful woman in her prime would shackle herself to a man three times her age if not to gain in consequence.

Had she done to Lord Cantle what she had done to him? Was that why the man had agreed to such a hasty union? He would have thought, with reason, that a woman so willing to use her mouth would make his nights as exciting as could be.

The idea of them together caused his stomach to lurch.

"Why are you so upset?" the minx had the gall to ask when he winced. "You didn't want to marry me, and now you won't have to."

"Why am I so upset? Let me see. Mayhap because you tricked me into fucking you, hoping to have the leverage to trap me into marriage afterward, and now I find out you never really wanted *me*."

"It's not what—"

"It is. Or are you telling me you suck the cocks of all the men you meet?" She'd been a virgin, but perhaps she'd not been innocent. The notion caused his gut to tighten further. "My. You must spend an awful lot of time on your knees if that is the case."

The way Siân blanched and fell on the bench behind her was enough to tell him it was not as bad as he'd feared. She was horrified at the accusation because he had been the first man she'd gifted with the use of her mouth.

Yes, but only because she wanted me to agree to marry her, he reminded himself before he could apologize for his crudeness.

And it had worked. He had agreed to do the honorable thing by her. He had been so honorable, in fact, that when his real place in the world had been revealed, he had done what he thought best for her even though his whole being had rebelled against the idea. He had given her a chance to free herself from a union that would signify her ruin and marry a man who could offer the life she would never have had with him.

He had not thought she would jump at the first opportunity to do so, so quickly, or so cynically. But there it was, less than a fortnight after she'd found out he was not, after all, a lord, she'd found herself a husband.

Why was he even surprised?

She had pretended to be Mildred in the hope that he would deflower her before he realized who she was so she could go cry to her father that Lord Ashton had to be made accountable for his actions. And when a man like Connor Hunter wanted to coerce someone into doing something, there was no stopping him. But her plan hadn't worked because upon discovering who she was, he'd refused to bed her. So she had resorted to the oldest trick available to women. She had dropped to her knees and taken him into her mouth, for Christ's sake. What lady did that unbidden? Wily, desperate ones, that was who. And he, stupid fool that he was, had allowed his cock to do the thinking.

Christopher shook his head. The oddest thing was not that he had allowed his lust to guide his actions, as that could have been predicted. What was truly surprising was what had happened afterward. Once he had finally come back to his senses, he'd found that he wouldn't mind being married to the little lamb, the only woman who had the ability to hold his attention. During his travel to Kent, he'd reconciled himself to the notion of marriage with her because he'd thought that perhaps, as her husband, he could have what he'd always dreamed of.

But then, it had all gone awry.

Christ on the cross, why couldn't his uncle have died a week earlier? Then he wouldn't have found himself in this mess. Even after his death, the man had made sure Christopher ended up all alone, uncared for and unloved.

Aye, that was the problem. With the little Welsh firebrand as his wife, he might well have been able to have what he'd never had growing up and still wanted. And because of a man who had never given him any thought, he'd been denied a chance at the life he needed.

"I do *not*—"

Siân could not finish, but he understood nonetheless. She did not use her mouth to pleasure all the men she met.

Small consolation.

She stood back up, indignation written all over her face. "As to my marriage, what did you want me to do? Pine after you all my life? Remain unmarried?"

No. *Yes*, damn it!

"You didn't have to rush into marriage with the first gullible fool who crossed your path, I'd say." A bare fortnight after their discussion, during which she had behaved as if his defection was the worst thing that could have happened to her, she had become another man's wife. If that didn't show he was replaceable, nothing did. "I thought ... I thought you might actually sympathize with me."

He had. More the fool he. And why in the name of Christ had he told her that? Wasn't the entire affair humiliating enough? He really was losing it.

Siân's eyes almost popped out of her head. "You thought I would *sympathize?*"

Pure fury distorted her features. In that moment, his little lamb looked more like an enraged bull than a meek woolly thing. The image should have made him laugh, but it did not because behind the rage blazing in her eyes, he saw pain. She was hurt, but he could not understand why.

"Yes, sympathize," he repeated. "You once did."

She had been the first woman to see under the façade he presented to the world, one of the few people he'd confided in. And she had seemed to understand and trust there was more to him than bluster. How could he forget the compassion he'd seen in her eyes when he had talked about his family, his father's disinterest? He'd imagined she would be devastated to hear about the man's last act of spite. Instead, she had used it to extricate herself from a marriage that had lost its appeal overnight. When she'd heard he was no longer Lord Ashton, she had probably thanked the saints they had not had time to speak to her father, after all. The inconvenience of severing her ties with him had been minimal.

"I did sympathize with you once, Christopher!" she spat, surprising him with the use of his name. "But that was before you told me you didn't want me, before you abandoned me to go to Kent, knowing I'd have to face my disapproving family on my own, before you informed me you had taken every precaution not to get me with child that night in the clearing so you wouldn't have to honor your worthless promise to me. Shall I continue?"

"No."

Christopher gritted his teeth. She wanted to hurt him? On her head be it. He might not be able to stop her from inflicting pain, but he could at least hurt her back. He didn't have anything to lose. If she ended up hating him, he would not be any worse off. It was likely the last time they would see one another anyway.

He leaned in to murmur in her ear, the darkness descending in the garden making their proximity even more dangerous. "Tell me, Lady Cantle, does your elderly husband please you in bed? Does he even manage to raise his cock for you? Or do you have to stroke him before he can do the deed, take him in your mouth? Do you scream for him like you did for me, or do you fake your moans because he cannot give you the kind of fucking you like?"

Each crude word was like a nail to his own heart. He'd meant to hurt her, but it was causing him indescribable pain to think of her in her husband's arms.

"Is that all you can tell me?" Siân had gone so pale he wondered whether she was not going to swoon. "You really *are* a horrid man."

Christopher straightened his spine. There was no point in prolonging the agony. He had to go.

"Yes, I am a horrid man. But surely, this comes as no surprise. Enough people have tried to tell you as much and warn you away from me. You should have listened to them."

Chapter Fourteen

"My lord, I am ready to leave whenever you are."

After the dreadful confrontation with Christopher the previous evening, there was only one thing on Siân's mind. Leaving Sheridan Manor as soon as possible. She could not risk another visit from him. That first one had inflicted a terrible wound on her already damaged soul; a second one might well kill her.

"Of course."

Her husband didn't comment on her change of heart and immediately started to make the necessary arrangements. The farewell with her family the following morning was deeply emotional, just as she had dreaded. Promises of frequent visits were made, kisses exchanged, tears shed.

Unable to bear it another moment, Siân climbed on Angel—Matthew and Branwen's wedding present to her—and trotted away without looking back. A chapter of her life had ended. She was a married woman now, and she would have to act as such.

A week later, the retinue arrived at Clearfield Hall, which was to be her new home. Situated at the top of a hill overlooking a prosperous town, it was everything Throckmorton Castle was not, warm and welcoming, decorated with taste. Siân tried to tell herself that her change of circumstances had been for the best and put her heart into becoming the mistress of the place. It would not be said that Lord Cantle's Welsh wife didn't know how to play her role.

At night, she slept alone and sometimes even managed not to cry.

One gray November morning, she found herself breaking her fast with her husband. It was a rare enough occurrence for her to want to make the most of it. When she had agreed to marry him, she had not imagined he would spend most of his time away from Clearfield Hall. Her days, busy as they were, were rather lonely, and she delighted in the prospect of a conversation with Lord Cantle, all the more so that there was something she wanted to discuss with him.

Smiling, she took her place next to him. "I hear from Master Ralph that we are to host a tourney at the end of the month."

"Yes, my dear." He raised her hand to his lips and kissed it with affection. True to his word, he had never touched her more intimately than that in the weeks since their wedding. "I was about to tell you myself. We organize one every year, a sort of family tradition. Three days of festivities. 'Tis our way to mark the end of the year. There will be two days of fighting in various melees, both on foot and on horseback, and then on the last day, a joust."

A joust ...

Siân had often fantasized about seeing Christopher take part in a joust. With his powerful physique, skill in the saddle, and utter fearlessness, he would be the perfect contestant. Except that, in his current circumstances, he would never compete in a tourney of any kind, of course. Lord Ashton would have been eligible but not ... whoever he was in reality. Who *was* that?

With decision, she pushed the question away. Damnation, she was constantly having to remind herself that she had decided not to think about him ever again. And it did not matter who he was since he didn't want her.

"Would you like to see the list of knights taking part?" Lord Cantle asked once the trout pasties in front of them had been reduced to crumbs. The food served here was exceptionally good, and Siân often wished she had the appetite to do it justice. But her despondency made her ignore many of the delicacies.

"Yes, please." Anything to prolong the moment with her husband, who provided a welcome distraction from her maudlin thoughts.

"Here." He led her to a trestle table to the side where a roll of parchment was being held flat by four earthenware jugs placed at the corners. "As you can see, we have over one hundred contestants this year. I am pleased to say we are gaining a reputation."

She nodded, not as excited by the prospect as her husband. Those tourneys, particularly the melees, were violent affairs, and she could not say she was looking forward to it. Then one name at the bottom of the roll drew her attention. Sir Alexander Rathbone. Where had she heard it before?

"Is anything the matter?" Lord Cantle asked when she frowned.

"No." She pointed to the last line on the parchment. "That name sounds familiar, though."

"I suspect it will, as the man lives not so far from Sheridan Manor, at Audley Castle." Audley? Siân shook her head. The name did not ring any bells. "Just east of Throckmorton Castle."

Of course! Now she remembered. Sir Alexander Rathbone was one of Christopher's friends, the friend he'd been on his way to visit the day he'd rescued the girls from the river. Her heartbeat instantly picked up.

Was this a simple coincidence? It could be. After all, she could see that knights from all over the county and even further afield had been invited. Sir Alexander might just be one of them. Or had it something to do with Christopher, as she could not help but think? Had he convinced his friend to take part in the tourney so that he could see her? Would he be accompanying him? But to what end?

She dreaded to think.

For the next two weeks, Siân barely slept, unsure what to do, unsure what to hope for, unsure how to prepare herself. Finally, the day of the tourney arrived. It was only then that she realized she had no idea what Sir Alexander Rathbone looked like, so she had no idea who to look for. She forced herself not to ask anyone to point her in his direction. If Christopher really had come with his friend, let him take the first step; she would not humiliate herself by going to a man who only meant to hurt her.

For two excruciatingly long days, Siân had to watch men in armor hack at one another with swords, spiky maces, and sharp axes. It was not a spectacle for the fainthearted, and, more than once, she wished she could have excused herself, but she was convinced Christopher was here somewhere and she could not resist the opportunity to see whether her instinct had served her well.

In vain. She never saw anyone that could match his height and bulk or rival his good looks amongst the squires and attendants at work around the castle grounds. She did, however, see her share of blood, sweat, and unconscious men. Thank the Lord she knew Christopher was not allowed to take part in the melee for she would have gone mad with worry. The leaden skies above and occasional downpours of icy drizzle only made the whole thing grimmer.

On the third day, as if in honor of the event everyone was waiting for—the joust—the sun finally broke out.

As the knights started to enter the field, Siân looked on with avid fascination. This, at least, she might be able to enjoy.

The first contestant to come greet her and Lord Cantle wore a flat-topped great helm, and she found herself wondering what type of helmet Christopher would have favored had he been allowed to take part in the tournament. The second knight seemed impossibly broad, even broader than Christopher, and even more muscular. The third one's horse was covered with a blue caparison, the color reminiscent of Christopher's left eye. The next one seemed young and barely able to control his mount, unlike Christopher, who had always had complete mastery over Warrior. The one after that carried his lance with as much aplomb as she had imagined Christopher would.

By the time the sixth contestant appeared, she had lost all hope of stopping herself from comparing the knights to the man occupying her thoughts despite her resolve to forget about him. They were smaller, less imposing. They lacked his presence and skill. They could not

Siân froze.

Tall, broad, and lean, with a rounded top helm and his lance held proudly aloft, astride a copper-colored charger caparisoned in gold, the last contestant thundered onto the field, causing the mud to fly from under his horse's hooves.

No.

Her heart started to drum impossibly loud in her ears. Surely, he could not be who she thought he was? Lord Ashton no longer, he had no right to be here. Was she dreaming?

"Who is this?" she asked her husband, who was standing next to her.

"Sir Alexander Rathbone, the last of the knights competing

today," he answered, consulting the list in front of him. "He's eager! This promises good sport. My cousin Lord Spelling is convinced he will be the victor. Maybe he will be, but it seems to me he will have to fight harder than he anticipated to claim his victory."

The dashing knight stopped in front of them, as the others had done, to offer his salute. All the bones left Siân's body when their gazes met even if, through the narrow slit of his helm, she could barely see his eyes. There was no need. She already knew one would be brown and the other as blue as the winter sky stretching above them.

This was not Sir Alexander Rathbone at all. It was Christopher. And it was not just any copper-colored horse. It was Warrior. Somehow, the wretched man had convinced his friend to let him compete in his stead. And why not? No one knew Sir Alexander round these parts. With his face hidden from view, who would know the difference?

She would.

He remained in front of them, holding his stomping horse in an iron grip, daring her to expose him, or so it seemed to her. She could do it easily. One word from her, and everyone would know he was not who he was supposed to be and had no right to be here. Once again, he had usurped someone else's identity. Was his friend, Sir Alexander, aware of the deception, or was he even now at Audley, oblivious to the fact that he was supposed to compete in a joust?

She had no idea.

"Is anything wrong, my dear?" Lord Cantle leaned toward her solicitously.

Could she reveal the treachery? It was now or never. Once the joust started, it would be too late. Did she want to expose Christopher? Was she brave enough? Would it serve any purpose?

"No." She forced a smile. "Everything is fine. Let the joust begin."

～

The first opponent, a youth who seemed barely able to seat his horse, was easily disposed of, but the victory afforded Christopher little satisfaction. He could have beaten him with one arm tied behind his back. The next rider, though older and sturdy enough, was sent sprawling to the ground on the second run. The third one's skill in the saddle made no difference; he soon joined the other defeated knights in the camp erected on the other side of the walls.

Christopher's heartbeat had barely picked up. He was amazed he could focus after seeing Siân next to her husband on the stand built especially for them.

Every inch the lady of the castle in a heavy, embroidered gown that made her look at least a decade older, with her mane of hair hidden under a demure veil, she had looked barely like herself, pale and quiet. Had she recognized him—or Warrior— when they had gone to offer their salute before the first contest? Though she had no reason to think he would compete today since he was no longer Lord Ashton, it had seemed that her behavior had changed when she'd seen him.

If she had recognized him, she had not revealed his true identity, which was all that mattered.

And now, he had another contestant to beat. A tall, dark knight had appeared at the other end of the field, his black stallion champing at the bit. At least, this one might pose a bit of a challenge ...

A moment later, the seemingly unconscious contender was dragged away by his men.

Christopher rode away to the tent where refreshments were being served. Just like he had the two previous days, he refrained from removing his helm to drink the ale and eat the pie until he was back in his sleeping quarters, away from everyone else. It would not do for anyone to see that Sir Alexander was not who he was supposed to be. Not that he expected many people to know his friend, but with his distinctive eyes, *he* could all too easily be identified as Christopher Harrison. It was not worth taking the risk, so he had drunk and eaten only in private since he'd arrived.

The afternoon was spent in much the same way as the morning had been, a succession of contests easily won. No one seemed able to touch him. At any other time, he would have rejoiced at his good fortune. In that moment, he felt nothing but cold and hollow.

Why had he come? He was not sure. But there had not been any other choice. As soon as he'd heard a tourney was being organized at Clearfield Hall, Siân's—Lady Cantle's—new residence, he had known he would compete.

At last, dusk started to descend. Only he and one other contestant remained. Lord Spelling, who was none other than Lord Cantle's cousin. Unfortunate, that. Christopher would have liked to humiliate the man just because of his connection to Siân's husband, but he would have to let him win. He shrugged. Let Lord Cantle have that small satisfaction as well. He had taken everything else anyway.

Lance at the ready, Christopher took a deep breath and kicked Warrior into a gallop.

Chapter Fifteen

" I was wondering how you would avoid being caught."

Christopher didn't move when the feminine voice cut through the silence of the night. Had he hoped Siân would dare come to his tent? Yes, of course he had. Had he lost hope of seeing her when the sun had set and, much later, the moon had come up? Yes.

And now, with dawn starting to gray the horizon, here she was at last.

He took his first real breath since he had arrived at Clearfield Hall three days ago.

"Quite a masterful stroke, was it not," the voice carried on, "to lose to Lord Spelling on your last contest and allow him to send you to the ground, then claim the dent in your helmet prevented you from removing it?"

A corner of his lips curled. Little Lamb ... still as sharp as ever. Not only had she recognized him despite the armor and all-encompassing helm, as he'd thought, but she had also seen through his ruse. There had been no other choice. Going to collect his prize from the lady of the castle's fair hand would have exposed his real identity to everyone.

Alexander would be furious when told Christopher had impersonated him to take part in a tourney he had no right to compete in, of course. He could almost hear his friend. The knight was the proudest man he knew, and he would not like to hear that Christopher had purposefully lost his last contest.

"If you had to compete under my name, couldn't you at least have won, like I would have done in your place?" he would argue. "Now everyone will think Sir Alexander Rathbone an incompetent fool."

"Worry not. Your reputation is safe," Christopher would assure him.

He had not been incompetent—far from it—and, fortunately, Lord Spelling had been skilled enough to make his victory appear genuine. Christopher was confident no one would suspect anything. He had intended to plead an injury of some sort to disappear into the background while everyone else was celebrating the victor and then ride away before questions could be asked. But an even better solution had presented itself when his helm had been damaged by Lord Spelling's lance.

It had not exactly been pleasant to have the blacksmith hammer away to free him from the metal prison, but it had meant he'd then been able to fake a cut to the head and wrap half of his face in heavy bandages. With only his right eye showing—Blaidd, as he secretly called him in his mind—no one would guess his other one was a different color. And with his most distinctive feature hidden from view, no one should be able to identify him as the former Lord Ashton.

The temptation to stay the night at the camp had been too strong to resist.

And the gamble had paid off because Siân had come.

"How do you know I 'allowed' Lord Spelling to unhorse me?" he asked, keeping his back to her. "Perhaps he was simply the better contender?"

Was it possible to know someone was rolling their eyes without looking at them? Apparently, it was because he knew that was exactly what Siân was doing.

"Please! Do you take me for a fool? Lord Spelling was good, but you could have beaten him three times over had you wanted to."

"I'm flattered."

"Don't be. I was not trying to flatter you, merely stating facts."

Yes. And she was right. He had been the best contender that day, but his aim had not been to win money he didn't care about since it could not buy him what he wanted the most, the woman standing on the platform at the end of the field—next to her damned husband.

There was a pause, then a whisper, which was somehow loud enough to penetrate all the way to his bones, causing warmth to spread through his body.

"You know you shouldn't be here."

"No."

In all senses of the word. As plain Christopher Harrison, he shouldn't be competing in a tourney reserved for lords. As the lady of the castle's former lover, he shouldn't dare appear in front of her husband. As a man whose pride had been hurt, he should have stayed well away. But there he was.

He turned to face her at last—and almost swooned.

Dear God, with her hair in disarray, her eyes huge in the light of the brazier, her hooded cloak wrapped around her shoulders—the same one she had worn that day in the clearing— she was a vision. A vision from the past sent to torment him. This afternoon at the joust, in her formal attire, complete with veil and precious jewels, she had been every inch the married English lady.

Right now, she was once again his mischievous little lamb, his wild Welsh girl, his Siân—*not* Lady Cantle.

"You shouldn't be here either, in my tent," he breathed, wishing he had his two eyes to look at her. "And yet you are. But then again, we've never been the kind of people to do what was requested of us, have we?"

There was nothing she could say to that because it was the truth. Of course, being the woman she was, she didn't let it deter her. And true to form, she said the last thing he had expected her to say.

"Why did you choose a gold caparison for your horse?"

He couldn't help a smile. *What did her elderly husband make of the unusual way her mind worked?*

"It reminded me of honey rather than gold, if you must know."

Honey. Like her hair. Like the honey he had pretended to lick from her fingers in the meadow. Like the honey he was dreaming of tasting between her thighs. It had been an obvious choice, and he was surprised she had not guessed it herself. Or perhaps she was shying away from the fact.

"Why are you asking?" he asked, coming a step closer. "Would you rather I had chosen another—"

"I prefer nothing!" she roared, finally breaking her unnatural stillness. "How dare you show your face here, in my husband's castle!"

"I did not. My face was hidden all the while, as you pointed out. It is still hidden." He gestured at the bandage. As he could have anticipated, she was not impressed by the taunt.

"You lied and pretended to be someone else, usurping another man's identity yet again. First, you pretend to be Lord Ashton, then Sir Alexander Rathbone. Whose place will you take next? What is wrong with your real identity that you keep changing it? Are you so ashamed of who you are?" She came to stand right in front of him, her face tilted upward. "And who are you going to seduce now, I wonder, only to abandon her when she finds out you are not the man you claim to be?"

Christopher's nostrils flared. Dear God, he had not posed as Alexander so that he could fuck his way through the ladies present at the tourney! And how dare she even suggest that he had *pretended* to be Lord Ashton?

"It wasn't like that, and you know it," he shouted, his own temper finally erupting.

"Do I?"

"Well, yes. I can hardly be blamed for being kept in the dark about my 'real identity,' as you call it. Believe me, I would have preferred to know where I stood from the start, but my bastard of a father only ever cared about himself, as usual! It's hardly my fault."

"W-what do you mean?"

All the anger in Siân's voice had vanished. Even in the dim light, Christopher could see she had become deathly pale. What was going on? Knowing her spontaneous nature, he doubted her reaction was feigned. She looked about to swoon.

He steeled himself against the impulse to draw her into his arms. She wanted to know what he meant? Well, she would.

He decided to explain the situation as if she hadn't heard it all from Thomas before. There was no knowing what the man had told her exactly, or rather *how*. When Christopher had heard from his uncle that he was not alone but had the brother he had always dreamed of having, he had hoped to find someone with whom he could enjoy a relationship such as Connor and Matthew Hunter enjoyed. He now knew it would never happen. Barely a day after their first meeting, he'd understood that Thomas was just as self-serving and pompous as the other Harrison men had been. Such a man would not have missed the opportunity to make himself look good in front of Siân.

Perhaps it would help to present his own version of the story.

"What do I mean? Let's see."

He started at the beginning, with his arrival in Kent and his uncle's deathbed confession. As he spoke, he could see something in Siân's eyes die, like a candle slowly extinguishing itself from lack of air. When he stopped, all that was left of the flame was the smoke of her last illusions—and his.

She hadn't known. Somehow, and though he could not understand why, she hadn't known what had happened in Kent.

"I ... I had no idea."

"How? You said you knew what had happened," he said in a whisper, appalled by the turn of events. That day, by the river, he'd asked her whether she'd heard, and she had said yes.

And now he was being told she hadn't known.

She swallowed and started her explanation. "Well, I knew that the man we saw in Throckmorton's solar was the real Lord Ashton. A man, who would have been his squire, I guess, led us to him when we asked to see Lord Ashton. There was no question in his mind who we meant, no indication that they had just arrived at the castle, no trace of you. And then the man called you a usurper." She paused, looking ill at ease. "It was all clear enough, or so we thought."

Christopher blinked. That was her explanation? That someone had called him a usurper? And she had thought it sufficient?

"After this extraordinary declaration, you didn't ask Thomas for any explanation?" He was incredulous. "You just accepted a stranger's word that I was a usurper and assumed I had impersonated a nobleman from the age of four, which was the moment I came to live at Throckmorton Castle? You really believed I had fooled everyone for two decades, with no questions asked, until the rightful lord decided to come back?"

Siân bit her lip. She had to admit that when he put it like that, it sounded ridiculous. But Christopher was forgetting something. He hadn't been around to contradict the rumors. And apart from her, everyone thought him a rogue; they had been all too ready to accept the worst of him. As awful as it sounded, no one had questioned the possibility of him doing something so dishonorable.

"Well, who would make such an extraordinary declaration if it wasn't true?" she defended. Why would she have assumed the man was lying about something so enormous? "This Thomas said he had all the proof we needed. And after he'd announced he was Lord Ashton, not you, I felt somewhat faint, so my father took me back to Sheridan Manor. We could have gone back for explanations, true, but we didn't, preferring to wait to hear it all from your own mouth. But you weren't anywhere to be found, and we had no idea whether we would see you again. It did look as if you had fled and abandoned me despite your promises."

"So it's my fault, is it?" he snarled.

"No!" She hadn't meant it that way, but the pain she had felt at that moment came rushing back, making her dizzy. The shock of being told Christopher had never been Lord Ashton and would likely never come back, of realizing she would never be able to find him again, had stunned her. "But we had come to discuss a wedding between us. And yet you had vanished, to be replaced by someone else, who was, by all accounts, Lord Ashton. You have to see how it was for us, how it looked."

"How it *looked*? How about how it—"

"And when you finally reappeared ..." she carried on, now as incensed as he was. She had made a mistake, but he was not exempt from blame. That day by the river, he had not given her the chance to tell him she was ready to hear what had motivated the deceit, ready to forgive him. "You didn't offer any explanation as to your change of heart. You just told me we could not marry."

"That's because I thought you would understand my reasons, because I thought you knew I'd been stripped of my title and fortune!"

Disbelief made her stare at him. "What does that have to do with anything?"

"Everything! When we agreed to get married, as Lord Ashton, I would have been able to offer you the life you wanted and deserve. Now, as plain Christopher Harrison, it is clear that I cannot."

Siân's head was spinning. The deluge of new, shocking information was hard to cope with. Christopher had not abandoned her because he'd never wanted to marry her. It was even worse than that; he'd rejected her because he thought she wanted the life of a rich, pampered noblewoman. He'd assumed she would prefer being a lady to being his wife and acted accordingly. He'd thrown their future together away before even speaking with her and asking her what she wanted.

"You think I only care about standing?" She could not hide the hurt in her voice. Didn't he know her better than that?

"But of course you do, and why should you not? It is what you're entitled to, have been raised to expect." He threw his hands up in the air. "And it's not just about you, can't you see? Your family didn't like me when I was a man of importance. I doubt Lord Sheridan would have agreed to see his beloved daughter married to an impoverished knight who'd been stripped of his title and possessions and become a laughingstock."

"My father will always want what's best for me. He will always want my happiness." There was no doubt about that, and Siân wanted Christopher to stop worrying about what her father thought and concern himself more with what *he* had done, what *she* might be feeling after his betrayal.

He did not take the hint. "He did not seem too happy to see me every time we met. I can't even say I blame him after the way I treated Jane and then Elsie, or so everyone thought."

It was true that, at first, her father had been none too pleased to hear who she had selected as her husband. Not only was he not well disposed toward the man who had made his daughter's life a misery as a child, but Christopher's extensive list of conquests had done nothing to help. His supposed defection had been the last straw. But Siân was confident her father would have listened to her had she explained what had actually happened in Kent and would have shared her dismay had he learned what Christopher had gone through.

Connor Hunter was nothing if not a fair man. He would have understood Christopher had never set out to trick her and that he'd not abandoned her, only done what he'd thought was best for her.

"You're wrong about my father. When I told him I wanted to marry you, he accepted my decision because he trusts me." Besides, whatever else had happened, Christopher had earned his eternal gratitude by saving his daughters from drowning. "He would have welcomed you as my husband had you shown him you wanted—"

"It's not about what *I* want! Jesus Christ, Siân, for once in my life, I'm actually trying to do the right thing! Can't you see?" He yanked at his hair. "And I'm having my efforts rammed down my throat for my pains. But I had to protect you—"

"Protect me from what? From you?" She could not stop the trembling in her voice. "It's too late for that. You could not hurt me any more than you already have by thinking I wanted your title more than I wanted you. You cannot hurt me anymore,

Christopher. You've already taken my heart, my maidenhead, the life I've wanted from the age of nine!"

When sobs choked her, she turned around and buried her face in her hands. This was a catastrophe. They had been kept apart by a dreadful series of events. And the worst of it was, they each had their own share of responsibility for it. Christopher had assumed she was a mercenary creature, and she was furious with him for that, but she was not entirely blameless either. She had not given him the benefit of the doubt, taking a stranger's word that the man she loved was a usurper without question. And as a result, she had married someone else. This marriage had placed her out of his reach and he out of hers. Even if she somehow managed to convince him she cared nothing about his loss of title, it was too late since she now belonged to another man.

It was all over.

Unable to cope with the scale of the disaster, she ran out of the tent.

The life I've wanted from the age of nine.

Once the shock of her words had dissipated, Christopher rushed after Siân. She couldn't leave, not now, not like this. He'd just found out that, contrary to what he'd thought, she had not married Lord Cantle out of greed but because her heart had been broken. Not knowing what had happened in Kent, she'd thought the man who'd agreed to marry her had tricked and abandoned her, safe in the knowledge he would never be made accountable for his actions.

They had to talk. After such a revelation, they could not part as enemies.

Outside the tent, the darkness was almost complete. Fortunately, the fair hair flowing behind Siân made it easy to spot her because he knew that even if he shouted at her to wait, she wouldn't stop.

He caught up with her easily and imprisoned her in his hold. "Siân."

"No! Let me go. We cannot be seen together thus," she whimpered when he buried his face in her hair. She was right; they could not be seen in such a compromising position, but he could not seem to let her go. She was so warm, she smelled so good, she fit so perfectly in his embrace.

"Then come back to my tent. This conversation is not over." There was too much still unsaid, so much he needed to understand. She couldn't leave yet. "Please. Come."

She stopped struggling. Seizing her by the elbow, he nudged her forward. At first, he thought she would resist, refuse to comply. Eventually, she followed him.

Once the flap of the tent was secured back into place and no one could see them, Christopher placed himself in front of Siân and frowned. Had she always been so small? Yes but not so frail. He knew she was on the slender side, but earlier, when he'd had her in his arms, he'd been shocked to feel her so slight. She had lost weight since the summer. In other words, since she'd thought he'd lied about his true identity, amused himself with her as he had with his other conquests, and then wilfully abandoned her.

Dear God.

Not knowing what to say, he started to undo the ridiculous bandage covering his left eye. He needed to be in front of her as himself after she'd accused him of being ashamed of who he was. He was not ashamed, not with her.

"Siân. Look at me." Her eyes were full of tears when she finally obeyed—tears he wanted to wipe or, even better, lick away. "Did you say you've wanted to marry me since the age of nine?"

The age of nine, when she had named his eyes, when she had planted a tree in the clearing. It all made sense suddenly. She had wanted him all that time. All her life. Or as near as. She had forced his hand that day in the clearing because she'd wanted *him*, not his title. She had not knelt at his feet because she'd wanted to trap him. She had not asked him to marry her because he'd taken her maidenhead. Their frantic coupling had not been an inexplicable impulse.

She had made love to him because she had wanted to for years.

"Yes," she said slowly. "The day we came to see my cousin Iorwerth for the first time when he was still a baby. I instantly fell in love with him and decided I wanted children of my own. Which, in my childish mind, meant only one thing. I had to get married. And later that day, you rode in through the gate, the perfect knight on his beautiful steed, like the answer to my prayers. It seemed like a sign. I could have dismissed it, of course, as the fanciful musings of a child, but every time I saw you after that, my resolve only grew, even if you ignored me. And then finally, this summer, I got to know you and understood you would be the perfect husband for me."

His throat was awfully tight, but he found the strength to ask. "How so?"

He could not think of anyone less suited to the task at that moment. He seemed to have brought her only pain, and he knew he would never be able to offer her what she was entitled to.

She shrugged, a gesture he found oddly moving. "Because you see me. You like me and never make me feel inadequate, clumsy, or transparent."

"That's because you're nothing of the sort! You're the most

intriguing person I've ever seen, the most generous soul, the most reckless rider, the most brazen lover. You are exceptional in every way. There is no one else like you."

"You see, that's exactly what I'm saying." She gave a sad little smile. "A man who sees me like this can only be the perfect husband. He will make my life a happy one."

Yes. Perhaps. Except she would never marry him since she already had a husband.

"Lord Cantle—" he stopped, not daring to ask the question, knowing it was disloyal.

"Is a good man but not the man I wanted," Siân said in a whisper, braver than he was.

They stared at one another, not knowing what to say or do. Around them, the camp was awakening. Daylight was slowly returning and the stark reality of the situation with it. They each had a life to go back to. A life they had never asked for but had to accept nonetheless.

Siân took a step backward, knowing if she stayed too close to Christopher, she would end up in his arms.

"I have to go."

She had to do more than return to Clearfield Hall. She had to leave the man she had never stopped loving and go back to the husband she should never have married.

Another sob escaped her lips.

It was all her fault. If only she had not rushed into a decision ... Had she waited but a few more weeks to exact her petty revenge on Christopher, the truth would have come out. She would have found out he'd not abandoned her, never set out to trick her, and she would have been able to tell him she cared not about his loss of title. Eventually, he would have had no choice but to believe her, and they would have ended up married, as planned all along.

Now, of course, that was out of the question.

Fate was cruel indeed.

"You're not really cut then?" she asked, placing a hand over his left temple. When she had seen him tumble to the ground, she had almost fallen into a swoon. For a dreadful moment, she'd feared she would have to watch him die in front of her.

"No. I only pretended I was hurt to hide my face, especially Ellyll, who would have given me away."

Oh. He remembered the name she had given his blue eye ... It could mean only one thing. She was special to him. The weight in her chest became crushing. How was it possible that so much joy could cause someone so much pain?

"It was an inspired idea."

"Aye." He scoffed. "I should have thought of this earlier instead of going to the tent every time I wanted to eat or drink something the first two days. I don't think I've ever been so thirsty in all my life."

Siân's heart almost stopped. He'd been one of the contenders fighting for their lives in the rain, stamping in the mud, avoiding dreadful blows? And all that time, she had allowed herself to relax, thinking he could not have been one of the knights in danger of being killed.

Shivers turned her skin to ice. "You mean ... You were in the melee?"

"Yes." He skewered her with a direct stare.

"Lord, have mercy. What was your weapon of— No, don't tell me." She didn't want to have to imagine him with a mace in hand, facing an opponent swinging a flail at his head or thrusting a spear into his gut. She didn't need to know. "Were you hurt?"

He shrugged. "Bruises everywhere, a few cuts, nothing more. 'Tis nothing."

No. But it could have been something. And he had done it for her. He had put himself in danger for her. He had risked discovery and punishment for her. Even after their argument, when he'd thought her a horrid creature interested only in his fortune, he'd not been able to stay away. Why?

What was he hoping for?

"Why did you come?" she breathed, wanting to hear it from his mouth.

Christopher smiled to himself. Trust little Siân to pretend she didn't know why he had come into her husband's lair. As if there could be many reasons for him to pose as Alexander and risk punishment.

He decided to indulge her. After today, in all probability, they would never see each other again. He could be honest. "I had to see you."

Even though she was married, he had not been able to stay away. He'd had to see her one last time. But what would they do? What could they do? She had found out he had never intended to trick her, and he had learned that marrying him had been a lifetime ambition of hers. It was a relief to know everything between them had been real, but the result was the same. They could not be together.

Christopher covered Siân's hand with his.

It was so small ... His heart constricted.

"I had to see you, and I know it was a mistake, but I do not regret it. I cannot. Because now at least I know you would not have forsaken me had I given you the chance to choose whether to marry me or not. I should not have assumed you would prefer a prestigious husband."

"No. I would never have forsaken you," she breathed. "But what good does it do us to know it?"

None. And yet ...

And yet, it changed everything. That she still wanted him in spite of his loss of title proved she truly wanted *him*, Christopher, not the prestige a union with Lord Ashton would have brought her. No one had ever wanted him, not even his own father, the person who should have loved him most in the world.

And so, even if it did not make their current situation any easier to bear—quite the contrary—Christopher was grateful to Siân for telling him she wanted him no matter what. It was what he had needed to hear all his life.

"I will leave in the morning," he murmured.

The rest of the sentence was left unsaid.

And we will never see one another again.

Chapter Sixteen

By the end of the day, almost all the knights had departed. The only one who had stayed behind, predictably, was Lord Spelling, Lord Cantle's cousin. Siân pleaded an indisposition to be allowed to stay in bed instead of bidding the men farewell. It was the only way she could ensure she would not throw herself into Christopher's arms in front of everyone and beg him to take her with him on Warrior.

A week later, unable to bear it any longer, she went to speak with her husband. She was finding it hard to shake off her profound despair. It had been seven long days since the tourney had ended and Christopher had ridden away, taking her heart with him. Her chest constantly felt hollow or too full to contain her overflowing grief; she wasn't quite sure which. She was like a person in mourning, which, in a way, she was.

She was mourning the life she could have had.

"My lord," she said once he had finished writing his letter. "If I may, I would ask you if I can go and visit Sheridan Manor."

He arched a brow, more surprised than disapproving. "We left barely over a month ago."

"I know. But Seren will turn eight next week. I would be with my family to celebrate."

How fortuitous that my sister was born in December, she thought, averting her gaze. It provided her with the perfect opportunity to go see Lord Ashton—the real one—without raising her husband's suspicion. She was determined to demand an explanation from the man. He was responsible for her and Christopher's wretchedness, and she could not let him get away with it. Instead of explaining what the situation was when she and her father had gone to Throckmorton, he had made it sound as if Christopher had consciously used a title he had no right to, fooling everyone in the process. He had called him a usurper. At no point had he told them what needed to be said, that he was, in fact, his half brother and innocent of any wilful deception. That omission had had terrible consequences.

If he had been honest, if he had explained the confusion, Siân would never have believed Christopher had set out to trick and then abandon her. She would have understood, if not agreed, with his reasons for thinking they could not be wed after the loss of his title. Most importantly, she would be free. Lord Cantle was a good man who didn't deserve to be married to a woman who wished she belonged to someone else.

Lord Ashton had to pay for ruining so many lives. How, she wasn't sure, but the first step was to ensure she told him exactly what she thought of his duplicity.

"Of course, my dear. "It's only normal for you to wish to be with your loved ones," Lord Cantle said, bringing her hand to his mouth in the familiar gesture. His eyes were gleaming with understanding—and perhaps something else. Did he suspect her of hiding the real purpose of her visit from him? Siân fought hard to stop the heat warming her chest from spreading to her cheeks. *Your loved ones*, he'd said. Not *your family*.

Had that been deliberate?

Did he think she was, in fact, planning to go to the man she should have married? Lord Cantle could reasonably imagine her lover lived near Sheridan Manor even if he didn't know who the man was. Was he sending her away knowing full well that while she was away, she might meet with a man who had bedded her? A man she desired and loved still? Was he ... giving her his unspoken agreement for—

No, of course not. Siân shook her head. She was getting herself into a state for nothing. Her husband had no reason to suspect her of deception. The day he had proposed, she had made it quite clear the man she had been betrothed to didn't want to have anything to do with her. Why would Lord Cantle suppose that had changed?

"I will provide you with an adequate escort, but, forgive me, I will not accompany you. We have just undertaken repairs on the barbican, and I would like to oversee the progress."

"Of course, I understand." Their wedding had already kept him away from home for longer than he had anticipated.

He tilted his head in consideration. "It will be Christmas soon. Mayhap you would like to spend the holiday at Sheridan Manor?"

This proof of solicitude pierced her heart. The tears she had fought for days sprang to her eyes. What was wrong with her? There she was, married to the best of men and all she could think about was Christopher.

"No. I thank you for the thought, but I will come back to Clearfield in time for the festivities." She owed this man at least the appearance of happiness. "And we shall celebrate together."

~

"My lady."

Lord Ashton was reading a letter when Siân was introduced

into the solar on a drizzly afternoon. He barely lifted his head from the parchment when his squire announced her. While she waited for him to acknowledge her presence, she looked around, and relief washed over her at the idea that she wouldn't have to live in the place after all. It was not just that the decoration was not to her taste; the castle was falling in ruins. It would never feel like a home, no matter what anyone did.

No, she was well away from Throckmorton Castle. She had never wanted to live there, only to be Christopher's wife and the mother of his children. And the man purposefully ignoring her had robbed her of the opportunity for a reason she could not fathom.

She straightened her spine. Before she left, she would know what had possessed Thomas Harrison to make her and her father believe Christopher was a usurper rather than explain he was his half brother and a victim in the whole affair.

"Good afternoon, my lord." Siân forced some warmth into her greeting. No sense in antagonizing him at that point. Recriminations would come soon enough. "Do you remember me?"

"I cannot say I do."

Why was she not surprised? Not only was she used to being overlooked, but he had also barely glanced at her. "I came some three months ago with my father, Lord Sheridan. I was not yet Lady Cantle then, of course, but we came to enquire about your brother."

This got his attention at last. He abandoned his letter on the table next to him and walked closer to her. "My brother?"

"Whose existence you were ignorant of until the summer. Christopher."

"I know who you're talking about!" he snapped, coming to stand next to her. He was just as tall as Christopher, she noticed, even if not quite as imposing. "I only have one brother.

Or half brother, actually. That doesn't make me a fraud. I am the rightful Lord Ashton."

"I do not dispute it." That was not the issue.

"You would be the first!" he sneered. "Every day, I am met with complaints. People who bemoan the loss of a man who was, by all accounts, a better Lord Ashton than me." He glared at the letter he'd just discarded. Another such complaint, Siân imagined, which would account for his foul mood. "Men want the competent ruler back when, surely, my judgment is as good as his, and women want the lover who made them quiver with one touch, as if my caresses were lacking in any way. I'm tired of it, do you hear? Tired of having to justify my existence. It's been months. Why can't they all just accept me! I am my father's true heir!"

She took a step back, worried at his vehemence. The man was getting himself into a state. It seemed she had chosen the worst possible moment to come to him, when he was already bristling with resentment. The light in his eyes had gone wild.

"It's not my fault I was kept in ignorance of my own importance and raised as little more than a peasant, with no idea of how to administer a domain as vast as Throckmorton! I should have been taught how to fight, how to read ledgers, how to talk to other lords."

At any other time, with any other man, Siân might have sympathized. Indeed, it could not have been easy for him to take the place of someone like Christopher, who was, as he'd said, an excellent ruler. But she was not disposed to sympathy toward a man who was acting like a petulant child and had ruined her life.

"Your brother was wronged too. He was also kept in ignorance, and—unlike you, who gained a title and everything that goes with it—he lost everything when the truth was revealed," she reminded him. "He never lied about his identity, never meant to enjoy a fortune he had no right to; he truly thought, as did everyone else, that he was the real Lord Ashton. The fault for the confusion lies with your father, who thought only of himself and did not think it appropriate to tell his own children the truth."

"Yes, yes."

He did not sound convinced, but Siân was not so easily beaten. "Now, to the reason for my visit. Why did you let my father and me believe your brother had wilfully wronged you when we visited in the summer? You should have been more honest, explained what the situation was."

There had been no misunderstanding his intentions. The man had made it appear as if Christopher had taken advantage of the fact that no one had known the real Lord Ashton, so far away from Kent, when he had only lived the life he'd been told was his to live.

"My decisions are my own. I will not allow anyone, much less puny little ladies who think they can come in here accusing me of deception, to question my rightful place in the world anymore, do you hear? I am Lord Ashton, my son will be Lord Ashton after me, and I will silence anyone who dares doubt it."

It was then that Siân understood she would not get out of the room alive if she didn't get out immediately. The light in the man's eyes was not only wild but also murderous. He was one provocation away from snapping. She ran to the door, but Lord Ashton caught her by the waist before she could reach it.

"No! Let me go!"

She started to struggle. In vain. The hands that closed around her neck were too strong for her to even dare hope to survive the attack.

~

It is odd to be back at the place I called home for so long and will never be mine again, Christopher reflected as he and Alexander trotted through the gate of Throckmorton Castle. Had it always looked so dreary, or was it the miserable weather that was making it appear thus?

No. It had always been that deary. He remembered thinking he would have to undertake significant repairs now that he was the new Lord Ashton. *Well,* he thought with no small amount of bitterness, *at least that is not an issue anymore.* Someone else was master of the place, it was his responsibility no longer. Thomas would have to see to the renovations. If he'd been inclined to such sentiment, Christopher might have pitied the man for inheriting the castle at the worst possible moment.

As he had come to Throckmorton filled with resentment, he thought it just retribution for what Thomas had done. Let his snake of a brother deal with a crumbling castle since he had destroyed his and Siân's life. It seemed apt.

A man welcomed them as they dismounted in the bailey—a man who obviously had no idea he was talking to his master's brother. Had Thomas even mentioned he had a brother? It was doubtful.

"I am Sir Alexander Rathbone," Alexander took it upon himself to say when he saw Christopher was too angry to speak. "My friend and I have come to see Lord Ashton."

"He already has a lady visitor with him in the solar."

"Well, let us hope he's finished with her, then," Christopher snarled. "The matter is rather urgent." He would not be made to wait while his pathetic brother bedded his latest conquest. In any case, he knew his way to the solar better than anyone else there. If need be, he could run to it before the squire could stop him. The man seemed to understand he would not win and led them up the stairs without another word.

As they approached the room, they heard a roar, followed by

a whimper. There was no mistaking the reason for it. The lady visitor, whoever she was, was being assaulted.

Christopher didn't stop to think. An excuse to pounce on his brother and beat him to a pulp was just what he needed. Before either man behind him could react, he'd kicked the door open and burst into the room.

The spectacle that met his eye was not quite the one he had expected to see. Thomas was indeed pinning a woman to the wall, but his intent was not to rape her, as Christopher had first feared. It was even worse. He wanted to kill her. Both his hands were around her slender neck. It took Christopher less than a heartbeat to recognize Siân. What the hell was she doing here? It didn't matter. What mattered was that he got to her before Thomas succeeded in killing her.

With a roar, he ran to his brother and plucked him off Siân's limp body as easily as if he weighed nothing. As soon as she was released, she fell into Alexander's arms, senseless. No! Was he too late?

"See to her," he instructed his friend in a panicked rasp. "I will deal with him."

For all his roguish ways and supposed villainy, Christopher had never thought he would ever kill a man in cold blood. Who would have thought that the first one to make him question that certainty would be his half brother, the sibling he'd wished to have all his life?

Someone was having a laugh at his expense; that much was certain. Probably a creature from hell who, tired after an eternity spent tormenting the disembodied souls of sinners, had decided to try his hand at humans of flesh and blood, starting with Christopher Harrison.

First, the demon had made sure to delay until the worst possible moment the life-changing announcement that he was not, after all, who he'd been raised to be, thereby preventing his marriage to the only woman who could make him happy. Then the foul creature had contrived a way to make Siân believe the worst of him and marry another man. As if all that was not enough, he had also made him see the only woman who had ever cared for him being assaulted. And now, he was offering Christopher the terrible, terrible temptation to kill his own brother.

Could he resist it? Should he? Surely, it would be just retribution for attempted murder?

Wild with rage, Christopher closed his hands around Thomas' neck.

"You shouldn't have hurt her," he growled against his ear. If the man liked to strangle people, let him see how pleasant it really was. "You shouldn't have *touched* her."

"I am Lord Ashton, not you," was the raspy answer.

"I know you are. What does that have to do with anything?" Did the man think his rank gave him the right to kill innocent people? It did not.

"She accused me of calling you a usurper when that's what you are. You were never meant to be the heir. I was."

So that was why Siân had come here? To confront Thomas about what he'd done? His brave, foolish little lamb ... Christopher shook his head. She should not have placed herself in danger for him.

As to him not being the rightful heir, he didn't bother pointing out, once again, that he had not willingly usurped the title. Thomas could think what he wanted of him as long as he didn't hurt the few people who mattered to him.

"Is she breathing?" he asked Alexander. If she wasn't, Heaven help Thomas. Brother or not, he would die.

"Yes." That one word allowed Christopher's blood to flow through his veins once more. "I think she fainted when she saw us and understood she was safe."

Thank the Lord. Siân was alive. He had arrived in time. Had Alexander not insisted they confront the man over what he had done without delay, she would most probably be dead by now.

"Come. We'll take her back to Audley and old Joan. She'll take care of her," Alexander ruled. "You'll need to carry her. My shoulder pains me too much."

That was the first Christopher had heard of his friend being injured. He suspected Alexander only wanted to drag him away from his brother before he could commit the irreparable and was using the best weapon at his disposal, Siân's well-being.

He let go of Thomas, fury still boiling in his gut. "If you ever find yourself in the presence of Si— Lady Cantle again, you will immediately excuse yourself and run away as fast as your legs can carry you." Unable to stop himself, he grabbed his brother again, bringing his face level with his own. "Have I made myself clear?"

A cough was all the answer he got.

Ignoring the man who would be an enemy to him from now on, Christopher strode over to Siân. Dear God, she was so pale ... He turned to his friend.

"Are you sure she's not—"

"Yes. She's breathing. She'll be fine., I think she's not really senseless, just too bewildered and in pain to do anything. Let's go."

To Christopher's relief, it was no longer raining outside. The last thing he wanted was for Siân to catch a chill.

With Alexander's help, he settled her in front of him on Warrior. Having barely the strength to sit, she would not be able to ride by herself. Once she was secure in his arms, his friend went to retrieve her horse. The mare would be taken to Audley; they could not leave her behind. When Christopher saw Siân had brought Angel, a small smile curled his lips at the memory of how he'd teased her the day he'd brought Warrior to Sheridan Manor. It seemed so long ago now.

Well, there would be no more teasing.

She was married to another man, as far from his reach as could be conceived.

Chapter Seventeen

When they finally rode through the gate of Audley a short while later, dusk was descending and Siân still had not said a word even though Christopher could feel she had regained some strength. But, of course, her throat would be frightfully painful.

Lifting her from the saddle, he carried her straight to old Joan, the castle steward's mother. The woman was a skilled healer, so he could only hope she knew of a remedy capable of easing Siân's pain and helping her to get over the shock of having almost been killed.

"Leave it to me. We'll have her ready to see you in no time."

After nodding his thanks to the old woman, Christopher went to the great hall and helped himself to a cup of mead, which he drained in a few gulps. Alexander stayed with him but was wise enough not to offer empty encouragement or ask inane questions. His friend would have guessed Siân was the mysterious woman he had almost married, but he mercifully kept his comments to himself.

Finally, after what felt like an eternity, old Joan came to announce that Siân had asked to speak to them. Christopher was out of the door and up the stairs before Alexander could move. He needed to see her to be fully reassured. She had been far too quiet during the ride here, nothing like her usual vibrant self. Was she truly all right?

He found her sitting in a large bed, looking pale but calm. The low-cut bodice of her gown allowed him to see the bruises that had started to form on her throat. Flames of hatred licked at Christopher's heart. Damn Thomas to hell and back. How dare he touch a woman thus? How dare he hurt *her*, his woman?

Except she was not his woman, was she? She belonged to her husband.

"I thank you for coming to my rescue," Siân said, looking at both him and Alexander. Her voice was slightly hoarse, and no wonder. She had barely avoided being strangled to death. "Your intervention was most timely."

"Please, my lady. What else would you have us do?"

Christopher was grateful to his friend for answering because his tongue was refusing to move. It seemed to be glued to the roof of his mouth. All he could do was stare at her—at her clear large eyes, at her hands nervously kneading the bed coverlet, at her neck and the bruises on her flawless skin. Bile rose in his throat. Why, oh why, had he allowed Thomas to get away with what he'd done? He was of a mind to ride straight back to Throckmorton and put an end to the bastard's life.

"I shouldn't have gone to him alone perhaps," Siân started, "but I never thought he would—"

"Of course you didn't," Christopher cut in, doing his best not to snarl. He was not angry at *her*, and she had gone through enough for one day, but he could not let her think that what had happened was in any way her fault. "How could you have supposed the man was deranged?"

Deranged, yes. That was what the man was. He suddenly saw it with clarity. Why else would Thomas not have relished finding out he had a brother? Why else would he have told strangers his brother was a usurper? Why else would he have attacked an innocent woman? Those were not the actions of a man of sound mind; they made sense only if his mind was unhinged. He should have guessed it before.

"It's all right. I'm fine now."

Yes, she really was his brave little lamb. Christopher could not stop looking at her. She was so ... bloody beautiful. Utterly perfect. After leaving Clearfield Hall two weeks ago, he'd not gone back to Audley Castle straight away. He'd wandered aimlessly from village to village for a while, unsure what to do, wondering how he would bear Siân's absence. He'd prayed for an excuse to see her again. Which went to show you should be careful what you wished for because, against all odds, he *had* been given a chance to see her again but only because she had almost died.

"I have sent my squire, George, to Sheridan Manor to explain you would spend the night at Audley," Sir Alexander told her, taking a step toward the bed. "We don't want your family to worry about you."

"No. Of course. Thank you."

Siân was grateful because in the aftermath of the attack, she hadn't thought that they would wonder about her disappearance. But he was right. No one might have noticed she'd gone at first, but with night setting in, it would not be long before they saw that she was not within the castle walls.

She looked at Christopher, who still seemed on the verge of an outburst. That he was doing his best to control himself so as not to worry her was obvious. The notion warmed her insides, but after her ordeal, she didn't want him to resist the urge to come to her. She desperately wanted to feel his arms around her.

Dare she ask Sir Alexander to give them a moment's

privacy? Did he know who they were to one another? Would he disapprove?

Before she could summon the courage to speak, he excused himself, mumbling he had to thank his steward's mother for taking care of her. It was just an excuse for leaving her and Christopher alone, she knew, and she was grateful.

As soon as the door closed, Siân sagged on the bed.

"How do you feel, really?" Christopher sounded racked with guilt.

"I'm all right," she repeated.

"I'm sorry."

"Why are you sorry?"

"You went there for— I should have been the one to— It—" He ran a hand through his hair, which was longer than she had ever seen it. "Dear God, Siân. You could have been killed."

Yes. She could have. In fact, she would have been had the two friends not arrived when they had. But it would do no good to dwell on that thought.

"What were you doing at Throckmorton Castle?" she asked instead.

"I told Alexander what you told me when I came back from the tourney yesterday, how wilfully Thomas had led you to believe I had usurped his title. He was incensed and insisted we confront him without further ado. Never have I been gladder to have followed someone's advice."

"Indeed." She would have to thank Sir Alexander in the morning.

Suddenly jerked out of his immobility, Christopher sat on the edge of the bed and took both her hands in his. "Siân, I beg your forgiveness for what happened. I'm so ashamed."

"Ashamed?" Whatever for? He had done nothing wrong. "But you didn't—"

"Yes, ashamed. Ashamed to be a Harrison, to be related to a

man like Thomas, who tried to kill you. Forget fish; the men in my family are nothing but filthy, dangerous, selfish rats. My father treated his children appallingly, my uncle tried to have me killed so he could take my place, my brother—"

"Wait," Siân cut in. Had he just said that his uncle had tried to have him killed? She stared at him. "What was that?"

Christopher sighed. "I will never be able to prove anything now, but I suspect the accidents I put down to clumsiness or bad luck these last few years were not, in fact, accidents. I think he might have wanted to kill me and become Lord Ashton."

Of course. The man from Kent pushing him down the stairs while exploring the castle, the saddle billets being damaged, the squire disappearing ... He was right. It was all too convenient. How had she not seen it?

"Anyway, what I'm trying to say is I'm sorry. An association with my family has brought you nothing but hurt and disillusion."

Yes. The men in his family had made his life miserable and ruined hers. Tears sprang to her eyes at the unfairness of it all. Without those despicable people, she and Christopher would have been married by now.

"Hold me. Please. I need—"

She was in his arms before she could finish the sentence, bathing in his wonderful scent. Closing her eyes, she let him hold her against his masculine heat and stop her from falling apart.

"Siân. Little Lamb. I thought never to see you again."

"I know."

For a long moment, she stayed huddled in his lap, her face hidden in the crook of his neck, her arms around his waist. Then, slowly, sleep started to steal over her, making her body slacken and her breathing deepen. The potion, of course ... Old Joan had given her a draught to drink earlier. How had she forgotten it? There was no use fighting the torpor numbing her body. A moment later, she felt Christopher draw away and deposit her on the bed. A fur cover was draped over her, a kiss grazed her temple, and a voice murmured in her ear.

"I'll leave you to rest now."

~

Siân woke up in the middle of the night to an odd sensation. Jane was holding her tight. Her sister's arms were wrapped around her middle, her chin was resting against the top of her head, her lower body was molded against hers. It was unusual, to say the least. They had often shared a bed, but they'd never ended up so entwined. At least not since they had been children.

She stilled. The arms were too strong, the embrace too possessive, the feeling it stirred in her own body too unsettling, the scent wrapping around her too reminiscent of ... Was it nutmeg?

This could not be her sister. But it could all too easily be—

"Awake, Little Lamb?"

Before she could answer, Christopher turned her to face him. Bare-chested in the moonlight, with his hair all in disarray, he looked like a pagan god, and his eyes, for once, appeared almost the same color. It made her see that she'd been right to claim she would not change them for the world. Without the distinctive feature, he was not quite her Christopher.

"Are you in bed with me?" she croaked. Her throat still felt somewhat sore from the terrifying attack.

An eyebrow arched at the admittedly silly question. "What does it seem to you?"

"It seems that you are. Did you remove my gown?" She could feel only the weight of her shift on her skin.

"Yes. I thought you would be more comfortable that way." He brought his lips to her ear. "Siân, I—"

"No, please. Don't say anything. We know you shouldn't be here."

And she should ask him to leave. But she could not. Even after her wedding to another man, he was at the center of her world, he was the heart of her soul, the light of her life.

She still wanted him, would never stop loving him.

Hadn't she run to him the day he'd been hurt at the joust? Hadn't she gone to Throckmorton Castle to confront Lord Ashton over what he'd done the first chance she'd gotten? Didn't that prove she couldn't let it go?

"I still want you too," he groaned, echoing her thoughts.

Yes. She could tell. He didn't want only her body even if she could feel his hardness pressing against her stomach. He wanted all of her. It was audible in the timbre of his voice, obvious from the way he was looking at her; it flowed from every inch of his body.

And she wanted him too.

"I am married now," she reminded him—and herself. Dear, oh, dear, how many times would she have to remind herself of it? How long before she succumbed to the temptation of forgetting it? "We cannot be together in ... that way. I will not betray my husband thus. He doesn't deserve it."

This was torture, testing her inner resolve to the limit. Siân had once thought that not knowing whether Christopher returned her feelings or not was the worst torture she could endure. It was not.

Hearing, seeing, feeling that he did return her feelings all the while knowing they could not act on them was a thousand times harder.

"I know you won't betray your husband." His mouth was still at her ear. What was it doing there? She wanted it on her cheek, on her lips. She was dying to taste him. They had kissed only once; it was not enough, nowhere near enough. "I would like to say that I care not, that you don't owe anything to him, but I won't. Because as much as it pains me, I admire you for your moral rectitude. In your place, I would be incapable of it."

"Does that mean you will respect my wishes?"

That surprised her. Why had he come to her bed if not to make love to her?

"Yes, if it kills me. I hurt you once. I won't do it again."

Christopher could barely speak. The pulsing in his veins was agony, the heat of Siân's body against him torture, the smell invading his nostrils temptation itself. And yet he could not surrender to it. Had he damned only his own soul by taking her, he would have gladly sent everything to hell. Siân would even now be writhing under him, begging for more, crying out his name again and again.

But he would not do that to her. She did not deserve the burden he would place on her shoulders because then she would have to live with the consequences of his loss of control. She was the married one, not him. She would have to face her husband knowing she had lain in another man's arms. She would have to worry about birthing a child whose paternity she could not be certain of because this time, he would not be able to stop himself from taking his pleasure to the full.

If he ever got inside her heat, he would not withdraw until he'd emptied every drop of his seed inside her. It would be more than sex, more than lovemaking even; it would be a claiming. A claiming he had no right to. In the eyes of the world, she belonged to Lord Cantle.

He, of course, knew differently, and she did as well. They belonged together, and nothing could change that, not a piece of parchment with names on it, not words pronounced by a man who did not even know them. The marriage certificate meant nothing to him. The priest who had conducted her wedding ceremony meant nothing to him.

But Siân did.

Her dignity, her ability to keep her self-esteem, and her future peace of mind were his priorities. His desire, his needs, didn't matter. *He* didn't matter.

"You won't take me?" Her voice was barely above a whisper, and he thought he detected a hint of disappointment in it. It brought a smile to his lips. The little lamb was hoping the wolf within him would give her no choice and force her to take what she secretly wanted.

"No, I won't take you. Because I know it's not what you want. In here." He tapped the side of her head lightly with his finger. "Even if you ache for me here." The finger landed on her breast, over the place where he guessed her heart was drumming in unison with his. Somehow, he found the strength not to squeeze. "And even if you burn for me here."

Christopher stilled before his fingers could touch the place between her thighs. She was wearing only her shift. If he felt her heat, her soft, intimate hairs through the thin fabric, he would not be accountable for his actions. He bunched his fist.

"I do," she moaned, as loudly as if he had actually slid his finger inside her. His blood started to sizzle. "I ache for you. I burn for you."

"And I for you."

"Kiss me," Siân begged. "My body may belong to my husband, but my every breath is yours. Take what's yours. No one can object to that."

Before he could protest or say anything, she fell on him, coming to straddle his hips, trapping his diamond-hard cock between their two bodies. Did she have any idea how alluring she was in that position? How close he was to lifting her and impaling her onto the hardness giving him no rest?

"Siân, please," he rasped. "You're killing me." She bit her bottom lip and straightened back up, as if understanding she was asking too much of him. He caught her by the waist and drew her back to him before she could slide off him. Having her sitting over him was torture, but having her leave would be death. His whole body slackened in surrender. "Oh God, kill me, then. I'll die anyway if I don't kiss you."

This kiss was the most intense one he had ever experienced in his life. It was not a kiss; it was so much more. Christopher made love to Siân with his mouth, did all he could not do to other parts of her body, took each of the breaths she offered.

All the while, he kept his arms by his side and she her hands by his head. There was no touching. Yes, perhaps it *was* just a kiss, after all. Surely, even the sternest, dried-up souls would agree he had earned the right to let Siân know how he felt about her. So he let her know, over and over again, using his lips, his tongue, his soul.

Then Siân started to undulate over him. He did nothing to stop her. He had promised he would not take her, and he would honor that promise, but he was a man, not a saint.

Let the demon from hell make what he would of his victim's actions. Christopher would let Siân get the friction she needed. Married or not, she was allowed to pleasure herself. That she chose to do it by grinding her folds against his cock rather than rubbing her own fingers against her flesh was neither here nor there, in his opinion. Knowing that by using him, she could still reach the release he was not allowed to give her was all that mattered.

"Christopher." One word tinged with panic. She was afraid of the sensations building in her body. He was not afraid. This was no betrayal; it was what she was owed, the least he could offer her for all he had made her endure.

"Yes, sweetheart, I know," he breathed against her lips. Her impossibly soft lips, swollen from their earlier kiss. His were tingling, as was the lower part of his body. He arched against her, increasing the pressure against her folds. He had never been so hard, so desperate. But he was desperate on her behalf. He needed to know he would not leave her unsatisfied. "I'm here. Take the pleasure you need. My body is yours. Use it. Use me. I'm here."

It was as if his words had pushed her over the edge. She cried into his mouth, a delicious, lust-filled moan that was his undoing. His seed shot out of him, pooling between them, soaking his clothes, scalding his skin, stealing his sanity. Siân whimpered and collapsed against his chest.

He did touch her then, to stop her from sliding off the mattress in a tangle of limbs and injuring herself. She was as limp and soft as a kitten. Kitten. Mm, yes, maybe she would like that better than lamb. He would have asked her what she thought if he could talk, but he could not. He couldn't move. He could barely lift his eyelids.

After a long moment, he deposited Siân next to him. He'd thought her half asleep, but she bolted upright as soon as he made to leave the bed.

"No! Don't leave!" she cried out. "Stay with me. This is the only night we'll ever have. You won't take me, and I understand why. But please, let me have this at least. A moment in your arms."

He stroked her cheek in a soothing gesture. Of course he would let her—and himself—have this night. "I'm not leaving. I was only going to ..." He cleared his throat. With anyone else, his loss of control would have been excruciatingly embarrassing. "I was going to wash."

Her eyes flicked over to his groin, and even in the moonlight, he saw her cheeks flush crimson.

There was a basin of water and a piece of cloth on the chest by the hearth. Christopher made quick work of discarding his clothes and wiping himself clean. Leaving everything in a pile, he walked back to the bed naked.

Siân, who'd been watching him all the while, nodded, as if to signify her approval. Then she took her shift off and lay back down on the mattress, waiting for him to take his place by her side. He slipped back under the covers and took her into his arms.

"Thank you," she breathed in his ear.

For a long moment, they lay side by side, skin to skin, soul to soul. Then Christopher spoke.

"When I saw Thomas's hands around your neck, I thought I would have to see you die in front of me, and I knew I would never—" He stopped, trying to control the pain slicing through his chest.

"It was the same for me at the joust. My heart almost stopped beating when I saw you tumble to the ground. For a dreadful moment, I thought you'd died, and I couldn't bear it." A sob escaped her lips, and she nestled closer to his chest.

"Hush, sweet. I didn't die. It's all right."

"Thank God you came to the tourney," she said, clinging to him. "If you had not, we would never have known the truth. We would still think we had betrayed one another."

Yes. But was it better that way? They both knew they wanted to be together but they could not be. It was perhaps even crueler.

Siân seemed to realize it as well because he felt her grow still. "Just ... hold me."

Yes, always, he almost said.

But they would have only ever that one night.

Despite their intention to make the most of the moment, it was not long before they were both asleep.

Chapter Eighteen

In the morning, Siân woke up alone. Though she was not surprised that Christopher had left before dawn, the pain of the loss was crippling, reminding her that she would wake up alone for the rest of her life. Well, she would at least make the most of their last day together.

As soon as she was dressed, she went down to the great hall, where she found the two friends breaking their fasts together. They stood up when they saw her in the doorframe.

"My lady."

"Good morning," she murmured, walking toward the table.

"I trust you slept well?"

Siân knew she had gone bright red from the heat blooming through her chest and the spark igniting in Christopher's blue eye. The tone of Sir Alexander's voice betrayed the fact that he had guessed the two of them had slept in the same bed. Still, he didn't sound disapproving.

"Very well, thank you," she said, sitting on the bench. "Having not eaten last night, I am rather hungry, though."

"Of course. You will find everything you need here. If you'll excuse me, I have to—" Instead of finishing the sentence, he gestured toward the door and bowed before leaving her and Christopher alone again.

"He knows we slept in the same bed," Siân whispered.

Christopher shrugged as he sat next to her, utterly unconcerned. Clearly, he thought his friend could be trusted with the information. "He strongly suspects. But don't worry, he will never say anything to anyone. Now, what do you want?"

You.

He arched a brow when she bit her bottom lip to prevent the word from bursting out.

"I meant, what food takes your fancy?" The low, sensual purr did nothing to ease the burning between her legs.

Slowly, she released her lip. "Some of the ... pie would be nice, thank you."

They ate in companionable silence, not sure what to say. Then Christopher shuffled closer to her. His eyes had gone dark as thunder. Anger was boiling under the surface, having replaced the earlier desire. A light finger landed on her neck, where she guessed the bruises were still visible.

"I will make Thomas pay for hurting you, never fear."

She placed her hand over his. "No."

She didn't want him to get hurt because she'd been foolish enough to go and confront the man on her own. Or rather, she feared the consequences of Christopher killing or even hurting Thomas. She didn't doubt he would have the better of him, but he was not Lord Ashton anymore. Who would take the defense of a man who had killed a lord and his own brother? No. It was better he stayed well clear of Throckmorton Castle.

"He is your brother, father to your nephew, the only family you have. I cannot be responsible for you hurting him."

She couldn't bear that burden even if, clearly, the two men would never be friends, for all they were related. Christopher had finally been given the family he'd craved, but, by a cruel twist of fate, it was not one he could ever enjoy. Brother or not, he was just as alone as he'd always been.

"I should get back home," she said, feeling guilty. Unlike him, she had a loving family who would be frantic if she didn't come back soon. One thing was for sure, she didn't relish the prospect of explaining the bruises on her neck to her father and uncle.

Christopher nodded. "Let me escort you."

They set off when the sun reached its zenith in the pale winter sky. Angel and Warrior made a striking couple walking side by side. Air and fire, silver and copper, mist and sunlight, each complemented the other perfectly. Did she and Christopher look as good together? No, she was under no illusion. She would never be a match for his magnificence. In any case, they were not a real couple, would never be.

Her heart stopped because, for the first time since her wedding, she realized that if she had married someone she didn't love, he could do the same, find himself a wife and a family at last. Could she make him promise never to marry? Of course not.

She clenched her jaw so hard she feared she might crack a tooth.

"Shall I race you?" Christopher asked once they had reached an open field. "Allow you to get your revenge on me for last time?"

Never one to turn down a challenge, Siân found herself shaking her head. She wanted to make the most of this stolen moment with the man she loved. All too soon, she would have to go back to her husband and her life away from Christopher. A walk was already too fast for her liking. She wished they could crawl back to Sheridan Manor. Or better still, flee together, far, far away, to a place where no one knew them.

"We are riding the same horses as we were that day, in case

you hadn't noticed, so there is little point in us racing again. You didn't win as much as Warrior outran Angel, who is not a strong destrier but a lady's palfrey. One was selected for speed and strength, the other for elegance and comfort. Those are their natures. Some things cannot be changed, as much as we would like to."

Christopher nodded. They both knew she was not talking about the horses anymore.

"If you must know, I was amazed you thundered through Sheridan Manor right on my heels. Even Alexander on his stallion would not have been able to keep pace with me. You are an exceptional rider."

"And if you must know, I appreciated that you didn't let me win, like too many men would have."

"I would never do that. Next time, we'll race on evenly matched horses so we know where we stand."

Before she could answer, he skewered her with a knowing look. There would never be a next time, and he knew it. Once she was back at Clearfield Hall, they would never meet again. It was for the best, as she could not risk a repeat of the previous night. She had managed to resist her desire for him this time, but she would not do it a second time.

They carried on in silence and all too soon came in view of Sheridan Manor.

Christopher brought his horse to a halt, forcing her to do the same.

"This is where we part. As much as I would like to, I cannot accompany you back to Sheridan Manor and see your family. They do not know we've met, and it's better that way. I will have to leave you here, in the forest, and let you ride to the gate alone."

He was right. It would not do for them to be seen together, though she was not worried about Uncle Matthew not wanting him to set foot in his home. Rescuing Gwenllian and Seren from the river had ensured he would never be refused entry again, but she would hate to see the pity in her mother's eyes, the compassion in her father's, the questions in Jane's. They all knew, even though the matter had never been discussed openly, that her marriage to Lord Cantle had not changed her feelings toward Christopher.

Siân was wondering what to do when Christopher jumped from the saddle and reached out to her, closing his hands about her waist in a proprietorial manner. A moment later, she was in his arms, her feet not quite touching the ground. He was holding her so tight there wasn't an inch of her body that wasn't touching his. It was just like it had been the night before, intimate and wonderful.

"Promise me you'll never place yourself in danger on my account again," he said, speaking with his mouth against her temple. "I need to know you're alive and well even if you cannot be mine."

"I promise." The word ended with a sob. This parting was going to kill her. "Don't let anyone tell you you're a rogue ever again, do you hear? You're nothing of the sort."

"I cannot stop what people say," he answered, placing her on the ground.

"No. More's the pity. But you're a good man."

"Ah, Little Lamb. You *do* say the oddest things." She heard the familiar amusement peeking through the gruffness. "I'm not sure many people would agree with you."

"People are fools."

His hold around her tightened. "I wish I could kiss you, but I can't," he rasped. "If I kissed you now ..."

"Yes. I know."

If he kissed her now, he would not be able to stop, and neither would she. They would make mad, passionate, soul-destroying love on the forest floor. It would be an utter disaster. Because then she would not resist fleeing as fast as she could with him.

She buried her face against his chest and inhaled his scent one last time. *Cardamom.* It hit her like a bolt of lightning. The man she loved smelled like cardamom. A sad smile tugged at her lips when she, at last, identified the elusive spice. Too late. Much too late.

"Christopher—"

"Goodbye, Siân." Her name was little more than a sob. "Forgive me, but I can't do this."

He pushed her away almost roughly and vaulted on top of Warrior. Before she could protest or do anything, he was thundering away, leaving her with a hollow shell for a body.

Two days later, Siân and her escort set off for Clearfield Hall under a cloudy sky. Snow was threatening, but she barely felt the cold. It seemed to her she had not been warm since she had watched Christopher gallop away from her.

For once, it was actually a relief to leave her family. Every waking hour since her return to Sheridan Manor had been spent reassuring them that she was all right and no real harm had been done to her. Their reactions when they had seen her throat bruised from Lord Ashton's assault had been as bad as she had feared.

Her father's hand had gone to his sword as soon as she had walked into the great hall. "Who dared?"

He exchanged a rapid glance with Matthew, who, in turn, stepped forward. "Don't tell me this is—"

"No," she instantly interposed.

She would not let the two men even suggest that Christopher was the one responsible for hurting her. Fortunately, earlier that morning, in agreement with Sir Alexander, she had imagined a story that would explain both why she had spent the night at Audley Castle and how she had ended up with bruises around her neck. Her family wouldn't like to hear it, but at least that way, she would ensure Christopher's name was not mentioned and her father did not rush to Throckmorton to murder Lord Ashton.

"Yesterday, I went for a ride, and as I stopped by the river to water Angel, two men jumped on me."

As she had expected, a chorus of feminine gasps and masculine growls greeted her announcement. "What the—"

"Mercifully, my shouts alerted Sir Alexander Rathbone, who was riding past. He came to my rescue before anything could happen." Remembering Lord Ashton's assault and her fear at the thought she was about to die, she did not find it hard to sound convincing. "He saved me. But I'm afraid I fainted once he'd sent the ruffians running, and, not knowing who I was or where to take me, he carried me back to his home at Audley Castle. By the time I came to, it was late and I was too badly shaken to attempt a ride. I believe he sent a messenger to inform you where I was?"

"He did," her mother confirmed, her voice trembling. "We are most grateful to the kind man for his timely intervention."

Jane seized her hand, looking sick with worry. Branwen had gone deathly white, and Matthew quickly drew her into his embrace, cradling her rounded stomach as he did. Guilt sliced through Siân. She should perhaps have tried to find a less shocking explanation for her disappearance, one that did not send her family into such a flurry of anguish. But with the memory of Christopher's body against hers, she had been unable to think, and Sir Alexander's idea had seemed as good as any.

"I'm truly all right," she said, giving Jane's hand a squeeze. "I swear."

"Sir Alexander Rathbone," her father muttered.

Siân's heart flipped inside her chest. Damnation, he was trying to remember where he had heard the name before. If he identified him as Christopher's friend, his suspicions would be renewed.

"Yes, though he is a complete stranger, he was most helpful," she offered, desperate to steer his mind back to her.

"And he let you ride back home alone despite what had happened the day before?" Her uncle sounded confused—and not best impressed. Of course, a chivalrous knight who'd just rescued a woman from assault would never have let her leave his home without a proper escort. It made no sense.

"He would have come with me—in fact, he was most insistent—but when I found out he was due to visit a sickly cousin in town, I declined his offer. He sent his squire and a groom instead. On my orders, the two men left me once we were in view of the gate."

Fortunately, as that did sound like something she would do, no one doubted her.

"I will have to ride to Audley tomorrow to thank him for what he did," Connor said eventually.

"Yes. I'll go with you," Esyllt added.

And so the following day Siân had accompanied them and been relieved to see Sir Alexander play his part to perfection. Her parents had left Audley fully reassured, and Connor had not seemed to remember why the man's name was familiar. Of Christopher, there had been no trace. He could have hidden in some dark corner when he'd seen her ride through the gate with her parents, of course, but it was more likely he'd left the castle altogether. The way he had galloped away from her the day before seemed to suggest he wanted to put as much distance between them as he could. It wouldn't surprise her if he had gone to the south coast and even crossed the sea in his bid to avoid her while she rode back north to her new home—and her husband.

Her chest tightened when she spotted the towers of Clearfield Hall in the distance.

This was it. The rest of her life was to be spent here, as Lady Cantle. It would have to suffice even if it was not what she wanted. Aged nine, she had elected to marry Christopher so that she could have children. And here she was, aged twenty, married to a man she didn't love who would never give her the babies she craved.

How cruel life could be.

But at least she had her dignity intact.

As hard as it had been at the time, she was grateful to Christopher for allowing her to go to her husband with her head held high and her conscience clear. She and Lord Cantle did not have a true marriage, and he knew she'd had a lover before their wedding—a man she was still in love with—but she guessed he would be gratified to know she had honored her vows to him if he found out she had spent the night in the same bed as Christopher after her ordeal.

Not that he ever would, fortunately. It would forever be their secret.

The retinue rode into the bailey just before dusk, as the first snowflakes started to fall. Young Peter, the steward's son, ran up to her as soon as she had dismounted, his face a mask of anguish.

"Oh, my lady! Thank the Lord you're back! We were about to send a message for you to Sheridan Manor."

"Were you? Why?" Her heart started to beat wildly as a hundred and one possibilities, each more dreadful than the last, crossed her mind.

"An accident. Lord Spelling and Lord Cantle. A j-joust.

The l-lance ..." Peter was stammering and shaking his head. "His lordship is convinced he will not survive his injury."

Siân blinked. Had she heard right? Had the man mentioned a joust? Had he just said her husband was *dying*?

"Take me to him." It was clear she would not get much sense out of the poor boy.

As she entered her husband's bedchamber for the first time since their wedding, Siân immediately saw that Peter might not have exaggerated. She could tell Lord Cantle had indeed been injured and that the injury was severe. The left side of his face was heavily bandaged, much like Christopher's had been after the tourney. Except this time, it was not a ruse destined to hide his identity. It was all too real.

"My lord," she said, her voice barely above a whisper.

"Ah, my dear," he said, turning his head to her. He sounded weary, nothing like his usual self. "You're back."

"I am." She nodded his dismissal to Peter and closed the door behind her. Alone with her husband, she sat on the edge of the bed and took his hand in hers, something she had never dared do before. "Now, what is this I hear about a joust?"

About him dying?

"Alas, 'tis true. I fear I will not live to see another Christmas, and my physician agrees, though he has not dared say as much out loud."

As he spoke, a grimace contorted his face. Her own insides twisted in turn. Was there nothing she could do to alleviate his pain?

Siân swallowed, utterly at a loss. What did one say to a man who knew he was dying?

"It's my own fault," he carried on. "After the tourney, I was filled with renewed enthusiasm and felt twenty years younger. A few days after you left, I accepted my cousin's challenge and agreed to ride against him in a friendly contest. As anyone could have predicted, I was no match for him. On the first run, his lance shattered against my breastplate. A shard flew up and embedded itself in my left eye. Herbert had promised we would take it steady to start with, so, fools that we were, we didn't wear any helmets."

A shard of wood had hit him in the eye? This was horrific. "I-I don't know what to say," Siân stammered.

"There is no need to say anything. My children have all been notified and should arrive soon to receive my final blessing."

Final blessing? She recoiled.

"No! It cannot—"

"It will. The wound got infected and ... Well." He patted her hand gently, resigned but firm. "I don't have much time left, and, in all honesty, I don't wish for it. I'm in too much pain." Another pause, ominous. Siân tensed up. What was he about to say? Did she want to know? "Forgive me for my bluntness, but there isn't much time. I saw your reaction when Sir Alexander Rathbone appeared in front of us at the joust, and I did not miss his attempt at hiding his features afterward. Unlike Herbert, I am not as foolish as to ignore that the man lost his last contest willingly. I imagine he wanted to avoid questions about his presence at Clearfield being asked."

Her silence was a confirmation in itself. Lord Cantle gave her hand a squeeze.

Heart in her throat, Siân waited.

"Now I understand why you asked me about him when you saw his name on the list of contenders. He is the man you love, is he not?"

The irony of it would have made her smile at any other moment. Her husband had guessed the dashing knight was the man who'd captured her heart, but he had attributed him a false identity. It seemed that the world was forever destined to think of Christopher as another man.

"He is." She didn't want to lie, and she didn't see the point in explaining the confusion behind the name. It would serve no purpose, and Lord Cantle was in too much pain for lengthy conversations.

"Well, I think you were mistaken to think he had abandoned you. It is clear to me that the man still has feelings for you. He came to the tourney to see you, nothing more, nothing less. Why else would he compete in the joust and then wilfully renounce the prize that should have been his? He is not as indifferent as you thought."

He was absolutely right. Christopher had not abandoned her; he still had feelings for her and she for him. Still, she could hardly admit to being in love with another man while at her husband's deathbed.

"You should not worry yourself about—"

"But I do. As my widow, you will be able to enjoy the happiness you deserve when you are finally reunited with Sir Alexander." He stared at her with his right eye, the look in it earnest. "I give you my blessing not to mourn me overmuch. Make Sir Alexander see what a gem he's losing in losing you. I think he will if he is half the man I think he is. And then, marry him. He will give you the children I never could."

Tears filled Siân's eyes. Had a more selfless man ever existed? She brought his hand to her mouth and kissed it fervently. "My lord, please do not talk like this. I cannot bear it."

"But you will, with his help." He attempted a smile. "Life is short, my dear. Make the most of yours, or you'll regret it. I have very few regrets, that is why I can leave in peace. I wish the same for you. Now, if you'll excuse me, I want to rest."

Chapter Nineteen

Lord Cantle breathed his last on Christmas Eve, surrounded by his wife and six children.

Siân was heartbroken, but she didn't feel she had the right to show her grief in front of people who had lost a beloved father. She had been married to Lord Cantle for only a few months and she was younger than all of his children save his last daughter, Anne. That was the first time she had met any of them. It made for an awkward situation, to say the least, but to their credit, they never made her feel as an intruder.

Still, it was a relief when they departed.

In the new year, Siân decided to leave Clearfield Hall as well. Edward, the new Lord Cantle, would be back with his wife and two sons within a fortnight. He had assured her she was welcome to stay, but she knew she would never feel at ease with such an arrangement.

And so, a week later, on a sunny January afternoon, she was back at Sheridan Manor. A letter had preceded her, informing her family of her new situation and pending arrival.

Sobbing, Siân fell into her mother's arms as soon as the two of them were alone. Esyllt would understand what she was going through better than anyone else. Her marriage to Gwyn had been much the same as Siân's with Lord Cantle, based on mutual affection. With two notable exceptions: it had lasted much longer, and it had borne fruit.

"Oh, Mam! I fear you might not believe me, but I was truly fond of my husband, who was the best of men!"

"My sweet, I know." There was no judgment in Esyllt's voice.

"He was so brave, so kind ... He didn't deserve so much pain."

"I know." For a moment, her mother just held her. Then she drew back and looked her straight in the eye. "But you're still young, and I think I have proved that it is possible to have a second happy marriage, one with a man you love and who loves you in return. That is the sort of marriage I wish for all my children."

"Like yours and Father's, you mean." Siân wished for such a marriage as well, had wished for it from the age of nine.

"Yes." Her mother's eyes softened. "When we met, things were very complicated between us. But we didn't give up because, deep down, we knew it would be worth it in the end. You have to fight for what you want in this life. And I think we both know what—who—you want." She took her by the shoulders and forced her to look at her when Siân averted her gaze. "You know what I'm going to tell you, *cariad.* If you still love your man, as I suspect you do, then go get him. Don't let anything stop you—guilt, conventions, people's malice. You two are made for one another. So just go get him."

Oh, she wanted to, but that was more easily said than done.

"I don't know where he might be," she whispered, not even trying to pretend she didn't know who her mother was referring to or that she didn't want him.

"No, but his friend, Sir Alexander, might know. Go ask him tomorrow."

Siân nodded—then her heart skipped a beat. It seemed that what she had dreaded had come to pass. "You know the two of them are friends?"

Esyllt gave a wistful smile. "After you left, your father remembered where he'd heard Sir Alexander's name. It wasn't long before we pieced everything together."

Siân shot to her feet. "I swear I never dishonored my husband!" The merit for that restraint was all Christopher's, of course, but the result was the same. "We only—"

"I trust you. What happened or did not happen between you is no one's concern. Now, listen to me. Enough with the past. Make sure Christopher Harrison understands how badly he's hurt you, but go get him. If you don't, you'll regret it for the rest of your life."

"He hurt me, aye, but it was not his fault."

During her last visit, not wanting anyone to know she had met with Christopher since her wedding day, she had kept his confession to herself. But it was time her family knew what she had found out the night after the joust, what had happened to him. She could not afford to have any of them ignoring that he had done nothing wrong and been badly used.

Once she had finished her tale, Esyllt looked aghast.

"That weasel Lord Ashton! How could he do such a thing? I have a mind to go to Throckmorton now and—"

Her gaze landed on her daughter's throat, and she stopped abruptly.

"Don't go to him. He's a dangerous man," Siân said, answering the silent question in her mother's eyes. Lord Ashton, not two strangers, had been responsible for the bruises on her throat. "And please, don't tell Father who really tried to strangle me. He would only kill him."

"Which is nothing less than what he deserves for attacking you!"

"Perhaps. But he has a wife and child, who are innocent of any deed, and he is Christopher's only family. A man who's always wanted a family should not have to hear that his only brother has been killed. And Father should not become a murderer because of me." She was adamant on both accounts. "In the end, there was no harm done. Sir Alexander and Christopher reached me in time."

Reluctantly, Esyllt nodded. "Very well. I understand. Let's hope the vile man meets his just deserts one day."

~

The following day, Siân rode to Audley Castle, accompanied by Jane and William the young squire. Her mother had agreed to keep the real purpose of the outing from her father but had insisted she take an escort. Though she knew her daughter had not really been assaulted by two strangers that day in December, Esyllt was not going to risk it happening for real. It had cost Siân little to agree to the condition.

"My lady. Welcome back."

Sir Alexander was delighted to see her again and offered his condolences on her recent loss, which made her frown. How had he heard about Lord Cantle's demise? As far as she knew, only her family had been told. She didn't have the opportunity to ask the question, however, because before she could open her mouth, he told her he had no idea where Christopher might be at present.

"He left the day he accompanied you back to Sheridan Manor, and I haven't heard anything from him since. I'm sorry. I wish I could help."

Siân could not pretend to be surprised, as that was exactly

what she had feared, but she was crushed nonetheless. Christopher could be anywhere, and if even his closest friend had no idea of his whereabouts, what chance did she have of ever finding him? That last blow threatened to undo her composure, and she bade Sir Alexander goodbye before she could crumple in despair. What had she done to deserve having fate beleaguer her thus? She wanted only a chance at happiness with the man she'd always loved. Surely, that was not too much to ask?

The ride back home was miserable. Siân could barely stop the tears from falling on her cheeks, and by her side, Jane didn't know what to say. That was hardly surprising. There was nothing to say.

Then, as they entered the forest, William called out to them, tension making his voice raw. "Halt!"

Before either woman could react, he had urged his mount in front of theirs and placed one hand on the hilt of his sword. It was then that Siân saw it.

Half-hidden in the foliage, was a man on horseback, his position making it clear he was waiting for them to round the bend to pounce. Her first reaction was to recoil in fear. Not an attack—not now! Then she started to wonder at the man's clumsiness. How did he hope to pass unnoticed so close to the road, sitting on a horse of such a vibrant copper color? It was almost as if he wanted them to spot him. It was almost as if ...

Almost as if ...

Siân kicked her horse onward before she could think. Behind her, she heard Jane tell William that everything was fine, that he didn't need to intervene. Indeed, it was more than fine. Because the conspicuous copper-colored horse was none other than Warrior and the attacker heedless of being seen Christopher, the man she most dearly wanted to see.

He dismounted when he saw she had recognized him, and she jumped down from the saddle as soon as she reached him, despite knowing her knees were the consistency of boiled mollusks. By some miracle she managed to stay upright. Distantly, she became aware of Jane and William trotting off together back to Sheridan Manor.

And then, the forest quieted.

At last, Siân was alone with the man she had never stopped loving—and with whom she was free to be. She took a step forward, then stopped, her heart thumping hard in her chest. There was only one reason for the fiery look in Christopher's eyes.

He had come back to claim her.

As if to prove it, thunder flashed in his brown eye. "May I offer my condolences?"

"Thank you. It was truly horrid. The poor man ..."

Pain sliced through her gut when she remembered her husband's last moments. No one, much less a man like Lord Cantle, deserved to endure that much pain.

Then the meaning of Christopher's words hit her. He'd heard. Despite being nowhere near Clearfield Hall, he'd heard about Lord Cantle's passing.

"Wait. How did you know of my husband's death?"

He stared at her for a long moment, as if unsure whether to answer or not, then he shrugged, clearly deciding he might as well be honest. "I befriended John, the groom at Clearfield Hall, during the tourney. I asked him to send me word if ... erm, anything happened."

She stilled. Far from washing his hands of her and fleeing to the continent, as she had supposed, he'd ensured himself a way of finding out what had happened to her. There was no prize for guessing what he meant by "anything." He'd wanted to be told the moment she was with child. Her chest tightened because, of course, that would never have happened.

"Where was John to send his messages to you?" she asked, lifting her chin.

"Here, at Audley Castle."

"But ... That's where we're coming from. Sir Alexander said—"

"I know. He lied, on my orders."

Siân remembered the man's pained face when he'd told her he was sorry he could not answer her questions. She understood then that he'd been sorry to have to obey his friend's orders when he would have preferred to tell her what he knew.

"Why did you ask him to pretend he had no idea where you were?"

She could scarce believe it. How could he have been so cruel?

"Because I knew as soon as I saw you, my resolve to do the right thing would be forgotten. I wanted to wait a few months, weeks at the very least, before I came to you, but in the end, I—" Christopher sent a stone flying with the tip of his boot and rounded on her, his face taut with anguish. "Jesus, but I really am the worst kind of bastard."

Siân recoiled at the harsh word. "W-what are you talking about?"

"Listen to me! Here I am offering my condolences on the death of your husband when, in truth, I am relieved you are not married to him or anyone else anymore." Another stone disappeared in the undergrowth, then another. "I've hated the man for months, did you know that? Ever since I heard about your wedding, I've hated him for being the one to see you every morning, the one allowed to taste your lips whenever he wanted, the one touching you, the one holding you in his arms, the one making you—"

"My husband never touched me."

The words were spoken in such a low voice that she wasn't

sure Christopher had heard her. He tilted his head and leaned in closer to her.

"Pardon me?"

"Ours was not that kind of marriage. Lord Cantle only asked me to marry him when he heard about your rejection of me."

A frown. "Who on earth told him about that?"

"Me. He visited Sheridan Manor two weeks after you came back from Kent and we had our argument. I was distraught, convinced no one would ever want me and I would never want anyone else. He was kind, he listened to me, he didn't judge, he wanted to help." Unbidden, tears sprang to her eyes. He'd been so understanding, offering her a way out of the despair she'd been drowning in. "He offered to marry me, to give me his name and his protection, but he told me he would never be a true husband to me because I reminded him of his dead daughter. I agreed to his terms because I could not imagine being in another man's arms. Our marriage was never consummated. The only part of my body he ever kissed is my hand."

Thunder falling on Christopher would not have stunned him more. Had he heard Siân right? For months, he'd agonized, imagining her in the man's bed, shouting her pleasure, doing all the things she had done to him and all the things they had not had time to do. He'd driven himself mad thinking she might one day swell with her husband's child, the child he desperately wanted to give her.

And now he was being told that it had all been for nothing, that the man had not even kissed her!

He looked at Siân, incredulous. She was crying, her arms wrapped around her waist, looking like a lost little girl. Everything within him collapsed.

"Jesus, Siân, and you let me torture myself all this time?" How could she have been so cruel? "In all those weeks, you never once thought to tell me I didn't need to imagine his hands on your skin, his mouth at your breasts, his cock inside you?"

In the blink of an eye, she became a different woman. Her arms fell to her side, her body stiffened, and her eyes sent out furious sparks.

"No, I didn't, because you didn't deserve it, you lout!" she cried out. It was as if the pain and resentment she'd felt for the last few months was finally erupting out of her, a feeling he understood all too well. He was overwrought himself. "After the way you didn't trust me and allowed me to believe you cared not about our promises to one another, after you assumed I would not want to fight for you, for us, you didn't deserve to be told. How could you even think I would not want you just because you'd lost your title when we'd already agreed to marry? When I'd already faced my family for you? You thought your fortune was all I cared about, but all along, I only wanted *you*! It was not—"

"Yes, I did deserve all you made me endure and more." Cupping her cheeks, he covered her face with hot kisses, stopping her litany. He saw how much he had hurt her with his lack of faith in her. "Punish me, then; take your revenge for what I did. Give me all you want to give me, everything I deserve. I want nothing less. I've been a fool."

"You have."

"I could have lost you."

"You could have, and you almost did, you horrid man. But you did not. I'm here. And I'm still yours. We can finally be—"

His mouth descended on hers before she had time to blink. The kiss was too rough, the hold around her much too tight. At the back of his mind, Christopher knew it, but he was powerless to stop. When he finally managed to slacken his embrace and soften his lips, Siân grabbed him by the collar and drew him back to her, ordering him to kiss her again, harder.

He obeyed. Then, finally, he fell to his knees in front of her. Siân had still not stopped crying. He took her hand and pressed it to his heart.

"Siân. Little Lamb. I'm so sorry. You're right; I should have believed in you. I should have seen something was not right. If you let me, I will spend the rest of my life atoning for what I did to you and what I didn't do, for what I should have done and what I didn't say."

Through her tears, she smiled the most beautiful smile anyone had ever given him. "That is a lot of atonement. You had better live to a hundred, or you'll never make it."

"Yes, I had better. And I will love you every day of my long life if you find it in yourself to forgive me, if you will just ... have me. Please." He placed his forehead against her stomach in a gesture of complete submission. He was hers to command, now and forever. His life made sense only with her in it anyway. The last few months had almost destroyed him. No stranger to unhappiness and solitude, without her, he had known true loneliness. "I beg of you, Siân. Have me. To make my life hell if you must, but have me."

After such a declaration, Siân could do nothing but fall to her knees in front of Christopher. He had never abandoned her, and he still wanted her; it was all that mattered.

"Of course I will have you, you silly man." How could she not?

He swallowed, looking nothing like his confident, arrogant self. "If we marry, you know you will not be a lady. You are Lord Sheridan's daughter, and you were Lady Cantle. Nothing I can offer will compete with that."

"You will give me the love my father gives me, the protection my husband offered, the pleasure no one else could make me feel, and the children I've always wanted. It is more than enough. I want nothing else."

A kiss, tender this time, came to seal her pledge. Then she placed her hand on his cheek and finally said the words burning her lips. "I love you."

"I know you do."

"Christopher!" A giggle escaped her throat, erasing the last vestige of her tears. "You're supposed to say 'me too' or some such."

"Forgive me, Little Lamb. I'm new to all this. I've never loved anyone else before, so I have no notion of how I should behave." Despite the words, he looked anything but contrite. "Tell me again."

"I love you."

He brought his nose to hers. "Me too, or some such."

Her heart melted. There were no two men like him, and he was hers at last. "You really are horrid."

"Yes. But fortunately, you love me and are going to marry me. With you as my wife, I will become a worthy man, one who can be trusted to raise the children you want."

Children.

Everything within her leaped at the thought of the babies she would finally have. "That's why I decided to marry you, you know, all those years ago. Because I wanted children. Even as young as nine, I knew I needed a man for that."

"I see." His left brow arched in the way she loved. "If you only wanted babies, any man would have done."

How she loved it when he teased her. "Mm, I suppose so," she teased back, making sure to appear as if she were considering the option. "But it just so happened that you were the first one I saw that day, so my choice fell on you."

"Lucky me." His smile was wolfish, a perfect match for the look in his brown eye. "And lucky you. Because if that's what you want, I will be sure to fill your belly with babies time and time again. In fact, I would like nothing more than to take you to

Audley right now and then on to bed, where I can start fulfilling the task I've been assigned."

Siân was practically panting. "Then why don't you?"

Christopher kissed the tip of her nose. "Because first, there is something I have to do. This time, I will do things right."

"I'm sorry for all I made you endure when we were young. I was jealous. It's no excuse, but there it is. I was a jealous fool."

Siân stood between Christopher and Jane, her eyes darting from one to the other, unsure what to say or whether she should say anything. Earlier, he had taken her straight to her father and, to her shock, had asked him for his daughter's hand. Instead of answering, Connor had turned to her.

"Do you want this man?"

"Yes!"

The word had burst out of her mouth. What else could she have said? She would never accept anyone else ever again.

She had not imagined Christopher would then take her to Jane so that he could apologize for his past behavior toward her. She looked on nervously as they stared at one another.

"This is not something you should be telling me but my sister," Jane finally said. "You should be sorry for what you made *her* endure."

"I am sorrier than I can ever express." He sounded uncharacteristically earnest. "I have already told Siân as much, and she was mad enough to forgive me for what I made her go through. Though we all know I don't deserve such generosity and she could find herself a better man, I don't have the strength to do the right thing. I tried to once and ended up causing us months of misery."

Siân took his hand and gave it a squeeze.

Jane turned toward her and said in Welsh, "Did he really apologize?" She sounded dubious, perhaps not unreasonably so. Christopher Harrison was not a man easily given to remorse, and it wasn't hard to guess not many people had heard him admit to his faults.

"Most thoroughly."

"And you've forgiven him, as he says?"

"I have." Her forgiveness had never been in question.

"Was that why he waited for you in the forest? To apologize?"

"Yes."

There was a pause, during which Jane subjected Christopher to a thorough examination. He withstood it with calm and dignity, something that seemed to impress her sister. Not only that, but he had not batted an eye at the use of Welsh in his presence when it was clearly meant to exclude him and he knew they were discussing him. This whole new attitude seemed to convince Jane that he was a reformed man, one who could make her sister happy. Siân held her breath. It would mean a lot to her if the two of them could become friends or at least learn to tolerate one another.

"What are you doing wasting your time talking to me, then?" Jane smiled. "You should be celebrating your betrothal in bed together. Or are you telling me you haven't agreed to get married?"

"We ... we have. Father just gave us our blessing."

"Then there is nothing for me to say. Go, and make sure to get all the pleasure he owes you."

Siân could only stare at her sister's retreating form.

"What did she say?" Christopher asked once they were alone again.

She was too stunned to even think of a lie to cover Jane's startling words. "That we should be in bed together right now instead of talking to her so that you can give me all the pleasure you owe me."

A laugh escaped Christopher's lips. "Perfect Little Jane Hunter is correct as usual. That is exactly what we should be doing." He swept her into his arms and nodded toward the keep. "Which one is your room?"

"No bed." The idea of lying with Christopher in a place where they could be overheard while they made love was not an appealing one. "The evening is not so cold. Take me to the meadow."

A feral smile uncovered his teeth. "*Our* meadow, as it will be known from now on. An excellent idea, my love. Take me to our tree."

Chapter Twenty

"Don't tell me you've gone all shy now?" Christopher's blue eye sent out sparks. "I rather liked it when you acted all brazen the last time we were here alone together, if you must know."

Siân bit her bottom lip. She wasn't shy exactly. But she could not deny feeling daunted because this time, she knew their tryst would end with marriage; this time, she knew there was no need to trick or seduce him. He was all hers. And she wasn't sure quite what to do with him.

Fortunately, he didn't seem to be suffering from the same predicament. "Come here," he said, spreading his cloak on the ground in a flamboyant gesture. "Before anything else, we need to get you comfortable, Little Lamb."

The nickname that had once grated on her wasn't a problem anymore. In fact, it had been months since she'd stopped objecting to it. Right now, it sounded perfect. In his arms, she felt small and deliciously vulnerable.

He settled himself next to her. "Not cold, my love?"

"No."

"Good. So tell me something unexpected."

She understood he was only trying to put her at ease, and her heart swelled. How well he knew her. As ever, she didn't have to look far for what to say. "Did you know you smell of cardamom?"

His throaty laugh sent goosebumps all over her body. "No. Do I?"

"You do."

"Does that bother you?"

Bother her? She buried her face in the crook of his neck and inhaled deeply, smiling as she did. Yes. Rich, floral, and earthy. Definitely cardamom. "It is the most mouthwatering scent I have ever smelled, and it took me a while to place."

"That's because you have not spent near enough time in my arms. Fortunately, that is something that we can easily remedy." He nudged her onto her back and rolled over her, caging her under his big body. "You're not going anywhere, my lady."

"I don't want to go anywhere," she breathed, all shyness finally gone. She was exactly where she wanted to be.

"Good, because as I recall, I owe you some pleasure. And I always honor my debts in full."

"Shall I get undressed?"

"Later. First, I need to taste you." He sounded so raw she shivered. "Spread your legs for me. Let me see your cunt."

Without having heard the word before, Siân knew what he was referring to, and she sensed it was the height of decadence to refer to that part of her body in such a way. The look in his eyes had gone wild, and this new, crude, commanding side to Christopher was enough to melt her bones.

"You want to see it?"

"I want to do more than see it. I want to devour it."

Siân had thought she'd been shocked before, but she realized she had not because *now* she was shocked. But it did not even cross her mind to deny him. She allowed her knees to fall apart as she lifted the hem of her dress slowly, never averting her gaze. If that particular wolf wanted to devour her, she would not stand in his way.

"Mm. Perfection." Christopher ran a light finger along her seam, up and down, groaning all the while. "So pink. So wet. So good." To her shock, he brought the finger he had used to stroke her to his lips and licked it with as much relish as if it had been smothered in honey. "Delicious," he rasped while she struggled to bring enough air to her lungs.

Having licked his finger clean, he knelt between her legs and placed his hands on her inner thighs to spread her legs as wide as they would go. She winced. How much more intimate could this get? Christopher's nose was inches away from her core, and his tongue was dancing along his lips, teasing her.

"Look at you, ready for me." He sounded almost agonized. "I'm going to lick you until you erupt in my mouth."

A moment later, she did just that. There wasn't any other choice because the heat of his kisses was pure ecstasy. He loved her with precise, deliberate licks that built her need to do what he intended her to do and erupt. Slowly he pushed a finger inside her sheath, then another, and the combination of his wicked tongue and his even-more-wicked fingers was too much. Flames burst under her skin, and heat seared the place Christopher was worshipping with everything he had.

"Christopher!" Her cry sent a flock of birds soaring into the skies.

It was a long moment before she came to herself.

"Now you can get undressed," he whispered before giving her a slow, languorous kiss that tasted of her pleasure. It was rather delicious, she had to admit.

"I can't move," she mumbled.

With a muffled laugh, he rolled her onto her stomach and

started to unlace the back of her gown. Then he turned her over again and lifted everything, the dress and the shift, over her head in one swift move. Siân was now naked save for her stockings and shoes. The notion was so decadent she barely felt the chill in the air. But would she have the strength to continue after the release he had wrung from her?

When Christopher cupped both her breasts in his hands, she understood that, yes, she would.

"By God, I have missed these." His voice was reverent, the look in his eyes awed. "I have dreamed of them many a night while I stroked myself to oblivion. I have imagined them jiggling while I fucked you almost as many times as I have longed for your hot mouth to engulf me."

Siân blinked. That he pictured her when giving himself pleasure came as a surprise. She'd hoped her personality would attract him; she'd guessed her willingness to pleasure him would be appreciated. But she had never thought her body could arouse him so much as to be what he thought of when he stroked himself. She knew she was on the slender side and her breasts were not as generous as men seemed to like.

"You like my breasts?" What else did he like about her body? Suddenly, she was desperate to know.

Christopher stared at her with such confusion that, for a moment, she wondered if she had not spoken in Welsh. There was an expression on his face she had never seen before. Dismay?

"Jesus, Siân, I cannot believe you asked me that question. I cannot *believe* my actions have left you in any doubt about that. I should have told you over and over again last time, with each of my thrusts, how beautiful you are." With more possessiveness than care, he rolled her nipples between his thumbs and forefingers. Then he bent his head and suckled her a long moment, making sure to give each breast equal attention. Siân squirmed and panted, feeling tension building in her body again. "Of course I love your breasts. They are the most perfect thing I've ever held in my hands, the most enticing sight I've ever seen, and the second-most delicious thing I've ever put in my mouth."

"Second?"

"Aye." He coaxed her legs open as he spoke so he could settle himself between them. "Shall I tell you what the first one is, my love? Or have you guessed it already?"

What little of Siân's body that had not been reduced to liquid by now dissolved at the words. Because, yes, she thought she might have guessed. Nevertheless, she wanted to hear him say it.

"I know you like honey."

"I do. Especially the sort I get from between your thighs." She whimpered. Were all men so crude while they were in bed with a woman? She had no idea, and she cared not. *Her* man was crude, and she loved it. "But it's not just your breasts that send me mad, or your pretty little cunt," Christopher growled, tightening his hold around her.

"Oh?"

"Oh, no. *Everything* about you sets my blood on fire. Your fingers, to start with, which I can't help but imagine wrapped around my cock." He took her index finger into his mouth and sucked like he had sucked his own earlier, causing her insides to melt into a puddle. "Then that navel of yours, which I remember filled with my seed." He swirled his tongue inside it in an impossibly lewd manner. "The beauty spots here, under your right breast, are pure perfection." Siân held her breath when he kissed each and every one of the large spots she had always disliked, as if they were as sweet as the honey he liked. "And let's not forget that wicked, damnably alluring crooked tooth."

Dear Lord, if he loved that, then he must really love her.

"The tooth?"

"The tooth," he confirmed sternly, as if he wouldn't hear of having it disparaged in any way by anyone. "Because it's in your mouth, and I adore your mouth. It says and does things that make me prick my ears in interest and my body roar with desire." Christopher's finger landed on her lips and pushed gently until it was resting on the tooth. "I only ever get to see it when you're surprised into revealing it. I hope to change that. I hope to see it every time you smile at something I say, every time you shout my name in pleasure, every time you take me between your lips to make me lose my mind."

Who is making the other lose their mind?

"Christopher, do you suppose it is possible to make a woman reach her peak just by talking to her?" she asked, going limp on the forest floor.

"I doubt it. But worry not, I know of other, sure ways to make it happen. After having to put up with all the disadvantages of dealing with a rogue, you are now going to reap the benefits. Come." He rolled onto his back, taking her with him. "You're going to ride me this time. Let us make the most of your exceptional skill in the saddle. This is the one race where I'll make sure you come first."

Siân watched in fascination as he freed his rock-hard manhood with deft gestures. Unable to resist, she wrapped her fingers around it, taking possession of what was rightfully hers.

"I'm not sure riding a man is quite the same as riding a horse," she mused, out of breath already.

"It's not, I expect. Not that I have ever tried. Why don't you tell me?"

It turned out that, no, riding a man didn't have much in common with riding a horse. It was much more scandalous, much more instinctive, and even more pleasurable. And she did reach her peak first, thanks to Christopher's skill as a mount.

"Ah! My beautiful little lamb, now it's my turn. Hold on."

The cry he gave when pleasure overcame him was unlike anything she had ever heard. It reached all the way to her soul. Each of the pulsations she felt within her was like the most precious gift. As wicked as it had been to watch his seed erupt, she never wanted him to pull out of her when he reached his pleasure. It was so much more satisfying that way.

Utterly spent, she collapsed on top of him.

"This will not do. I still have to see you fully naked," she drawled. Though they had made love twice, he had kept his clothes on for both occasions. The only part she had seen was the one capable of giving her indescribable pleasure.

A chuckle answered her. "Worry not, my love. When we are wed, you will complain that you want to see me fully clothed, as I plan to spend all of my free time naked and on top of you. Or under you. Or behind you."

Behind her? Like Warrior with Angel, she suspected he meant. She did not ask for clarification, however, as she feared it would only lead to more lovemaking and at the moment, there wasn't an ounce of strength left in her body.

"I don't think I could ever complain about such a thing," she said instead, nuzzling closer to him. A naked Christopher touching her with the intention of making her swoon in ecstasy was not something she would ever object to.

"Good," he growled.

"What happened last time? I don't remember making my way back to my bed, so I guess you must have taken me home?"

He let out a soft laugh as he wrapped the cloak over her naked body. "I did. There was no other choice. I could not leave and trust you to make your way back alone. You were all but senseless, unable to stand straight."

"I wonder why."

"I don't. If you recall, you had just forced me to ravish you in a most thorough way."

Forced him? She didn't remember much coercion.

Wrapped securely in the cloak, nestled against Christopher's warmth, Siân could feel herself falling asleep, just like the last time, but she fought the torpor stealing over her body. She had waited for their reunion for too long; now was not the time to sleep.

"I guess I should thank your father," she told Christopher, placing a hand over his heart.

"You do?" Even if he was used to her unusual comments, he seemed astounded that she should express such a sentiment, as well he might be.

"Despite my numerous entreaties, Jane only ever called you Lord Ashton," she explained. "Now that you don't have the right to the title, she will have no choice but to call you Christopher instead, like I urged her to."

He stilled, and she held her breath. Had she gone too far? Then, to her immense relief, he let out an exasperated sigh. "Dear God, what on earth am I going to do with a vexing wife like you?"

"Love her?" she suggested. "Make her wild with desire? Fill her belly with children?"

The hold around her tightened. "I can do all that. But first, I will have to actually marry her."

Suddenly, Siân wasn't so tired anymore. Rather, she was full of anticipation. Finally, she would be Christopher's wife.

"When do you suppose we can get married?"

She had been widowed for just over a fortnight. When could she decently remarry? A hasty second marriage would set tongues wagging, but she cared not. Waiting for another six months or even another six weeks would achieve nothing. Aware she was in love with another man, Lord Cantle had given her his blessing before dying, and it was all that mattered to her. Let people who didn't know her say what they would; the ones who loved her would understand.

She and Christopher were destined to be together. She had always known it, and she would not be denied a second time.

"The sooner the better."

Epilogue

"**I** do."

Two little words. The two most important of her life. Siân felt peace descend over her as they passed her lips. That she had pronounced them for the second time did not matter. That she had waited longer than she should have to say them did not matter. All that mattered was that she *had* finally pronounced them.

She was Christopher's wife.

He'd said his vows just before her, and, of course, their union had already been consummated. They were husband and wife; no one could dispute the fact. And it was exactly like she had always imagined it would be. With one difference.

She was Mistress Harrison, not Lady Ashton.

Lifting her face, she beamed up at him.

"I love you," her new husband said, his blue eye twinkling.

"I know you do."

The smile she got for her answer was dazzling. And there would be a lifetime of such smiles. She couldn't wait.

Outside the chapel, Jane was the first to offer her congratulations. To Siân's delight, she even called her new brother-in-law 'Christopher.'

"Thank you, Jane. I will strive to deserve your generosity by making your sister happy." Never had any oath sounded more solemn.

"That will be the best way to earn my affection," Jane confirmed. "And somehow, despite all your failings, I trust you to be equal to the task."

Christopher nodded, seemingly delighted by the fact she had not been able to suppress a last barb. Her parents came next.

"I would say this has been rather hasty, but I suspect I would be wrong," Connor said wryly. Siân couldn't help but smile. Indeed, her union to Christopher had been more than ten years in the making. "I will ask, though, what are your intentions regarding my daughter?" he added, turning to address her groom. "Where will you two live if not at Throckmorton?"

"Father!" Siân's smile wavered. What was he doing reminding him of his reversal of fortune at such a moment? Her mother, seeing her unease, gave her a quick, reassuring smile. She seemed aware of what her husband was doing and clearly approved.

"I have no home left, it is true, but I believe my wife does," Christopher said calmly before wrapping a hand around her waist. Siân melted against him. Dear God, but it felt good to hear him call her his wife and behave so possessively. "I will gladly follow her wherever she wants to go. And I think she would be happiest in her home country, so we'll make our home in Wales."

"As I thought." Connor nodded. "There is a cottage near Esgyrn Castle in need of new tenants. I would like to offer it to you."

A cottage! Siân stared at her father. Did he mean what she thought he meant?

"The one at the foot of the hill?" she asked, barely able to contain her excitement. "With the stream at the back and the rosebush around the window?"

"The very one," her mother answered, smiling in turn. She knew the place had always held an irresistible appeal to Siân. Had she been the one to suggest that the newlyweds should make it their home? It was possible. "We'll leave you to explain everything to your husband."

Siân turned to face Christopher. "'Tis perfect. You'll see! We will be so happy there."

He dipped his head, placing the tip of his nose against hers. "We will be happy anywhere, Little Lamb, as long as we're together."

Siân smiled as joy pierced through her heart, lighting her whole being. She had been right after all.

Love *was* just like sunshine.

Next
A Lover for Lady Jane

About the Author

As far back as I remember, I have been attracted to the Middle Ages, to knights in shining armour and their ladies in spectacular dresses. Now I get to write about them, I feel like the luckiest woman in the world. Being French and married to a Brit makes each book I write extra special, as our countries share a long and sometimes painful past. But in the end, in life as well as in fiction, love conquers all!

I have published several medieval romances under my own name, including series, and also have a pen name, Judith Falcon, for spicier projects, still in historical romance.

Join my newsletter and check out my other books on virginiemarconato.com.

Also by Virginie Marconato

The Welsh Rebels

A Husband for Esyllt

A Savior for Branwen

A Second Chance for Carys

A Rogue for Siân

A Lover for Lady Jane

The Noble Norsemen

Taming the Wolf

Soothing the Beast

Wooing the Devil

Baiting the Bear

Tempting the Saxon

Seducing the Warrior

Loving the Blacksmith